THE
MYRIAD
RESISTANCE

THE
MYRIAD
RESISTANCE

THE TESLA GATE: BOOK 2

JOHN D. MIMMS

Cover design by Michael J. Canales

ISBN: 978-1-5040-2804-2

Distributed in 2015 by Open Road Distribution
345 Hudson Street
New York, NY 10014
www.openroadmedia.com

For our brave military men and women, past, present, and future. Thank you for your service to our country. This book and millions more would not be possible without you.

ACKNOWLEDGMENTS

Thank you God for all I am and all that I will be. I will always do my best to put you first in everything.

Thank you Andrew Bequette, LK Griffie, and Aimee Mimms for your invaluable editing. You helped make this book shine.

Thank you Michael James Canales for another incredible cover.

Thank you to my family, friends and agent for your unwavering support.

And finally, a huge thank you to everyone who read book one and asked me, "What happens next?" This book would not have happened without your desire for more.

THE
MYRIAD
RESISTANCE

"When you are in the eye of the storm, you are often not aware of the whiplash around you."
~*Hugh Bonneville*

"Our virtues and our failings are inseparable, like force and matter. When they separate, man is no more."
~*Nikola Tesla*

PROLOGUE

"The greatest deception men suffer is
from their own opinions."
~Leonardo da Vinci

Do the dead have rights?

The debate over this question has raged around the world since the cosmic storm arrived a few months ago. This storm revealed the lingering souls of the deceased known as Impalpables or Impals.

The United States Supreme Court handed down a unanimous ruling on this hot, late September day. The decision made it difficult to imagine that Hell could be any more stifling in temperature or tyranny.

It was hard to believe the decision could be unanimous, given the great divide in the world on the standing of these souls. Impals are people. These people once loved, once worried, once cried, once laughed and worked as contributing members to society. Some might say that they once lived, but the past tense no longer pertains to those referred to in the court decision as Impals. They are very much alive, though perhaps not in the flesh-and-blood sense. Nevertheless, their legal standing now is no better than a dog's. The court declared open season to round up and detain these people in the name of national security, while it guaranteed to protect the privacy rights of the living.

The Supreme Court is traditionally a political court with majority decisions usually falling along party lines. There was something wrong, something nefarious with this decision . . . something orchestrated.

The vast majority of the public has no idea that the current president's administration now found itself hijacked by the Chairman of the Joint Chiefs of Staff. This was not accomplished by brute force, but by slick finesse and opportunistic posturing. It was a junta based on misplaced trust and masterful manipulation. The three-star general and chairman had the president's ear in which to whisper his conspiracy theories and deceitful pleadings. The need of military assistance to protect the Impals would be imperative to their security and the country's. The chairman gained the president's trust with benevolent claims of aid to the Impals. These proclamations were all lies.

It had now gone too far to turn back; the military solution too entrenched under the fanatic watch of General Ott Garrison. Even though the president was not conquered by force, the highest court in the land probably was. What Garrison did, or threatened to do, to get a unanimous decision was unknown. It didn't matter now because the damage was done. The Impals were now fugitives.

The Tesla Gate, nicknamed the Shredder, awaits the Impals. Its design was not intended for its current purpose, but it is performing its present task with terrifying efficiency. The official word from the government is that it will send the Impals back to where they were before the storm arrived, back to their level of existence. This is only one theory. Another is the Tesla Gate will *not* send the Impals back, but will in fact 'shred' the soul out of existence. No one knows for sure, and no one who made the decision to use this horrific device cares.

On all of the radio talk shows, the self-proclaimed experts debated whether these entities truly are the souls of the deceased, mass hallucinations or demonic deceptions. In either case, should they have rights? Legality, morality, racism and political correctness are redefined by this event. According to the pundits, the Constitution must be reexamined along with international law. The global implications of this event begin to unfold as the people who fight this battle for Impals risk becoming Impals themselves. The battle now facing humanity is not a battle for hearts and minds . . . this battle is for the soul.

CHAPTER I

THE SUPREME COURT

"Of all tyrannies a tyranny sincerely exercised for the
good of its victims may be the most oppressive."
~C. S. Lewis

AN EIGHTEEN-INCH CONCRETE WALL and a half-mile of military base separate me from the condemned Impalpables, but I can still hear them. Their cries of sorrow, despair and terror pierce my soul as easily as it pierces the distance between us. The Shredder is being fed today and it has a voracious appetite. I know these pitiful cries will haunt me for the rest of my life. God give me strength.

I have been told the Impals don't feel physical pain, although the iron restraints used to hold them seem to cause a degree of discomfort. In any case, I can't help but believe the soul is capable of feeling pain far beyond the threshold of our earthbound existence.

I tried to rescue a young Impal named Seth today with the help of his father, Thomas Pendleton. Seth was only six years old when he died a couple of months ago. His father brought him to Washington D.C. to see the Air and Space Museum because he wanted to fulfill a promise made to Seth before his premature death.

Thomas gave his life to be with his son. They went through the Shredder together shortly after the MPs brought me to my prison cell.

7

Deep down I knew my plan was flawed. Sending Thomas to destroy the Tesla Gate while I tried to remove his son from the horde of Impals was foolhardy, yet I saw no other options. We were out of time. Thomas knew what he did was the only thing he could do for Seth. To be together as they faced whatever fate lay before them.

My name is Cecil Garrison and I was a major in the United States Army. I say it in past tense because I am sure to be stripped of rank and imprisoned. I may very well become an Impal myself. Death is one penalty of treason, which is one of many charges I will face in the morning.

My father, General Ott Garrison, is the president's chief military adviser. He is also one of the early proponents of the government's policy for rounding up Impals. I'm sure his influence will not get me out of this, not that I want it to. We have not enjoyed a strong relationship in years. Judging by his vehement hatred of Impals and my vehement hatred for the perpetrators of this covert genocide, I do not think we ever will again.

I sit alone in my small eight-foot-by-eight-foot cell, listening to the pleas of the Impals in the distance as they enter the hangar. My hammering heart beats against my ribs like a caged animal trying to escape and flee what is to come. I reach up and touch the dry, sticky blood from the broken nose I received in my rescue attempt.

I gingerly touch each side of my nose with my fingertips; the pain is excruciating. With one swift motion, I squeeze my fingers on the bridge of my nose, shoving the bone and cartilage into place. White-hot pain flashes through my head and radiates all the way to my toes. I heard a scream, but I am unsure if it was from a terrified Impal or me. I fall back on my cot, breathing in heavy gasps with tears streaking down my cheeks. My head swims as I bite my bottom lip and wait for the pain to subside.

The scream *had* come from me because a minute later I heard the heavy thump of boots coming up the hallway.

"What the hell is that racket down here?" a sarcastic, juvenile voice sounded from just to the right of my cell door.

I didn't reply, I lay there with my eyes shut tight.

"It's the damn traitor . . . you know, daddy's boy!" a deep booming voice said from somewhere to the left of the door. "I guess he's hollering for his ghost buddies."

He let out a snort before breaking into a fit of laughter as if his comment was the most hilarious thing he had ever heard. He muttered something else which I couldn't hear between his snorting guffaws.

I could hear and feel the presence of someone hovering at my cell door, but I kept my eyes closed, waiting for the pain to go away. I was glad I wore my boots when I felt a nightstick slam down on my toes.

"Was that you, traitor?" the sarcastic juvenile sneered. "You asking your spook buddies for help?"

He let out an obnoxious laugh then ran his nightstick back and forth against the metal bars like someone swiping a xylophone.

"I don't think they can help you get out of this," he said then busted another boisterous laugh.

I felt drops of spittle mist my arms and face as he cackled; I knew his head must be between the bars. I could imagine his adolescent face, pocked with pimples, jeering at me. In my mind's eye, he was an obnoxious Alfred E. Neuman, fresh from the cover of a sadistic Mad Magazine. He wrapped my toes a little harder. When he realized he wasn't going to get a reaction from me he gave up and went to talk with his buddy. Thank God for patience and steel-toed boots.

I heard them laughing and talking in low tones, but I paid them no attention. My mind focused on the travesty occurring outside. The distant shrieks in the unearthly tinny pitch of the Impals sent chills through my body. At least it distracted me for a moment from my physical pain.

I was about to sit up when something else caught my attention. Someone turned on a radio. A broadcast on the government radio channel echoed off the concrete walls of the prison. An unfamiliar radio announcer delivered the news in a deep, matter-of-fact voice. He reminded me a little of James Earl Jones. What I heard made me feel as if all hope had run out of me, leaving my insides a hollow shell of despair.

". . . reme Court ruled today in a unanimous decision that the beings now legally known as Impalpables or Impals have no legal rights under the Constitution. The opinion written by Chief Justice Paul Keith explains the courts position in detail as we will relay to you now:

"The court has reviewed this matter concerning Impals on the basis of Petition for Certiorari Before Judgment. This allows a dispute to bypass the lower courts and come straight to the High Court on the basis of a national emergency. The recently passed Impal Relief Act was in dispute and the court deemed it to be in the nation's best interest to review this law quickly and decisively.

In a unanimous decision of 9-0, the court's opinion says the Constitution of the United States only guarantees rights to living human beings. Since the Impalpables do not fall in either category, it is this court's determination that they have no rights under the law. The government is free to detain the Impalpables in the interest of national security and privacy. It would still be an immoral act if these beings are harmed in any way, much as it is if an animal is abused. Since there is no law governing the moral treatment of Impalpables, this court strongly suggests that Congress address this issue at their earliest convenience.

The Court has not taken this decision lightly because we believe there to be many of us, including some presiding justices, which have a present Impalpable from their family or know someone who does. We want to express nothing but sympathy for these individuals but unfortunately, our Founding Fathers did not write the Constitution with the dearly departed in mind. There is over two-hundred years of estate and inheritance court decisions to backup this opinion.

Furthermore, on the second point of the appeal regarding the laws against corpse desecration, the Court finds that corporeal desecration laws and decisions have always pertained to the mortal remains of the deceased, which in this case is not in question. This is a decision that has always and should continue to be left up to each individual state as to what constitutes desecration and what is the appropriate penalty for such an act. Since this is not a Federal matter and due to the fact that the issue is not against mortal remains but rather, for lack of a better word, immortal remains; the court will not make a ruling on this second motion."

"The opinion went on to name a number of precedents over the years regarding estate and inheritance cases," the radio announcer continued. "The bottom line is, they upheld the president's decision to detain the Impalpables."

Cheering erupted from my two guards. You would have believed someone just scored the winning touchdown in the Super Bowl. The rest of the news story was drowned out by their hoots, snorts and pounding on the desk. I heard enough. I found it unconscionable that Congress could have passed such a despicable act, but now I was in complete and utter shock. Nine people hammered the final nail in the eternal coffin of the Impalpables. What made it even more frightening was the decision was unanimous . . . not one dissension in the group. At least it passed the House and Senate by only a narrow margin. Evidently, several people believed this was wrong. However, influencing all members of Congress is a much taller order than the nine members of the Supreme Court. My father is a shrewd strategist and he got what he wanted.

A smothering dread crept to every extremity of my body as I considered what I believed to be a terrible certainty. They were influenced. There was no other explanation. I could picture my father and eight other armed soldiers with their weapons pointed at the justice's heads. Did it really happen like that? Maybe not in the literal sense but at least metaphorically. A well-placed subtle threat is all it would take. Two months ago, I would not have believed my father to be capable of sedition. However, now I wouldn't put anything past him.

I was sad that my father found himself on the wrong side of the moral equation. He believed himself to be absolute in his moral justification. In his mind, he was ridding the world of an abomination. His cause was just. Didn't every evil perpetrator in history believe they were doing the right thing? Atilla the Hun to Adolf Hitler believed they were doing the best thing for their people, even though their methods were sick and misguided. I hated to think of my father in the same vein, but there was no denying the similarities.

I don't have the luxury of blaming the president and claiming my father is just carrying out orders because it is not true. The president is a weak man. He reached office not by his ideals and accomplishments, instead it was a fat family bank account. He surrounded himself with those who he believed to be the best in their profession. This ensured the Executive branch would run effectively while he acted as a figurehead and cheerleader. I knew he would do whatever my father said when it came to dealing with Impals. The president was not a bad man; he was an idle one. In this case, idleness was just as terrible.

My father was raised a 'hard-shell' Baptist. As a denomination, they traditionally hold a very narrow and literal interpretation of scripture. This was true in a number of beliefs taught by the church. None of the teachings were so relevant than what was occurring now. Any mention of the existence of ghosts is met with viral scorn and rebuke. It is not scriptural. When we die, we go to Heaven or Hell . . . end of story. Ghosts are nothing more than an attempt at deceit by Satan.

Years of this heavy-handed dogma left very little room in my father's heart for anything else. I understood where his hatred and motivation came from. Nevertheless, it still did not excuse his actions. I parted ways with this type of thinking years ago. I do not believe that God, in all his wisdom and glory, would expect us to have such a narrow and stubborn view of the universe, a view darkened by the lens of animosity. Religious idealism is probably the greatest contributor to atheism in the world.

I wasn't sure where God played into this now or if he was even a part of it at all. I don't believe God actively sends hurricanes, tornados or floods to destroy, kill and maim. He allows them to happen for a greater purpose. I believe he allowed this cosmic storm to come to Earth. For what purpose, I am not sure. If nothing else, I would say we have been given definitive proof of the existence of the soul. However, it has also given definitive proof of the atrocities human beings are capable of committing.

I said a short prayer as I lay there with my eyes closed. I prayed for the Impals, and more important, I prayed for my wife and daughters . . . they are now my primary concern. I didn't think my father would harm them to get to me. There was no doubt he would definitely use them. In all honesty, I had no idea how far his righteous indignation would take him.

I forgot about any pain in my nose as my heart ached. The vision of them sitting blissfully at home made me crazy. What would my actions bring down on them? I sat up with a jolt, my heart racing with panic in my chest as if I awoke from a terrible nightmare. What was I thinking? Did my own righteous arrogance made me lose sight of the potential consequences of my actions? The only honest answer was yes. I needed to get out of here . . . now.

I grasped the bars to my cell and yelled at my captors.

"Hey! Can someone tell me what time it is?"

The volume on the radio dropped and I heard faint whispering coming from down the hall. A moment later the heavy footsteps of my captors approached. Their footfalls echoed rapid and deliberate. They were not those of happy or carefree people. I stepped to the back of my cell to be out of striking distance when they arrived.

I felt as if I experienced a psychic premonition when the first one arrived at my door. He was definitely a dead ringer for the face of *Mad Magazine*. The second man was tall and slender with a receding hair-line, which made his military cut seem somewhat ridiculous. His features were sharp all the way to his blade like nose. He held the rank of sergeant, while his *Mad Magazine* reject counterpart was a private. Two enlisted men tormenting an officer . . . I made their day. If looks could kill, I would be dead on the floor of my cell.

"Why the hell do you care, Major Turncoat?" the sergeant sneered.

"Yeah, why the hell do you care, Major Asshole?" the private asked then cackled with sadistic pleasure at his cleverness. The sergeant didn't think it was clever or funny and gave him a slap to the back of the head for his troubles.

I didn't know whether to laugh at my guards as they carried out their sadistic Laurel and Hardy routine or worry about their cruel unprofessionalism. The sadistically stupid could often be much more dangerous than the sadistically clever. In any case, I was not in a laugh-ing mood.

"Stand at attention when you address me!" I barked, more testing the water than expecting compliance with my command. I soon had my answer when I saw the malevolent grins on their ugly faces. Their countenance did not show a shred of respect, only hatred. As far as they are concerned, I am guilty. In their eyes, I am no longer a human being, let alone their superior officer.

The sergeant raised his right hand and poked it through the bars while extending his middle finger.

"Address this," he jeered before he took his nightstick in his left hand and smacked the bars for emphasis.

I returned the salute, which was a mistake. I was hot, I was angry and I was desperate to get to my family. If only I could get them to open the door and come after me, I might have a fighting chance to get away before it was too late.

His buddy didn't say anything as he gave me the 'what, me worry?' smile, only it was devoid of any humor. I realized trouble was eminent. He slowly reached in his pocket and retrieved the keys.

"Okay, Major Smart Ass, you want to play? We can accommodate you there." He said with spittle flying from his lips. I could tell he wanted to hurt me, hurt me bad.

Even though they were about to smash my face in, I experienced a moment of pity for my captors. How had these two men arrived at such a frenzied state of hatred towards me? All I was guilty of was trying to save two lives, two possibly eternal lives. Now I am a traitor to the country I have loved all my life. I pitied the Impals in their current situation, yet I felt these two men deserved a modicum of my compassion. That feeling was short lived, however, as the private unlocked and threw open the door. The sergeant charged like a raging bull, knocking me into the wall. I straightened up, ready to respond, until the private clubbed me in the gut. I doubled over as every measure of air vacated my lungs.

The two men continued their barrage with alternating blows to my head and body. I collapsed to my hands and knees. I was beaten and kicked for what seemed an eternity. I was certain the fatal blow would crush the back of my head at any moment, ending my physical life.

Just as hope was about to leave my mind, along with consciousness, I heard two popping noises closely followed by high-pitched whines. A second later, the thud of two bodies hitting the floor echoed in my cell. I slowly raised my head, my vision swimming from my pounding head. The blood and sweat pouring over my eyes blinded me. I could just make out the blurry outline of two bodies lying in a V shape in front of me.

I managed to rise to my knees and then sat back on my haunches against the cell wall. Wiping my eyes with the sleeve of my shirt, I tried to shake the cobwebs out of my head and focus on what was in front of me. When my vision cleared, I gasped through my throbbing, broken nose.

Lying face down in front of me were the sergeant and the private. A large bullet hole centered each man's back as their blood slowly pooled beneath them. My gaze was drawn upward with foreboding assurance of what I would see next. Standing beyond the feet of their respective body was the shimmering form of both men. They both wore mixed expressions of shock and horror on their faces. The men were now what they seemed to despise more than anything. They were Impals.

CHAPTER 2

JAILBREAK

*"It's necessary to have wished for death in order to
know how good it is to live."*
~Alexandre Dumas, The Count of Monte Cristo

I TRIED TO PUSH MYSELF OFF THE FLOOR to see the source of this attack, but my struggle to catch my breath left me dizzy. I fell in a heap beside my cot. I glanced up in time to see iron chains lasso the new Impals and then jerk them backwards with a violent tug through the door of my cell. Both men let out a tinny high-pitched scream making hackles stand up on the back of my neck. It was hard enough getting used to the way Impals talk; their screams were terrifying. I didn't think I would ever get used to it.

Two shadowy figures walked up behind the Impals and pulled the chains hard. The newly minted Impals let out a blood-curdling howl.

"Doesn't feel too good when you're on the other side of it, does it private?" a voice growled behind the Impal who was now a *former* private.

"I'm shocked at your behavior, sergeant," another voice said with sarcasm.

The sergeant's chain tugged violently again. He let out another disturbing cry of agony.

"Don't you know that assaulting a superior officer in a time of war can carry the death penalty?" the sarcastic man said.

"We're not at war," I croaked, finally regaining my breath.

"Maybe not declared," the man said, this time his voice sounded a little more familiar. He walked in the cell door where I could see him.

"Make no mistake, this is a war, major," he said.

My heart leapt when I saw my friend and colleague, Captain Burt Golden. He never liked the military hair cut so Burt kept his brown hair in a neat trim parted on the side. His blue eyes and square chin always reminded me of an old Alec Baldwin. We had been friends for years, having graduated West Point and then served two tours in the Middle East together. He served as my unit leader for the past two years.

Burt is a good man who can be over zealous, but he is loyal to a fault. The other man walked forward and stood beside him. He gave the Impal private's chains another hard yank. I didn't recognize him. His brown eyes, dark hair and olive complexion suggested he might have some Hispanic blood. He held the rank of first lieutenant; a lieutenant who was a little too familiar with an unknown superior officer.

"Geesh, you look like Hell," he commented, staring at me and then at the bodies on the floor.

"You look like Hell, sir," Burt reminded him with a sharp tone suggesting he quickly make amends.

"Sir, sorry, sir," he said with a flushed face, and then reached out his hand in offering to help me up.

"What's your name soldier?" I asked through squinted eyes.

I was not trying to intimidate him; instead I fought back the pain of my broken nose. The throbbing now returned with a vengeance, not only to my nose, but also my body from the bruising my two captors inflicted.

"Sam, sir, Lieutenant Sam Andrews," he responded withdrawing his hand and standing at attention.

"Will Sam, do?" I asked, holding out my hand.

"Yes sir!" he said with enthusiasm then took my hand and helped me to my feet.

I forgot about my nose as the rest of my body screamed in agony when he helped me up. The private and the sergeant did quite a number on me and, for a moment, I wasn't sure if I was going to be able to walk.

"Thank you, Sam," I said as I steadied myself against the cell door.

He nodded and then reinforced his grip on the private's chain. I winced as my hand accidentally touched the Impal shoulder of the sergeant. The cold sent chills down my back for more reasons than one. In my limited experience with Impals, this was the first time I ever touched one. The best way I can describe the experience is like touching thick frozen air. The sergeant Impal shifted in his restraints, causing my hand to sink further into his form. It was the damnedest feeling, like putting my hand in a hot fudge sundae as warmth began to envelop my fingers the further they penetrated. I jerked back involuntarily and without thinking wiped my hand on my shirt, even though there was anything to wipe off. If my touch bothered the sergeant, he didn't show it. He continued to stare with a vacant expression at his lifeless body on the floor.

"Sam, put the sergeant's body on the cot in this cell and then put the private's a couple of cells down. Cover them up like they are asleep," Burt ordered.

"What about the blood, sir?" he asked.

"We'll worry about that once the bodies are in place. Give Major Garrison the chain in the meantime."

He thrust the chain in my hand and sprang into action. As he worked, I observed my two jailors. The two Impals were a stark contrast from their flesh-and-blood selves. They were quiet, still and docile, not a single shred of violence was evident on their shocked, shimmering faces.

"Where are we going, Burt?" I asked.

He regarded me with satisfaction.

"Somewhere we can do some good, my friend . . . somewhere we can do some good."

Sam pulled the body of the private out of the cell then down the hallway. I watched the trail of blood smearing across the floor then turned and whispered to Burt.

"Was it necessary to kill them?" I asked.

Burt was shocked. "They were about to kill you, Cecil. I really don't think we had much choice."

I knew he was right; they *were* going to kill me. My aching and throbbing body was a testament to the fact. I decided not to give voice to my question of why they hadn't restrained the men and locked them in a cell. The world was not a cut-and-dried, black-and-white place anymore . . . not that it had ever been. I am sure he made the best decision possible under the circumstances.

"Where *are* we going?" I whispered again.

He glanced at the Impals before responding. "Let's just say that there are several in the military who feel the same way as we do. We are going to join up with a group not far from here," he said in a serious tone.

"We're rebelling against the government?" I said, probably a little too loud because I heard my echo coming from the other end of the hall.

"In a manner of speaking," he said. "Nothing as foolish as starting a war. However, we will fight and kill if necessary to reach our objective."

"What is the objective?" I asked. It had been three weeks since Burt and I last talked. My trip to Arizona to visit my grandfather in an Impal relocation camp took most of my time as of late. Not to mention my inexplicable obsession with the plight of Thomas and Seth Pendleton.

"To save Impals," he said in a tone suggesting it should be as obvious as the swollen nose on my face.

"How are we doing that exactly?" I asked. I honestly had no idea. I knew there to be several supporters in the military who are afraid to speak out.

"You'll see," he said with a wink.

"What about my family?" I asked.

"Way ahead of you Cecil, way ahead of you," he said patting my shoulder. I winced from the pain. I wasn't sure there was a safe place to touch on my body at the moment.

A couple of minutes later, Sam had the bodies of both men tucked away, so to speak. He mopped up the blood with spare bed sheets and hot water from the nearby restroom. I was both impressed and disturbed by his efficiency. It almost seemed as if he were a pro at this. He finally took the chain back from me and they pulled both Impals out of the cell and closed the cell door. The two-chained souls offered no resistance; the shock seemed to have them paralyzed. I still marveled at the ability of Impals to pass through almost anything, except iron. Iron was their Achilles heel.

"So what do we do with them?" Sam asked.

"You take Major Garrison to the truck and hide him in the back while I take these two to the tarmac," Burt said.

I stopped in place, almost tripping over my own feet. Ice shot through my veins making me feel as cold as any Impal. For a moment, I thought I must have misunderstood Burt. Take them to the tarmac? It wasn't because I recently smashed my nose on its hard surface. What troubled me is the thing waiting on the other side of it.

"You're going to put them in the Tesla Gate . . . into the Shredder?" I asked, horrified.

This got an immediate reaction from the two Impals. Their faces snapped towards me in unison, terror frozen on their frigid features. They didn't utter a sound. Their mouths moved without forming words like a beached fish gasping for breath.

"Well what the hell else are we going to do with them?" Burt asked impatiently as he began dragging his Impal towards the door. "We can't take them with us!"

"Why not?" I asked, keeping a calm and even tone.

Burt stopped and turned to me. He was as speechless as his captives.

"You said you were saving Impals, well these two are Impals without a doubt. Isn't it kind of hypocritical to put them in the Shredder?" I said.

"They tried to kill you!" Sam blurted.

Burt shot him a scathing glance, causing Andrews to amend his statement.

"They tried to kill you, sir," Sam said.

"So are we any different? Can we summarily pass judgment on them as those in our government have? Are we going to help some Impals and then decide to condemn others?"

"But . . . they are a liability," Burt said. "They'll turn us in the first chance they get."

It was obvious he did not put a lot of effort into his plan. Dealing with collateral damage was an afterthought.

"Why would they? If they turned us in, we would go to jail and they would go to the Shredder."

Burt frowned with embarrassment when he considered my logic. They wouldn't do anything to turn us in because the consequences would be far worse for them. The sergeant Impal emphasized this point.

"That's right, we won't say nothin'," he said with pitiful desperation. "We'll do whatever you want!"

"You're damn right you will!" Burt responded, giving the chain a hard yank.

I was glad the Sergeant spoke up, thus allowing Burt to save face.

"Can all three of us fit in the truck?" I asked.

"I think so. I don't know how the hell we're going to explain them when we get searched at the checkpoint," Burt said.

"Leave it to me," I said as I limped across the hall and opened a supply cabinet. I found two flashlights and I unscrewed the end on each and slid the D batteries into the palm of my hand.

A little trick I learned in my conversations with Thomas Pendleton. He told me how he had gotten his son, Seth, and other Impals out in public without being noticed.

Not bothering to screw the caps back on, I tossed the flashlights back into the cabinet and slammed the door. I walked back to the sergeant and private then held out one hand to each of them.

"Here," I said.

They both sheepishly stretched out their right hand, palm up. I deposited two batteries in each man's hand and watched the silvery Impal shimmer vanish. Even though they were not, the two men appeared as flesh and blood as the rest of us.

"I'll be damned," said Burt.

"Incredible," Sam said. "So, they're solid now?" He asked, poking the private in the arm. He jerked it back as if he reached into a nest of angry snakes.

"That is freaky!" he exclaimed.

"They are not solid, they just appear that way," I said.

"I hope it will be enough," Burt said. "Just pray the guards don't start literally poking around."

Burt turned to the Impals.

"Okay, tough guys, if I take these chains off are you going to behave yourself?" he asked.

Both of them agreed. I have never seen such sincerity in my life. As the chains dropped to the ground, I noticed the two Impals still clutched the batteries in their hand.

"Put them in your pocket," I suggested. "It will be more comfortable and less conspicuous."

They agreed and shoved the batteries in their pants pocket. In death, the two men still wore their military fatigues. Most Impals wore clothing and it was usually a favorite or comfortable garment or outfit from their life. I guess these two were the most comfortable and happy in the military. Considering the thrashing I received, I suspected they were in it for the wrong reasons.

"What are your names, soldiers?" I asked.

"Staff Sergeant Tim Beeson, sir!" he said, showing me considerably more respect than he did a short time earlier.

"Private First Class, Jack Readnour, sir!" the Private said with the same submissive enthusiasm.

"Well Tim and Jack . . . even though you beat me pretty good and tried to kill me, I'm going to try and get the two of you out of here. I wouldn't know how to apply a court-martial to these circumstances so we are going to let it slide for now, understand?"

"Yes," they responded in unison.

"The slightest slip-up from either of you and we will leave you back here on this base's front porch, all trussed up in iron chains and gift wrapped for the Shredder . . . agreed?"

"Yes, sir," they said with much more enthusiasm.

"All right, let's go," I said to everyone.

Sam collected the chains and coiled them up under my old cot, then closed and locked both cell doors.

Before we left, Burt grabbed a black Sharpie off the desk down the hall. He proceeded to draw something on the concrete wall directly across from my cell.

"What are you doing?" I asked, my impatience growing.

He didn't answer until he finished. He then stepped back with a satisfied expression on his face. At first, it seemed Burt had drawn a large thick letter 'S' on the wall, until I moved a little closer. Burt continued the 'S' with two parallel dotted lines, connecting each tip of the 'S' making it appear like the number '8'. While the 'S' part was colored in, the connecting area was devoid of color except for the narrow dotted lines.

"What is that . . . an eight or an 'S'?" I asked.

"Neither," Burt said with a grin. He then turned and walked towards the door.

I glanced at the symbol one last time then turned to follow him.

"What the Hell is it then?" I said.

"A screw you to the government!" he called as he and Andrews reached the door.

Burt and Sam slipped out the door first and made sure the coast was clear. When they gave the signal, I followed with the Impals close behind me.

It was sunset. The orange glow over the distant tree line gave a surreal quality to the evening. The night began to descend with its eerie ultraviolet radiance . . . another by-product of the cosmic storm.

I was both surprised and relived to see no one else was around. The jail was in the far corner of the base and there was never anyone in it. I was probably the first person to do time in over a year. Now outside, I could hear the cries of the Impals now unfettered by my prison wall. I turned and watched as they marched to the Tesla Gate. My guts twisted with anger and remorse. They were not in pain; they were beyond physical pain. Sheer horror struck them at the sight of the Shredder. Who wouldn't be terrified? I couldn't imagine the concept of dying forever.

Burt drove the personnel carrier and Sam climbed in the passenger seat. I slipped under the large canvas cover on the back with the Impals and closed the flap. I sat delicately by the tailgate because I was still in a great amount of pain and opened the flap enough for me to peer out. A moment later, the truck roared and a black cloud of exhaust drifted past the canopy opening making my eyes water again. With a lurch and grinding of gears, we pulled onto the road leading to the west gate.

CHAPTER 3

DOWN AND OUT

"What fugitive from his country can also escape from himself?"
~Horace

IT WAS NOT LONG BEFORE I CAUGHT MY FIRST GLIMPSE of other Impals. In many ways, these were the most disturbing of the Impals, and perhaps, the most fortunate. The people who committed suicide remain here. They are like every other Impal except for one important detail. Their spirit immediately falls into a state of deep sleep. They slumber for an indefinite period and, to my knowledge, none have woken up yet.

These Impals had been placed on their backs in an open field next to the tarmac. They lay in perfect symmetrical rows; head-to-toe and side-to-side. Their silvery luminescent glow against the backdrop of the ultraviolet night sky was a beautiful sight. Unfortunately, the heinous circumstances made it impossible to appreciate anything about it.

Were they the lucky ones? Their unconscious placement into the Shredder did seem preferable. The alternative is to be part of the cattle herd. I couldn't imagine the horror of watching others go first as you wait your turn. The most inconceivable notion of all is the prospect of permanent death. This cold finality comes as their soul dissolves in the crackling blue electric arcs of the Tesla Gate.

Or, were they the damned? Staring across the perfect silvery rows, I estimated there must be at least one-thousand Impal 'sleepers.' Each one slumbers with their own unique story and reasons. Now they all suffer the consequences.

Had they sought the easy way out when life got tough or maybe they were manic-depressive? Alternatively, was it a conscious decision, a decision made with the goal of being together with their loved ones, the loved ones now here as Impals? Whatever the reason, I felt sorry for them, I truly did. I felt sorry for *all* the Impals.

I realize Thomas Pendleton faced the same dilemma when it came to his Impal son, Seth. I knew deep down that getting both of them off the base was a long shot; nevertheless it was something I must try. Thomas was smart enough to know that the only thing he could do for Seth was to be with him. Committing suicide would do no good because he would now be one of the sleepers in the field. He made a valiant attempt to destroy the Tesla Gate and was fatally shot in the process. It wasn't suicide any more than it is when a soldier storms the field of battle. Thomas made a tremendous sacrifice for his son; I hope I could be as bold for my family if the time came.

Beyond the field of sleeping Impals rests the large hanger where the Tesla Gate resides. The doors are open enough for about three or four people to fit through standing shoulder to shoulder. They don't dare open it any wider for fear of stirring up the Impals lined up outside. One would think the shrieks of terror coming from within would worry them. I guess either they don't hear them or are too trusting of their captors. I think most believe that, outside of the iron restraints, they are invulnerable. This belief holds until they get inside and then, well . . . seeing is believing.

The line had dwindled considerably since earlier today. Perhaps a couple of hundred Impals were yet to be herded inside, a couple of hundred too many. The cries dwindled with the line, yet each one sends a piercing stab through my soul as we drive past. Man, woman, child . . . the full spectrum of ethereal voices resonates with eternal sorrow from inside. The government makes no distinctions and neither does the Shredder.

The blue, flickering light of the Tesla Gate emanates through the crack in the door. It reminds me of a television's light viewed from outside a window with sheer drapes. An ironic comparison considering the fact television signals and internet have not been possible since the storm began. As I watched the door, I can't help imagining I was witnessing the entrance to Hell with blue flames instead of smoldering red ones. All of my emotions oozed into the pit of my stomach as I considered the horror inside the massive building. I wanted to get out, to run, to rescue the Impals; we could fit a lot in the truck, especially the children.

I could see two little girls in the back of the line and they curiously turned and looked over their shoulder as the truck drove past. They both wore naïve girlish grins on their shimmering faces as if this was another day at the park. These girls were innocent children and they didn't deserve this. I knew any action on my part would be fruitless, so I forced myself to withdraw from the opening in the canvas. I bit my lip then carefully placed my head in my hands. In my mind's eye, I saw my daughters . . . my father's granddaughters. The whole damned mess made me want to cry.

We bounced along for about ten minutes until I felt the truck starting to slow. I pulled up the canvas about an inch on the side and peered out. We were approaching the guard post at the west gate. There were at least five armed guards on duty, all carrying M16 assault rifles. The truck creaked to a halt and I heard Burt talking to one of the guards.

"We're going for another Impal pick up in Fredericksburg," he said, attempting to sound boastful. "Heard they netted about a hundred of them in an old house near the battlefield."

There were a few moments of muffled conversation then what I heard next made my blood run cold.

"Private Sanders, you check underneath the truck and I'll check the back!"

I could hear the sound of boots walking around the truck. A long dark silhouette twisted around the canvas as the soldier walked in front of the guard post spotlight. When he reached the back, the flap flew open and a head crowned with a Kevlar helmet protruded through the opening. His gaze fixed on me. I was about to attack when he turned his attention to the interior of the truck. The soldier unceremoniously swept his flashlight beam back and forth a couple of times before withdrawing. The ambient light from the spotlight caught the soldier's face for an instant. I could swear he winked at me.

"Nothing back here," he said. "Private, you find anything underneath?"

I could hear the sound of someone scampering to their feet then dusting their clothing.

"No sir, it's clear," the Private reported.

"Okay Captain Golden, you are free to pass. Good luck to you!" the unknown soldier said.

As the truck began to rumble forward, I pressed myself hard against the bed, not daring a peek. I didn't want to do anything to derail our good fortune. Unfortunately, it happened anyway. I estimate we were only twenty yards beyond the post when the unthinkable happened. Private Readnour, for some unknown reason, felt the need to get down in the bed of the truck with me. When he did, the batteries dropped out of his pocket with a clatter.

I don't think the soldiers could hear the noise over the diesel engine of the truck. Nevertheless, I knew they could see the shimmering light shining through the loose back flap. A moment later, I heard shouts and a couple of warning shots, and then the truck began to accelerate.

Grasping the bed of the truck desperately for purchase, I was thrown about a foot in the air when we ran over a large bump in the road. I screamed in agony, as every injury on my body seemed to flare at the same time. Intense pain paralyzed me, making it difficult to breathe. Even as pain overloaded my senses, I couldn't help feeling lucky. My travelling companion was not as fortunate.

Private Readnour was a victim of his own stupidity and perhaps dumb luck. For the most part, Impals can control their movement through solid objects. However, it takes a small amount of concentration. His panicked reflex to hide on the floor with me, coupled with the loss of his batteries, sent poor Private Readnour into a state of utter shock. When the truck bounced, he flew airborne like me. However, when he landed, he didn't land in the bed of the truck. He went straight through it and landed on the pavement beneath. A couple of his batteries bounced off the bed after he passed through it.

Despite my pain, I managed to pull myself up and pull back the flap. Private Readnour was on his hands and knees in the middle of the road a short distance behind. As we rounded a corner in the road, my heart stopped as a pair of headlights appeared on the other side of the private. They didn't have time to stop. Tires squalled as the Jeep passed through the Impal and skidded sideways before coming to rest on its side.

It is a good bet the occupants of the jeep were injured, how severe I did not know. The one thing I was sure about was nobody died because the only shimmering form in the vicinity was Private Readnour. He stood in the road for a few moments, staring at the wreck, then turned and bolted full speed into the woods. I hoped he made it and I said a silent prayer for him. In spite of what he did to me, he didn't deserve what would happen if he got caught . . . nobody did.

To my relief no other vehicles pursued. Ten minutes later, we pulled off the highway onto an overgrown path, which once served as an old logging road. When we were out of sight of the highway, Burt stopped the truck and he and Sam got out and came to the back.

"All right, change of plans," Burt said throwing open the flap. "I don't know what the hell happened. We were made. They'll have MP's and the Virginia State Police out searching for us." He paused for a moment and pointed at us with his index finger as if he were counting heads.

"Wait a minute, weren't there three back here?" he asked.

I told him the story of what happened to Private Dansby. Burt shook his head with solemn respect. In contrast, Sam's face flashed extreme anger and satisfaction. He remained silent even though he might as well have commented, "Good, he got what he deserved."

I glanced back at Staff Sergeant Beeson for the first time since the ordeal. He sat in utter silence in the corner near the cab. His expression suggested he might be sick at any moment.

"Come on sergeant," Burt said. "We've got more traveling to do."

To his credit, he managed to hang onto his batteries. He seemed as solid as the rest of us, until his right hand accidentally sank through the tailgate as he climbed out. I suppressed a shudder. As much as I believed in the rights of Impals, it was hard for me to get used to their physical characteristics. In a way, it made me feel like a hypocrite or even sometimes a racist. Although I am not certain the latter term applies to this situation. The Impals weren't a different race, were they? I guess the answer to that question lies in a person's individual belief of what it means to be human. Flesh and blood does not make a human any more than a milk carton makes milk. Unfortunately, the Supreme Court, in all its wisdom, disagrees.

"Readnour was a good man," Beeson muttered, shuffling the batteries in his pocket.

"Good at brutality," I thought.

Sam turned in disgust and started walking towards the road. Burt and I followed with Beeson close behind. For the first time since I had been outside, I realized how oppressive the heat and humidity were. Mid-September in Virginia is rarely pleasant, and tonight was exceptionally uncomfortable. I reached in my pocket and retrieved a handkerchief then began dabbing my head and neck as we walked and listened to Burt's plan.

It was simple; he was going to call someone to come pick us up, which would require at least an hour of lying low and hiding in the bushes. Of all the other troubles facing us, the first thing I thought of was snakes and then poison ivy.

We found a small thicket to the side of the road where we would be well hidden with a good view of the road. The freakish ultraviolet light emitting from the night sky provided as much light as a full Moon. I was reasonably certain I wasn't about to step on any snakes. Burt sat down on a fallen tree and pulled a cell phone out of his pocket. He hit a few buttons then held the phone to his ear, within a few rings someone answered.

"We got four bags of groceries and don't have enough money, can you help us out?" Burt asked. He paused for a few moments as the person responded. "That's great, that's great," he continued. "Send the check to the address on file." He then hung up, pressed a button on the phone and placed it back in his pocket.

"Well, gentlemen," he said. "I suggest you get comfy because it's going to be a little while."

"Who did you call and what were the groceries?" I asked.

Burt winked at me. "That, my friend, was the leader of our little resistance and I couldn't very well say, *hey, come pickup me, my two friends and an Impal*, could I?"

"What is the address on file? Did you make arrangements for us to be extracted from here?" I asked.

"Not in my wildest dreams," Burt said. "I didn't expect anyone to figure out you were missing for at least a couple more hours . . . by then we would have been safely back to base."

Burt took a breath to continue before Sam interrupted.

"Then that stupid Impal screwed everything up. I told you we should have left them there!" he snapped.

The comment offended Sergeant Beeson. He got up and walked a short distance away with his back to us. Burt held up a hand to his subordinate in a gesture suggesting he understood his aggravation, however now was not the time to express it. Sam scowled and fell silent with his arms crossed over his chest.

"Back to your question," Burt continued, "the address on file is the tracker on my phone, a simple app which is on millions of smartphones. It locates the phone by pings off the cell tower."

"Huh, and I figured you would have some high tech military GPS," I prodded.

"Are you kidding?" Burt asked in disbelief. "Anyone in the government or military would be able to track us with those!"

"Yes, I'm kidding," I said with mock exasperation. "So, how long have you been with this resistance?"

"Three weeks," Burt said.

"And I'm just now hearing about it?"

Burt cleared his throat and stroked his chin as he decided how to couch his answer.

"Well, Cecil . . . you've been a little out of pocket lately. With your trip to Arizona and the time you spent interviewing the Pendleton guy . . . we haven't had much of a chance to talk."

"Who your father is didn't help things either," Sam offered. "Quite frankly, we didn't know if we could trust you."

The lieutenant's words stung, yet I knew they were the truth. If I was in their position, I wouldn't trust me either. Burt started to reprimand him for his brutal honesty until I held up my hand.

"No, it's okay, Burt," I said. "I completely understand. It's going to take me a long time to distance myself from my father. How did you know you could trust me now?"

Burt shook his head as if I asked the stupidest question in the world.

"Uh . . . because you got yourself thrown in jail and beat up for trying to rescue an Impal from the Shredder. Either you're completely trustworthy or completely insane."

I couldn't help laughing.

"Well, I think the jury is still out on the insane part," I said.

I put the humor aside; there were more serious issues to address.

"You said you were 'way ahead of me' when I asked you about my family, Burt . . . where are they? Are Barbara and the girls safe?"

"Fine," Burt said. "Barbara is at the base where we are headed. I had her moved there earlier today when I heard about your rescue stunt."

"The girls . . . Abby and Stefanie . . . are my daughters all right?" I asked. It worried me that he did not mention them. Abby was capable of taking care of herself. She is in her first year of college. Steff wouldn't even be a teenager for another year. Steff was smart, but she possessed the maturity level of a second grader. She required a little special supervision sometimes.

"Yes, I'm sorry," Burt apologized. "I didn't mean to imply otherwise. I talked to Barbara. She told me she would take the girls and go."

"And . . . you confirmed she was there?" I asked, my stomach starting to twist in knots.

"Absolutely," Burt said. "Right before we broke you out of jail."

"Did she say anything about the girls?"

"No," Burt said, scratching his chin. "You and I both know she wouldn't go without them."

I knew he was right, except it didn't make me feel better. I wouldn't feel better until I held them in my arms again. I hoped that moment would be coming very soon.

"Who was the soldier that let us pass through the gate?" I asked.

"Lieutenant Zach Gomez, a good friend and an ally," Burt said with a worried frown. "I hope he's okay . . . I hope they don't suspect him for letting us through and I really hope he wasn't in the jeep." He sighed and folded his arms. "He was supposed to defect first thing in the morning and join us at the base."

"Defect . . . sounds like an old Cold War term," I observed.

"Is our government any better than the old Soviet Union?" Burt asked.

I shrugged.

"In many ways, I think what they are doing is worse," Burt said quietly.

He was not quiet enough to avoid being overheard by Sam as he continued his highway vigil across the clearing.

"Amen!" he called in a hushed shout.

After several minutes of alone time, Sergeant Beeson finally returned to our huddle. Sam gave him a cutting look, which I found disturbing me. I wasn't sure if his resentment toward the Impal was because he assaulted me or if it was more deep-seated. Someone with his attitude could be very detrimental to our cause. I trusted Burt and Burt trusts him, so for the time being I would give him the benefit of the doubt.

For the next hour, Beeson talked with Burt and me. Sam seemed completely disinterested in conversation. He stood up and moved into the tree line closest to the highway after the second state trooper blazed past with their lights flashing. The blue lights cast weird, undulating reflections on the ultraviolet night sky. Considering where we were in relation to civilization, they could only have been searching for us.

Beeson's Impal side turned out to be a stark contrast to his flesh-and-blood persona. He was polite with a rather dry sense of humor.

"I've got your back through thick and thin," he said, poking the index finger of his right hand all the way through his left palm. I guess it was his way of demonstrating thick and thin. However, it came out as disgusting and creepy.

We were so engrossed in conversation; I almost forgot we were hiding out in a thicket. I was rudely reminded when a voice behind us boomed out, causing my heart to leap into my throat. Dread flooded into my stomach like a noxious liquid as the words of the unseen person sank in.

"Nobody move! You are surrounded!"

CHAPTER 4

THE RESCUE PARTY

*"And the LORD God said unto the serpent, Because
thou hast done this, thou art cursed above all cattle, and
above every beast of the field; upon thy belly shalt thou
go, and dust shalt thou eat all the days of thy life: And
I will put enmity between thee and the woman, and
between thy seed and her seed; it shall bruise thy head,
and thou shalt bruise his heel."*
~Genesis 3:14–15

SEVERAL THOUGHTS RAN THROUGH MY HEAD in the span of a few seconds.
Run, fight, bargain, surrender; all seemed like viable choices for a frac-
tion of a second. I was about to choose one when Burt stood up.

"About time you jerks got here!" Burt boomed. "These damned
mosquitos are eating me alive!"

I heard several footsteps behind me. I slowly stood up, and turned
in their direction. I expected to see a small squadron of soldiers
approaching. Instead of soldiers, I saw what appeared to be civilians.
Four men approached, each wearing blue jeans and an inconspicuous
shirt. They all carried rifles.

The leader of the small band wore a plaid shirt, untucked with
the sleeves rolled up past his elbows. A solid black baseball cap sat

crooked on his head. He wore a large, illuminated watch on his left wrist. He pushed a button to extinguish the light before stepping forward. Before the light went out, I caught a quick glimpse of something drawn on his hat. It was only a couple of inches long and appeared to be painted on with white paint or liquid paper. The resemblance to the symbol, which Burt drew on the jail wall, was uncanny.

"What the hell kind of trouble have you gotten yourself into now, Burt?" he said with mock exasperation.

"Oh, you know, the usual. Ran a jailbreak, killed two guards, brought their ghosts with me then lost one of them. All in a day's work."

Sam walked back over to join us and the leader studied each one of us carefully. After several long moments of scrutiny, his gaze fell back to Beeson.

"You're the Impal, aren't you?" he asked in a soft voice.

"How did you know?" Beeson stammered, checking to see if the batteries were still in his pocket.

The leader touched a finger to his nose and gave a wry smirk.

"I have an Impal sense," he said in a cryptic tone as if he was about to reveal the secrets of the universe.

Beeson and I stared at him in disbelief. A few seconds later, everybody burst into laughter. I started to laugh too, not wanting to be left out of the inside joke. I quickly stopped when my ribs and nose reminded me of my injuries.

"No, I know Burton, and Uncle Sam over here, and you," he said pointing at me. "I know who you are, Ott Jr."

"Don't call me that," I said as I felt my cheeks flush red with anger. "My name is Cecil; I have nothing to do with my father."

He studied me for several seconds through narrowed eyes before extending his hand.

"I *was* Colonel Daniel Bradley. Now you can call me Danny or Bradley . . . either works for me," he said. "May I call you Cecil, Major Garrison?"

"Absolutely," I said. "Just don't call me Ott Jr. again."

"And lay off the Burton, Danny. You know I can't stand that," Burt said as he strode over and shook Danny's hand. He cocked his thumb back at Sam. "I'm pretty sure he doesn't care for the Uncle Sam either. Right, Sam?"

"You're damn right," Sam barked, a little too hostile for the mood.

Danny blinked at Sam with impassive curiosity, and then turned his attention back to me.

"Cecil, I would like you to meet my associates," he said turning to the person on the right as they stepped forward. He wore a similar plaid shirt with rolled up sleeves. Instead of a cap, he wore a red bandana.

"This is Taylor Farris," he said. "He is a civilian. I've never met anyone so brave and loyal and a true patriot."

Taylor and I shook hands and exchanged pleasantries.

"I guess we're all pretty much civilians now," he said. "In any case, thank you for your service to our country. It seems you took one hell of a beating."

I acknowledged his thanks and shrugged off his second remark.

The two individuals on his left wore T-shirts in contrast to their plaid companions. The first one stepped forward. I could see he was wearing a dark-green cap turned around backwards and a green T-shirt. A screen print of skulls arranged into an interesting rose garden pattern decorated the shirt. He introduced himself as "civilian first class" Derek Vandeputte.

His counterpart then stepped forward, wearing a plain white T-shirt and blue bandana on their head. I expected to meet another guy. I was surprised when the individual stepped into the light and spoke. There was no doubt I was addressing an attractive black woman.

"I'm Charlotte McVey," she said, shaking my hand. "I am military, but I am just a paper pusher in a general's office in Richmond . . . no bigee."

"Thank you for your service to our country, Charlotte," I said.

Her mouth gaped open in shock. She acted as if this was the first time anyone ever paid her respect. She blushed and then stepped back a few feet behind Derek.

"Okay, don't tell me you guys walked all the way here," Burt said. "What gives?"

"Transportation is about five klicks that way," Danny said. He turned around and pointed to the northwest.

"Someone want to remind us civilians of what the heck a klick is?" Derek asked.

"A klick is about one-kilometer," Danny said, "so five kilometers in that direction."

"Someone want to remind us of how far a kilometer is? This is America and the last I checked we deal with miles here," Charlotte huffed.

"One kilometer is about .62 miles," Danny said with exasperation. "You kids need to take notes so I don't have to keep repeating myself. I hope you can do the math."

"A little over three miles," Taylor muttered.

He sounded frustrated and I'm sure he was. He was a civilian and he seemed the oldest and most mature aside from Colonel Bradley. While Charlotte was military, she had very little field experience and was more or less still a kid. Her comrade, Derek, had no field or military experience and was likely the youngest one in the bunch. Acne and high school were probably less than two years in his past.

This was going to be an interesting hike back to the vehicle. At least everyone in my group is trained military, including our Impal Sergeant. We started with the complaints of the two young ones having to walk another three miles. This bickering continued until we reached the far side of the clearing and under the canopy of the woods again. Danny turned on them.

"Listen up you two snots!" He growled. "I didn't hear you gripe a single time on the way here! Suck it up, keep your eyes and ears open and above all else . . . SHUT THE HELL UP!"

They fell silent and glared at the colonel who now looked his age as veins pulsated on his temples and forehead. After a few long moments, he took a deep breath and finished. "If you don't, you can both walk all the way back to base . . . all one hundred twenty-five klicks. I'll let y'all workout the math; it'll give you something to think about the next three miles."

He turned and marched out in front of the group with great purpose and anger. We walked in silence for a long while. There were no sounds other than the crunch of brush and leaves underfoot. The hoot of an owl offered an occasional distraction. The tension was palpable the whole journey. Every time a siren ripped through the night air, it caused a noticeable slowing of our pace and an even greater slowing of breathing. The crunching under our feet was like walking on eggshells as we trudged forward.

We must have been about five minutes from our destination when I noticed a strange, ethereal light. I turned and saw a faint glimmer from my left-hand side. Sergeant Beeson glowed like a dying light bulb. His batteries were almost expired. When that happened, his glow would intensify giving away his identity as an Impal and our position in the woods. I guess batteries did have a limit with Impals. No telling how long those batteries had corroded in the flashlight.

"Anybody got a flashlight or anything with batteries in it?" I asked in panic, pointing at Beeson.

They all stared at me incredulously for several moments until understanding started to sink in.

"No crap, batteries makes 'em seem normal? I'll be damned," Derek said.

Taylor, who remained silent most of the journey, reached behind him and retrieved a large Mag Lite flashlight from his belt. He unscrewed the cap and dropped the batteries into the sergeant's hand.

"Here, Sarge," he said.

Beeson extended his hand. The second the batteries dropped into his palm, the glow was gone. I chuckled when I considered that Impals would give the Energizer Bunny a run for his money as a spokesperson.

A few minutes later, we reached the truck. I expected another military truck like the one we abandoned. I was pleasantly surprised when I saw a large luxury SUV. We each got a seat in the gargantuan vehicle, well, almost all of us.

The roomy interior would seat seven people in comfort; however we were a party of eight. So . . . Sergeant Beeson was relegated to the cargo hatch. I felt ashamed of the terrible discrimination going on in the world against the Impals. The similarities with the Civil Rights movement were undeniable. Sergeant Beeson may as well have been Sergeant Rosa Parks.

The trip turned out to be uneventful. I rode it out with an empty knot in my stomach and thoughts of seeing my wife and girls again.

After an hour-long zigzagging, back road tour of rural Virginia, we made it to our destination. Under normal circumstances, it would have taken about thirty minutes. I wasn't sure exactly where we were. I guessed we were somewhere between Culpepper and Charlottesville. A fifty-mile stretch of woods and mountains with a plethora of potential hiding places. I was sure there was also an abundance of critters, including snakes. Not many things frighten me, but snakes paralyze me.

When I was twelve years old, I went on a church retreat with a bunch of other kids. I can't remember the name of the park. It was on a large lake surrounded by campgrounds and cabins. One afternoon, me and a few other kids went out exploring in individual canoes. I paddled to the farthest cove; imagining I was the first person to go there in centuries. I think I actually expected to find the ruins of an ancient civilization. I would be a hero. My fantasy vanished in an instant.

All I found was a shallow inlet full of marsh grass and a nest of water moccasins. There must have been twenty of them, large and small, as they writhed and slithered through the water in a determined attempt to get in my canoe. I yelled and thrashed at the water with my paddle, trying to fend them off, but there were too many. By the time I managed to paddle a safe distance away, three of them slithered in the canoe, hissing like angry worms. I managed to smash two of them in the head with my paddle, before the third one got me on the calf. I screamed in pain as I kicked upward. The snake's fangs still dug into my flesh and his body snapped like a whip as he tore free of me and flew into the water.

All I knew to do was to remove my camp T-shirt and tie it above the bite and then try to remain as calm as I could as I paddled back to our camp. Tears blinded my eyes and I wasn't even certain I was headed in the right direction. I turned to look at the bodies of the deceased snakes and my heart jumped into my throat as one of them twitched. It was only a death spasm, a posthumous nervous impulse. I didn't know that.

I screamed and swung the oar at the dead snake. When I did, I brought the edge of it down like an axe. My fear and adrenaline caused a momentary burst in strength. I broke the oar and I also fractured the fiberglass bottom of the canoe. Water started to seep in through the crack that seemed to grow larger every time I moved. I yelled and began paddling with my hands as the water, which was now an inch deep, sloshed one of the snake's bodies over my calf. I screamed, kicked, and paddled harder. That was the last I remember until I came to and our youth minister was loading me in the back of his car to take me to the hospital. His tan face was ashen white and his eyes and mouth seemed drawn and gaunt with worry. I was sure that I was going to die.

Ever since then, I have been terrified of the slimy, slithering abominations. It didn't matter what kind. A snake was a snake as far as I am concerned. I survived the day and kept my leg. Otherwise, I would have never gotten in the military, not even with my father's influence. Even after the unimaginable horror, I think my father's visit to the hospital was the most troubling event of the day.

He came to the hospital a few hours after I was admitted. The first thing he did was pull up the sheet covering my swollen leg and then he began to laugh.

"Hmmmm, what did you do to get evil so riled against you, boy?" he said in a very judgmental tone.

I regarded my father stupidly, not certain if I understood him. Surely the venom dulled my hearing.

He reached down and poked my leg above the bite. Pain shot up my leg like fire. I was determined not to show any weakness in front of my father. He always taught me that the weak, those who do not carry out God's glory, are condemned to an eternity of hellfire. I imagined the pain now radiating up my leg covering my whole body for eternity. The thought terrified me as much as the snakes.

My father was and still is a Baptist, yet I think his eccentric attitude towards right and wrong goes far deeper. He grew up in the backwoods of West Virginia. His church was in an area where paranoia against anything or anyone different is the norm. In these rural areas, religion was often hardcore. He never spoke about his childhood. It would not surprise me if some of his church services involved a box of snakes.

I should have seen what kind of man my father was then, but I held him up on a pedestal. Now that I see him with my adult eyes, I realize pedestals aren't as high to us when we are grown. In fact, some of them are now quite small.

As we descended into the valley containing the resistance base, I felt fear bubbling up inside of me once again. A large lake, much like the one at my church camp, shimmered like a black light painting. It reflected the eerie night sky and full Moon. Soon, I found it hard to breathe, so I rolled down the window and took several deep breaths of summer air. The scent of the cedar and pines was refreshing as I closed my eyes and took it all in.

"You okay, Cecil?" Burt called from the front seat.

"Yeah, trying to get some air. I think I might have a cracked rib or two," I lied.

I was still very sore, however I have experienced a few cracked ribs in my life and I knew mine were fine. I wasn't going to tell the truth about my fear of snakes. I wondered how I ever made it through basic training. We did our share of woods and swamp hikes, yet somehow I was able to channel my apprehension. Perhaps it was the additional stress. My fatigue was allowing my old phobia to get the best of me. Although . . . I couldn't help feeling it was something more . . . perhaps a warning. A warning about *what* I wasn't sure. I had the terrible, ridiculous feeling this was a harbinger of something terrible.

I didn't dwell on this prospect long because a few moments later, my spirits lifted. As we rounded a corner and leveled out on the bottom of the valley, our headlights fell on a group of people. My heart leapt when I saw, waiting underneath a large sycamore tree, Barbara, Abby and Stephanie.

CHAPTER 5

THE MINE

"I stayed in a really old hotel last night. They sent me a wake-up letter."
~Steven Wright

I EMBRACED MY GIRLS FOR A LONG TIME. Steff was a little less enthusiastic than the other two; I guess it's not cool to hug your old man in public. There was little danger of her pals seeing her way out here in the boondocks. She didn't agree with my assessment. At least I got a hug from her, which was more than I managed most of the time.

"What did you do, Cecil?" Barbara asked with her hands pressed against both of my cheeks. "They came and got us without warning. We didn't even have time to pack anything much."

"I tried to help some Impals," I said. "I'm sorry I didn't plan it better."

I knew she was upset about the position I put the family in. I didn't realize how much until I saw the fear in her eyes. She knew how seeing my grandfather at the Impal camp in Arizona affected me. It was after I returned home when I learned of the Tesla Gates going online at different locations around the country.

Barbara kissed me on the cheek. "At least it wasn't Ott who came to get us," she whispered in my ear to where the girls couldn't hear.

Arizona was the first base to put it into action. A colleague of mine there confirmed my grandfather was one of the Shredder's first victims. I'm sure if I had known I would have gone back and tried to save him even though it would have been futile. If I did, I am sure I would not be here now and no telling where my family would be.

"Come on," Barbara said, "I'll show you our fancy digs."

We walked towards the lake as everyone else in the group said their good nights and went on their way. I waved to Sally, Burt's wife, as they disappeared, arm in arm, down a dark trail. I had the surreal feeling I now existed in some bizarre fairy tale at the mouth of the wood elves' lair. The ultraviolet sky enhanced the mystical ambience. The mystery of this place contributed too.

"Where are we?" I asked as Barbara and I walked hand-in-hand with the girls on either side of us carrying large flashlights.

"Brentwood Springs," Abby said.

"It's an old coal mining town," Steff interjected with enough disgust in her voice she might have said an old crap-mining town. "Love my new room . . . thanks Dad," she said, sarcasm dripping from her words.

Barbara turned and glared at her. It didn't seem to have any effect. Steff gave her an exaggerated apologetic smile. She then stared at her feet for the duration of our walk. It was not a submissive gesture; she didn't want to make eye contact.

I don't blame her for the way she felt and I was in no mood to reprimand her for disrespect. I let it go and addressed Barbara with a playful, curious tone.

"So, are we bunking with the seven dwarfs?" I asked.

"Hardly," Barbara said with giggle. "Maybe the seven rats . . . Steff is right, it's not the best place in the world, but at least we are together and safe."

Steff huffed and kept her eyes down.

"It's not bad, dad," Abby said. "I've been to Girl Scout retreats with cabins much worse."

"So, no amenities at all?" I asked.

"See for yourself," Barbara said as Abby shone the flashlight beam in front of us.

The girls didn't exaggerate. The place looked like a bunch of sheets of plywood tacked together with a roof thrown on as an after-thought. The roughly hewn front door rested off center between two small black windows. I couldn't tell if the window openings contained glass panes or were empty holes. In any case, the place was not very inviting except to maybe a member of the Sawyer family, the chainsaw wielding clan from Texas. I forced a smile and squeezed Barbara's hand.

"Home sweet home," I said.

It was obvious from the absence of light that electricity was not present in this old mining village. Whether or not my resistance allies brought any generators I did not know. I guess it made sense because we were hiding out from the military and electric lights would make us easy to spot.

The door creaked like it would fall off its hinges as we entered the small cabin. Dust rained down like brown snow. I saw something move out of the corner of my eye and much to my relief it was a mouse. There were no furnishings inside except for four camping cots, an ice chest and a gas lantern. The clean, new cots with fresh sleeping bags seemed completely out of place in the dusty, musty interior. I considered the bright side; it was preferable to a tiny prison cell. I was free and my family was with me. I counted my blessings and stepped inside. Taking the flashlight from Abby I walked around the small room, inspecting for more vermin and for any easy access points. I spotted a small hole in the far corner opening under the house. I found a discarded flag-stone, which someone tried to cook on it ages ago. It was the right size so I slid it over the hole. I turned around to see Steff watching me with folded arms and a smirk.

"There are snakes," she said. "I would stay out of the outhouse if I was you . . . oh, and we're pretty close to the lake here."

Abby grabbed her hand and pulled her towards the pair of cots on the opposite side of the room.

"Come on Steff, you need some sleep," she said, pulling the deliberate dead weight of her little sister.

Steff plopped down on her cot with a huff and turned her back to us. Abby gave me a faint smile. Her sister's attitude embarrassed her.

"I haven't seen any snakes, Dad," she said. "I wouldn't use the outhouse because it is about to fall in and well . . . there isn't much of a hole anymore."

Necessary body functions were the last thing on my mind. Now it seems they would soon be foremost on my worry list.

"Thanks, sweetheart," I said. "Pleasant dreams."

"Love you Dad," she said before lying on her cot.

"Love you girls," I said. As expected, I got no response from Steff.

I sat down on my cot on the opposite side of the room. I watched my daughters until Abby turned off the flashlight, plunging them into darkness. Barbara sat down beside me and wrapped her arm around my shoulders.

"She'll get over it," she whispered. "She's going through one of those stupid stages."

Barbara took Steff's flashlight and rested it across our laps; the beam shown into the corner of the room a few feet away. A brilliant array of spider webs reflected the light making them sparkle like strings of crystal. The ambient light shown upwards and highlighted Barbara's strong chin and wavy dark hair. It was too dark to see the brilliant color of her hazel green eyes, still, I could clearly make out her form. She gained a few pounds over the years, yet still managed to keep her sexy feminine shape.

I am indeed lucky to be in my forties and have a wife who is still a head turner. Burt's wife was a sweet, sweet woman, but she resembled a Weeble with her oval shaped form. I shared this thought with no one. I felt guilty for making such a cruel comparison with such a nice woman. The damned Weebles pitch song from the 1970s resurfaced in my head every time I saw her. *Weebles wobble but they don't fall down.*

"I know, I don't blame her for being upset," I said. "I'm sorry I got y'all caught up in this."

She grabbed my chin and turned my head towards her then planted a big kiss on my lips. When she pulled back, she left her hand under my chin and gazed deep into my eyes.

"You are doing the right thing," she insisted.

I saw the love and the sadness in her eyes; I felt guilty. She had lost someone too.

Barbara's mother passed away a couple of years after we married. She was a widow the last ten years of her life and lived alone in a small farmhouse outside of Hagerstown, Maryland. Two days after the storm arrived, Barbara got a call from the Yarnells. They were the people who purchased her mother's house after her death.

"Your mother is here," a terrified voice said on the other end of the line. "Please come and get her." They hung up and refused to answer when Barbara tried to call them back. By the time she was able to drive to Hagerstown the Yarnells were gone and so was her mother. We heard rumors that she was captured by the military. We were never able to confirm this.

"I love you," I said and kissed her on the cheek.

We both almost jumped out of our skin when a loud knocking echoed through the cabin; someone was at the door.

"Cecil, it's me, Burt . . . you decent?" said the hushed voice of my friend on the other side of the door.

I took the flashlight and walked to the door, opening it a crack. I shone the light in the opening. Burt squinted back at me.

"You trying to attract every bug in a three county radius?" he said, shielding his eyes with his hand.

"Sorry," I said and lowered the light. "What's up?"

"If you're settled in, I have something I want to show you."

Barbara shrugged. "We'll be right here," she said, patting the cot. "Leave me the light." She paused for a moment, "You do have one, don't you Burt?"

"How do you think I got here?" he asked with a huff.

Barbara loved messing with Burt because he often didn't get her sense of humor. Handing her the light, I stepped out the door and closed it behind me. Burt motioned for me to follow with a couple of quick jerks of his light then we set out down an overgrown trail behind my cabin. I wished I controled the light because he didn't keep the beam low enough for my taste.

The heavy canopy of trees surrounding our cabin did not allow any light in. We could not see anything outside the range of our flashlight. I could hear very well though, and I heard the unmistakable sound of water lapping gently on the shore to our left. We were close, too close;

I took a deep breath and focused my eyes on the forest floor in front of us.

"Okay, Burt . . . you want to tell me where we are going? It's getting kinda late," I finished with a yawn.

"You always were a sissy at parties," Burt said. "Always asleep on the sofa by ten o'clock."

I glanced at my watch to verify, however I forgot it was confiscated at the prison. There was too much on my mind to remember to retrieve it as we broke out.

"Yeah, it's a lot later than ten," Burt confirmed, noticing my futile motion. "Trust me; this is worth staying up for."

I was anxious to get back to my family, yet I wasn't keen on getting back to our dusty rattrap of a cabin. I knew this was going to be our home for the foreseeable future. It still didn't mean I had to like it. At least my wife and daughters were there. Their presence made it bearable. I would live over a pit of snakes if that were what it took to be with them.

"All right, buddy . . . whatever you say," I said. "What's the joke?"

"No joke," he assured me.

A few moments later, we came to an abrupt stop. Burt turned and beamed at me like a kid who was about to present his award-winning art project to his parents.

"Okay, step to the side," he said, motioning to his right with the flashlight. "Now give me a hand here," he said grabbing at a pile of brush and limbs in front of us.

It was so dark it seemed the only things in the world were this suspicious brush pile and us. I obliged Burt as I grabbed a handful of pine branches and hoisted them to the side. After several moments of clearing I was no more enlightened than I was before, all I could see was more darkness in front of us. When Burt shone the light where the brush pile had been, I noticed something very unusual. It was as if the darkness somehow reflected the light back at us.

Burt stepped forward and stuck out his right arm. He moved it in a motion as if he were drawing a curtain. I heard the sound of rustling material, like canvas. A moment later, my eyes adjusted. I could see he moved aside one corner of a massive tarp. It was at least fifteen feet wide and extended upward about ten feet before disappearing into the blackness. I saw only darkness behind it.

"What the hell?" I whispered in awe.

"Wait," Burt said. "We aren't in yet."

He stepped inside the tarp and motioned for me to follow. Once in, he let the corner fall back to its original position. It soon became obvious we were in an enclosed space. Every breath, every step seemed to echo as if we were in close quarters.

"Burt . . . I'm getting a little freaked out now," I said. "Where the hell are we?" He might as well have taunted me by singing, "*I know something you don't know.*"

"One more tarp!" he whispered. His whisper was almost as bad as a shout in our cramped environment.

He walked a few steps ahead and then bent down and grabbed what appeared to be the corner of another tarp.

"Ready?" he said with almost giddy excitement.

I shrugged; I was as ready as I was going to be.

When Burt switched his flashlight off I experienced a moment of panic. However, the panic did not have time to sink in before another sight froze me in place as he withdrew the tarp. What I saw blinded me.

CHAPTER 6

VIRGINIANS

"Words do not pay for my dead people."
~Chief Joseph

THE BRIGHTNESS WAS BLINDING to my light deprived eyes, but that was not what struck me with awe. We were in a subterranean passageway full of hundreds of Impals. Most of them did not notice our presence as they stood, laid or sat about. The ones lying or sitting were doing so on one of the small cots lining each side of the passage. I always pictured a mine tunnel as being a small passage with a single track. Mine cars hauling out the commodity harvest in never-ending succession. This was different.

We were in a large room, twenty to thirty feet wide and about fifteen feet high. The chamber seemed to narrow the further back it went until it was almost a V-shape. At the tip of the 'V' I could see the beginning of a stereotypical mine tunnel where several more Impals resided.

The few Impals who noticed us gave us a mixed reception. Some smiled and waved, while others ignored us. I felt as if we were in the presence of living history and I guess, in a sense, we were. The Impals inhabiting the mine ranged from dress styles of Colonial times to the present day. I even noticed a few American Indians in the group.

Their presence could potentially expand the historical timeline much further. The group was an even mix of men, women and children. I couldn't help thinking of Seth Pendleton when I saw a group of little boys about his age sitting nearby.

"My God, this is incredible!" I stammered.

"I told you, didn't I?" Burt said.

"So, all the Impals are living in the mines?" I asked.

"Yep," Burt said.

"Why?"

If I could take the time to think it out, the reason would have been obvious. My brain was too tired.

Burt folded his arms and seemed a little disappointed. He sighed and gave me a textbook answer. "Well . . . the Impals can be a little bright, especially at nighttime, so hiding them in here made the most sense. We put the two layers of tarp in so you could enter and close the first one before entering the second one, thereby not letting light out."

"How did you pull this together so quickly?" I asked.

"It wasn't that quick. We started prepping this place two weeks ago and started moving the Impals in last week. Before then, they hid out like a bunch of outlaws. The poor folks were scattered all over the countryside. Some took refuge in basements, back rooms, caves and about any hole they could find. This place was easy. We brought a bunch of cots in, a couple of dozen buckets and bulk food items like cheese, crackers and canned meats."

I was familiar with the Impals' desire to eat. There didn't seem to be any physiological need for it, yet they craved it all the same. I figured the buckets were probably for the end result.

A single little girl, sitting on a cot about twenty feet away, found it very amusing. She could have stepped out of an episode of *Little House on the Prairie*.

"My momma calls these squenching buckets!" she giggled, pointing at a stack of buckets in the corner.

I have never heard anyone use the term other than Thomas Pendleton. I wondered if this was someone who crossed paths with him and Seth. Curiosity got the best of me. I walked over to the little girl and knelt down.

"What's your name, honey?" I asked.

She stopped giggling and studied my face for several moments.

"Rebecca . . . Rebecca Fiddler," she said in a sweet tinny voice

"Where's your mom and dad?" I asked.

She pointed to a woman in similar nineteenth-century apparel. The woman held her hand over one of the buckets, dropping something out of her palm resembling breadcrumbs. A moment later, she walked toward us.

"Hello . . . Mrs. Fiddler?" I asked, extending my hand.

My hand felt like ice as she grasped my fingers. I did a good job suppressing my discomfort. Touching an Impal has always been akin to jumping in a cold lake. You know the water is cold, you know the moment is coming, but nothing ever prepares you for the shock of the initial plunge.

"Yes I am . . . and you are?" she said with gracious Southern charm in her voice. She reminded me of Scarlett O'Hara speaking into a tin can.

"My name is Cecil Garrison, ma'am. I would like to ask you a question if I may."

She shrugged and then sat down next to Rebecca on the cot.

"Did you come up with the term, squenching?" I asked. I felt a flush of embarrassment for asking.

Even though Impals can't blush like flesh-and-blood people, a sheepish smile washed over her face. Her eyes fell to her lap. As she began to speak, I believe I saw a noticeable bloom in her glowing features.

"I don't know . . . maybe," she said.

"Did you ever run across a man named Thomas Pendleton and his son, Seth?" I asked.

She blinked with surprise. "Why, yes . . . a little over a month ago we enjoyed a picnic with them . . . back in Arkansas," she said, and then her eyes widened with fear. "Are they okay?" she gasped.

I glanced at Rebecca who was watching us with great interest. Therefore, I decided to lie.

"Well, yes . . . I believe so," I stammered. I was never very good at lying, especially doing it on the spot. "Saw them not too long ago."

Rebecca seemed to buy my bogus story as she rolled over on

her stomach on top of the cot and began to sing a soft lullaby as she clutched her pillow like a doll. I'm sure it was a beautiful and innocuous song in her day. It sent a chill up my spine. I guess my affinity for horror movies coupled with the reality of my present company got the best of me for a moment. I jumped as I felt cold encircle my hand; I looked down to see Mrs. Fiddler grasping my hand and beckoning me to follow. She was not as gullible as her daughter. When we walked a few feet away, she stopped and regarded me with stubborn resolve and terror swimming in her luminous eyes.

"What happened?" she asked.

I glanced at Rebecca and then back to Mrs. Fiddler. I knew I needed to answer her, however I needed to ask a question of my own first.

"Where is the rest of your family?" I asked.

I immediately wished I hadn't asked. The balance in her eyes of stubborn resolve and terror shifted. My throat tightened into a knot as large silvery tears began to stream down her cheeks.

"We . . . my husband and my son . . . we got separated this side of Memphis. I think the Army took them away. We were trying to find my oldest son, Nathan. We wanted to see if he stayed behind like we did . . . that's all we were doing," she sniffed then quickly turned her head away. I noticed Rebecca was watching us again.

"I'm sorry," I said, patting her upper arm. "I'm sure they are fine."

I saw the balance in her eyes shift back to stubborn resolve. "I heard about the Shredder, Mr. Garrison," she said. "I don't think any of us who get captured will be all right, do you?"

I didn't want to lie to her and I didn't want to tell her the truth of my opinion. The truth was, her son and husband had probably already entered the Tesla Gate, just like Thomas and Seth. I said nothing and stared at the floor.

"Is that what happened to Thomas and Seth?" she asked.

I didn't answer for a long time. Finally, I told her the truth.

She turned and walked away through the crowd of Impals, leaving me with a curious little girl. She stared up at me with growing suspicion. "What's wrong with my mother?" she snapped.

"Nothing sweetheart, she is okay. Give her a minute," I said with as much assurance as I could muster. It wasn't enough.

I don't think she believed me because she got up with a scowl and ran after her mother. Turning, I saw Burt standing a few feet away smiling and shaking his head.

"We are doing the right thing helping these folks," he said. "You can't get emotionally involved on a personal level. Every single one of them has got a sad story to tell and it will eat you up if you stop to listen to all of them." He pulled me closer and whispered. "We are their rescuers, not their shrinks."

Burt was right. Nevertheless, it was hard not to listen and care, not for anybody with half a heart. It made it even more difficult when an Impal was as compelling as the one I was about to encounter. I felt a cold tap on my shoulder and turned to see a tall, imposing Native American man watching at me expectantly. His raven hair cascaded over his shoulders, framing his wise and aged face. He was bare chested and wore a garment around his waist resembling a buckskin kilt. An unusual beaded necklace hung around his neck.

"Have you seen my daughter?" he asked.

I was overcome by a sudden feeling of déjà vu. Strangely, it was much more bizarre than experiencing something I have already seen. The man spoke with a commanding tone in spite of his Impal timbre. He also spoke in his native tongue. The crazy thing was, I could understand him. I never heard this language before, yet I could understand it as clearly as if he were speaking English. When I recovered from the shock, I answered.

"No, I don't think so. What's her name?"

"Matoaka," he answered, his eyes sad and distant.

I shook my head.

"No. I'll let you know if I do. What is your name?"

"Wahunsunacawh," he said with deep appreciation.

I was not going to try to pronounce it, at least not on front of him. I felt it might be insulting if I screwed it up. Instead, I patted him on his cold and shimmering arm.

"I'll let you know, I promise," I said.

He bowed his head with deep appreciation then turned and walked back to a group of Native American Impals nearby. They all seemed to regard him with a great deal of reverence. I turned to see Burt smiling at me and winked.

"Did you have a good talk?" he asked.

"I guess, why . . . who was that?" I asked.

"You don't know?" Burt chided.

"Should I?" I asked, a little annoyed.

Burt shrugged.

"I met him a couple of days ago, took me a while to figure it out myself."

"He was wandering around the Mattaponi Reservation near King William County since the storm started," Burt said. "The government does a much better job of keeping their hands off of reservations than anything else. The people there knew it was only a matter of time before that trust was broken. The living residents of the reservation helped sneak him and a few other Indian Impals here."

"Okay . . ." I said. "It still doesn't tell me anything."

Burt motioned for me to follow and we headed back towards the entrance of the mine. I suddenly realized how tired I felt. In any case, my fatigue didn't dampen my curiosity to know the man's identity.

"It's weird how you can understand him even though you shouldn't be able to, isn't it?" Burt said.

"It sure is."

"I think it's the same with all Impals, they kind of have some sort of universal translator I guess. There's a French guy in here." He said motioning back over his shoulder as we walked. "I talked to him the other day and completely understood everything he said, even though I knew he was speaking French." Burt chuckled to himself. "I made a D in French when I was in high school."

"Okay . . . so who was he?" I asked as we approached the tarp.

Burt stopped and turned as he pulled up the corner of the tarp. He motioned me through and I stepped inside. As the corner of the tarp fell, total darkness descended on us.

"You ever heard of Chief Powhatan?" Burt asked in the dark as he flicked his flashlight on.

I scanned my brain for recall on my basic American history, a moment later it clicked.

"Jamestown?" I said.

"Yep," Burt replied.

"Well, that would make his daughter . . ." I said, trailing off in amazement.

Burt finished my sentence for me.

"Pocahontas."

CHAPTER 7

THE EUROPEAN INITIATIVE

"Do not let spacious plans for a new world divert your energies from saving what is left of the old."
~Winston Churchill

"He called her Matoaka . . . and he said his name was Wahunsuna-cawh," I said, probably bungling the pronunciations.

"Right," Burt said as we stepped under the outer tarp and back into the dark, humid air of the woods. "Those were their real names, not what the English called them."

I wore a stupid expression in the ambient glow of the flashlight; history was not my forte in school.

"He was chief of the Powhatan people, hence the name Chief Powhatan," Burt explained.

I laughed.

"Isn't it like calling the president . . . President America?"

Burt shrugged as we continued our slow march through the woods. "There's a lot of things I would like to call that cowardly idiot," he muttered. "He's the whole reason we are out here."

"Him and my father," I added.

Even though it was dark, I could see the expression on Burt's face, as if he had just stuck his foot in his mouth.

"I didn't . . . you know," he stammered.

"It's okay," I said. "I think he ceased to be my father a long time ago. I put it behind me. He always believes he is doing the right thing, no matter how bizarre or hurtful. After many painful years I finally realized that his right and wrong and my right and wrong come from different places and arrive on different buses. He is a misguided asshole."

I shared this with sincerity in my heart; I meant it more than anything I have ever said. The problem was, there was one point I did not share with Burt, the one thing that made my job all the more difficult. Like him or not he was still my father and just as bad, he was my daughters' grandfather. It hurt like Hell.

We couldn't help sharing a laugh about him being a misguided asshole. The most humorous things in life often contain the most truth. The truth in the world now was darker than it had been in a long time and one of the best weapons against dark truths is laughter. Didn't Mark Twain once say that against the assault of laughter, nothing can stand? While history was not my strongest subject, English was. I couldn't help wondering if my favorite author, the scribbler from Hannibal, Missouri, might be around. If he was, I hoped he found a safe location like this one.

After getting back to the cabin, I found Barbara and the girls sound asleep. I lay down on my cot, careful not to disturb them, and stared into the darkness. It was so black I might as well have closed my eyes. The dark was my whole world for the moment, which was also an appropriate metaphor for the world's present state. Earth might be experiencing a miraculous event. Many would even say it was wondrous and joyous. However, humanity had once again shut its eyes out of fear. The ignorance of man turned a miracle into something despicable, something dark, and something terrible.

"My father's ignorance," I whispered.

I am not certain when I fell asleep. I awakened to see Abby leaning over me.

"Come on Dad," she said. "You're gonna miss breakfast."

The sun was streaming in through the window above her head, the lavender tint from the cosmic storm made her appear as if she wore a purple halo. Sitting up slowly from my cot, I surveyed my surroundings in the daylight. The cabin did not seem quite as foreboding in the light, it just looked filthier. Every speck of dirt, dust and rodent excrement was on brilliant display in the radiant lavender morning light. It was evident that a thorough cleaning was in order. This task would come later after breakfast and a walk-through of the camp. I had just swung my legs over the side of the cot when Abby pressed a cold towel to my nose.

"Your nose is swollen and it bled last night, dad," she said.

I winced in pain causing her to recoil. I forgot about my broken nose. My abrupt dismount from the bed not only reminded me of my nose, it also reminded me of the beating I endured last night.

"I'm sorry, honey; I didn't mean to scare you. I fell yesterday and it is still pretty tender."

She examined my nose with a frown. I could see tears start to well up in her eyes. I was thankful she could not see the cuts and bruises currently concealed by my clothing.

"Oh Daddy," she sobbed. "I didn't mean to hurt you."

"It's okay, Abbs," I said as I stood up and gave her a hug. She seemed as if she had grown in the past few days, her forehead was now even with my chin. She is about an inch taller than Barbara now.

I felt a lump in my throat as I lamented the loss of my little girl; she was now, for all intents and purposes, a young woman. I still didn't have any problem addressing her by the nickname she carried since she was old enough to walk. We were heading towards the door when I noticed something hanging around Abbs's neck glinting in the sunlight. I screwed up my weary eyes and it was as if a light bulb switched on in my head. Hanging around her neck was a familiar pendant. It was a golden 'S' about two inches high. The two ends of the 'S' were connected with a small piece of clear plastic tubing, roughly making the 'S' into an '8'.

"What is that?" I asked, pointing at the charm.

She grasped it in her hand at first then held it out for me to see.

"It's the infinity symbol dad," she said as if she couldn't believe I didn't recognize it. "It's the symbol people started using to represent the resistance . . . to represent what we are doing."

"Why?" I asked.

She stopped and stared at me with disbelief for several long moments. She then removed the chain from her neck. I guess I have been out of the loop. It seems everyone is familiar with this symbol except for me.

"All of our lives are eternal," she said, watching me for agreement.

I nodded.

Abbs held out the pendant in her left hand, then traced the golden 'S' with her right index finger.

"This part of eternity is our physical existence," she said. With her index finger, she traced the area with the clear plastic tubing. "This represents our spiritual existence," she said then traced the entire symbol with her finger. "Our physical and spiritual existence makes up our eternal life or infinity."

"So the solid part is us," I said, tapping my cheek with the palm of my hand. "And the Impals are the clear plastic tubing?"

"Well . . . yeah, I guess," Abbs said. "We are no different than the Impals, just at a different point on the symbol."

"That's cool, honey. Did you come up with it?" I asked.

"No, dad!" she said with an impatient huff. "Everybody's using it! It is called the Myriad."

"Why not infinity?" I asked.

Abbs shrugged. "Not sure. I think it's because it represents more than a single infinity, it's kinda like a multitude of infinites . . . you know, a multitude of people."

My head already ached this morning from yesterday's activities. The prospect of entering a deep philosophical discussion wasn't going to help matters. I understood the gist of what the symbol represented and Myriad sounded like as good a name as any. "Come on, Abbs . . . let's go get some breakfast, I'm starving." I said, smiling and wrapping my arm around her shoulders. She slipped the chain over her head as I held her long black hair up for her. I knew my nose wouldn't allow me to taste breakfast very well, yet it didn't change the fact that I was famished.

"Where are your mom and sister?" I asked, noticing their absence as we stepped out the door.

"Mom is at the mess hall already; she didn't want to wake you up this morning and Steff . . ." she trailed off then smirked. "She refused to eat any of the 'slop' we were serving and disappeared into the woods."

"Is she all right?" I asked.

Abbs shrugged.

"Yeah, she'll go off and pout for a while then come home when she is hungry."

Steff was always the whiney, persnickety child growing up. Her twelfth birthday seemed to put those characteristics into overdrive. I loved her more than anything, but damn she could be difficult. I didn't blame the girls for being upset about their new living conditions. I was not crazy about them myself. At least Abby seemed to be handling it in stride.

By comparison, the outside of our cabin was pure paradise. Gently sloping forested mountains surrounded us on all sides. A large clear lake shimmered through the woods about a quarter of a mile from the cabin. The surface reflected the trees, giving the strange impression of Impal trees. I have heard Impals described as if they were a shimmering lake in the morning sun. For the first time, I could see the correlation. The lavender sky coupled with yellowish clouds completed the surreal setting.

The woods surrounding the cabin provided a thick canopy. A small percentage of sunlight could penetrate the dense vegetation. In fact, the only opening I could see was where the sun was shining through the front window of our cabin. Several cabins peppered the woods around the lake. Most were similar to ours, some larger and some smaller. All of them shared the ancient appearance of years of exposure and neglect.

We made our way down a winding trail through the woods and down a steep slope. When we reached the bottom, we emerged in a clearing centered by a large rectangle shaped building. It was every bit as old as the cabins. I could hear the sound of voices inside, like several people having a muted conversation. Barely audible over the voices was the electronic buzz of a radio broadcast. As we got closer, a strange scent caught my swollen nose like something was cooking. I wasn't sure if it smelled good or not.

The building once served as the old mess hall for the miners. The inside was filled with several rows of long tables framed on each side by long wooden benches. There were about a dozen people huddled on both sides of the table opposite the door. Barbara, Burt, Danny Bradley, Charlotte McVey, Derek Vandeputte and Taylor Farris occupied the table closest to me. They were mixed with six people I did not know, four men and two women. Burt waved and motioned toward a table at the back of the room. There was a small propane camping stove set up beside a stack of paper plates and a row of bottled water. A solitary man stood behind the table.

"Get you some breakfast and come on over!" Burt called.

Abbs patted me on the back, strolled over, and set down next to Barbara. I walked over to the man at the stove to see what was cooking. It turned out my nose would not have made a lot of difference. The only things on the menu were fried Spam or Vienna sausage, grilled toast (plain) or dry cereal.

"We can't store anything perishable," the cook said with an apologetic frown. "There's no power out here and the nearest ice machine is at the country store a few miles away."

"That's fine," I said as my stomach growled, "I've always been partial to Vienna sausages and Froot Loops," I said, pointing to the colorful box with the toucan.

"Vienny weenies and Fruity fowl!" he proclaimed as if calling out an order in a restaurant. He dumped a can of Vienna sausages on an iron skillet and they began to sizzle. It wasn't exactly bacon or sausage, but I was so hungry I didn't care.

The cook reached down under the table and produced a large bowl covered with a white cloth. He set it on the table then leaned forward and whispered as if he held a deep secret.

"I picked these this morning. Want a scoop or two on your cereal?"

He lifted the cloth and revealed a bowl brimming with blackberries. I enjoyed wild blackberries as a kid and I jumped at his generous offer.

I sat down by Barbara and Abbs while I finished my breakfast. I listened with great interest to the conversation. It seemed things were going to be moving a little faster than I anticipated.

"Europe is a little more humane than us," Derek said. "They are sending Impals to the island of Cephalonia and Lemnos off the Greek coast. The British and French are sending theirs to the fourteen Channel Islands, half of which are uninhabited."

"What are they doing about the ones that *are* inhabited?" Burt asked.

"I hear the European Union is offering anyone who has to relocate a very generous settlement. Most will probably be living better than they were," Danny said.

"What about the rest of the world?" Barbara asked.

"Not really sure," Danny said. "We haven't had a whole lot of contact lately from Asia or Africa. All we can hope for is that they handle the situation by keeping the best interest of all involved in mind."

"We are the only ones who have anything like the Tesla Gate?" Charlotte asked.

"Yes, I believe so," Danny replied.

I decided to jump in because I asked a question burning at me since I first heard of the infernal contraption.

"Where did the Tesla Gate come from?" I asked.

Danny stared at me for several moments with a stoic frown. He then he jerked his head to suggest later was a more appropriate time to address it. I saw by the disappointed faces around the table that the question was on everyone's mind. It seemed strange to me that these things, these Shredders, could have come into existence and implemented so fast.

"So what does Europe have to do with our situation?" Taylor asked.

Danny finished the last swig of his water bottle before he answered. "I have been in contact with an old buddy of mine, Admiral Jack Dyson of the British fleet, since this whole thing began. I've kept my ear to the ground in Europe, so to speak. I talked to him a few days ago and he was horrified by what I told him our government was doing." The colonel paused and took a deep breath before continuing.

"He told me that whatever Impals I could get out of the country; they would be welcomed at the island of Guernsey in the channel. It is the only place where any space is available."

"How many do we have here?" I asked. I calculated a rough estimate in my head based on what I saw last night.

"Roughly about one hundred-twenty," Danny said.

"Good God, the government has been putting that many through the Shredder every fifteen minutes . . . and we only have one hundred-twenty?" I asked in disbelief.

"It's the best we can do in a short time, Mr. Garrison. We don't have the resources the government does when it comes to rounding them up. Besides, every Impal here is here by choice."

"So how are we getting them out of the country?" Taylor asked.

Danny turned his agitated gaze into a wide smile as he turned to face the rest of the table. "Boats," he said.

Before anyone could ask him to elaborate, he did. Sam Andrews's brother owned a sightseeing tours company, which operated small cruise ships around the Chesapeake Bay area. He owned two ships in his fleet that he believed could make a transatlantic voyage.

"They should be more than big enough to hold all the Impals coming for the journey," he said.

"All of them . . . coming?" Charlotte chimed in. "There's more than the ones we shelter here?"

"There are three other camps I am working with . . . one in Pennsylvania, one in New Jersey, and another in North Carolina. We are going to meet on the determined night and facilitate one big extraction," Danny said.

"How many in those camps?" Derek asked.

"I'm not sure. We should be evacuating close to four hundred, give or take a few," Danny said. "Don't forget, we have another shipment coming in today . . . all the way from Washington!"

Everyone began to talk at once before Danny put a decisive end to it.

"Okay everyone, pack out you trash and let's get ready for the next shipment!" he proclaimed. He then turned and winked. "It's cleaning day for you, Cecil," he said pointing to a bucket, mop, and an assortment of cleaning supplies in the corner.

When I considered our dirty little shack, I was thankful to receive an order to perform clean up duty.

"Don't worry, they clean up good," Burt whispered, poking me in the ribs. "Ours was a regular crap hole when we first moved in last week."

I started to make a sarcastic comment when I heard a commotion outside. Several people darted about the mess hall and I could hear the sound of approaching vehicles. My heart leapt into my throat until I saw Burt's amusement.

"Relax chief," he said, reading the panic on my face. "It's just our new Impal pals."

We walked outside to find a group of people talking excitedly and watching the road with anticipation.

"Are you serious? It's really him?" one elderly woman asked a chubby young man with sunglasses and a large scar on his cheek.

He shrugged and said, "I don't know, I guess we're about to find out."

As if on cue, two large SUVs came into sight around a bend in the woods. A minute later, they skidded to a stop beside us. Everybody stepped back as if one of the vehicles might be radioactive and then stared in excitement. The front doors opened and a man and a woman got out of the front seat of each. They were either Impals carrying batteries or fleshers like us. They opened the back doors, including the cargo area and a number of Impals poured out of each vehicle. They all radiated with a 'batteries not included' shimmering glow. They always seemed much more surreal in the daylight.

The people began whispering again. I couldn't figure out what the commotion was about, until I looked a little closer. A group of Impals headed towards me. There was one man much taller than the rest. I felt a jolt of excitement as I recognized our new refugee. Thomas Pendleton told me about his encounter with him before his capture. I never dreamed I would be coming face to face with none other than Abraham Lincoln.

CHAPTER 8

MAN DOWN

"Beware of false knowledge; it is more dangerous than ignorance."
~George Bernard Shaw

THE TALL, LANKY FORMER PRESIDENT tried to blend in with everyone else, but it was impossible. His stature was too recognizable both in the historic and physical sense. He loped past without a word. I stood frozen in place, dumbstruck. I had met two famous names from history in less than twenty-four hours. I must admit, Lincoln is the ultimate. He may not be my favorite president, yet I was an admirer all the same.

The drivers of the SUVs along with Taylor, Derek and Charlotte accompanied the new arrivals. They led them into the woods along the path leading to the concealed mineshaft. I turned to see Burt and Barbara watching me with amusement. Abbs grin didn't last too long, however.

"Bye, Dad!" she said and ran after the group.

I started to protest, and then reconsidered. She was eighteen and I imagined she was as safe here as she would be anywhere.

"That's incredible!" Barbara said. "Do you think there will be a chance to meet him?"

I looked to Burt. Barbara and I were the rookies to the camp.

I didn't know what Danny's policy was about interacting with the Impals. Besides, Burt introduced me to the Impal quarters last night.

"Probably, later . . . you and I have something big to do today." He said, poking me in the chest in a playful manner. I think it was for Barbara's benefit because I could see the seriousness in his eyes.

"What?" Barbara asked with suspicion in her eyes.

"Nothing to worry about," Burt assured her. "Just a little roundup we need to prepare for."

I knew what he meant. He wanted me to come with him to collect another group of Impals.

"Not without me," Barbara said. "I am part of this group too."

I knew the main reason she wanted to go was not to be one of the guys. It was because she still hadn't given up hope of finding her mother.

"You certainly are," Burt said. "That's why we need you here to help watch over the camp."

Barbara started to argue until he brought up his next point.

"Besides, every flesher we take is one less Impal we can bring back."

Barbara could be emotional with the best of them when the time came. She was also a very rational and logical person. Burt's logic was flawless and she couldn't argue.

"Where are we going?" I asked.

"Can't say just yet for security reasons. I'll let you know when we are en route." He patted Barbara on her on the arm and said, "He'll be fine, I promise."

The words barely exited his mouth when a deafening crack rang out, echoing like rolling thunder around the valley. It was as if time ran in slow motion. I saw Burt spinning away like a top with shock in his eyes. I felt something warm and wet spray across my face. I turned to Barbara and saw crimson sprayed across the side of her face. I knew it was blood. Instinct took over and I dove forward, tackling Barbara to the ground. Another bullet whistled past my ear as the shot rolled around the valley like thunder.

I was unarmed and my only thought was to protect Barbara. Spreading my body across hers, I heard another gunshot as a bullet kicked up a plume of Earth mere inches from us. Dirt rained down on my head as I heard the voice of a strange man.

"You damned Pythonians! I saw you takin' your demons in there! I'm going to make sure you join them!" called a deep voice, distorted with rage. The breathing sounded like a marathon runner. The second voice belonged to a woman. It carried the same viral hatred and labored breathing.

"I'm gonna blow your damn head off, demon lover!" she screamed.

I braced myself and prepared for the shot. I covered as much of Barbara as I could, hoping that they, whomever they were, would be satisfied after they shot me. I heard her panting beneath me, my chest vibrating with every shuddering sob of her body.

"I love you," I whispered and closed my eyes to prepare.

I flinched as two shots rang out. Convinced that my life was over, a crazy idea ran through my mind. *Would I have to live in the mineshaft now?*

I waited . . . for what I was not sure.

Would my spirit, my Impal part, rise out of my body or would I need to make a conscious effort to stand up? A second later, two more shots rang out. These were immediately followed by two hard thuds a short distance away. I opened my eyes and turned my head in the direction of the gunshots. My stomach lurched as I saw the face of a red-haired, middle-aged woman lying a few feet away from us. Her milky lifeless eyes seemed to stare straight through me. There was little doubt that she was dead.

"Coast clear, it's over!" the familiar voice of Danny called. "Man down!" he yelled.

I rolled off Barbara and was about to tell him I was fine when I saw Burt lying face down a few feet away. I glanced down at Barbara as she rolled over, my heart seized when I saw the blood splashed across her face.

"Sweetheart?" I said, reaching out and touching her blood covered cheek.

She sat up and then rubbed her fingers over the blood. "It's not mine," she said.

Simultaneously, we turned back to Burt and then crawled to our wounded friend. As we reached his side, Danny appeared. He carried two Beretta M9 pistols, one in each hand. Small tendrils of smoke coiled from each barrel. The colonel was our savior.

"Thank God he has two guns," I thought to myself. If he hadn't, he may not have gotten off another shot before one of them did.

"Taylor, Andrews . . . restrain those two assholes!" he yelled at Taylor Ferris and Sam Andrews, as they sprinted out of the woods in response to the gunfire.

The man and woman who tried to murder us now stood dumb-struck. Their shimmering faces stared in shock at their lifeless bodies. Their ethereal forms were a surreal contrast to the lake behind them in the distance.

The man resembled like a middle age hunter. His eternal wardrobe consisted of a hunting jacket and jeans. The woman bore an uncanny likeness to Jessica Rabbit, Roger's sultry girlfriend. She wore jeans and a striped tank top. Their corporeal bodies bore the clothing of two rednecks who had not bathed since the cosmic storm started.

Taylor and Andrews each produced two large iron chains from behind the mess hall. Andrews was the largest and fastest and the most temperamental. He unloaded on the man with a swing reminiscent of Barry Bonds. The hapless Impal flew backwards and landed flat on his back. The man's shocked expression turned to one of horror as Andrews menaced the chain above him. Taylor clocked the woman a second later producing similar results. If the Impals tried to get up, they would be beaten back to the ground by the two iron wielding behemoths.

Turning my attention to Burt, I thankfully saw his chest rise and fall as he lay on his stomach; he was breathing. Copious amounts of blood soaked his shirt on his right shoulder. Danny reached down and touched his left shoulder. I moved around to his right, the direction his head was facing. With great care, I touched him on top of the head.

"Burt . . . are you hit?" I wheezed. It seemed my lungs were as much in shock as the rest of me.

His eyes remained closed as a faint smile creased Burt's face. "Who-ever punched me is about to get my boot in their ass," he mumbled.

Blood continued to pour from the wound on his back so I pulled off my T-shirt and put pressure on it as Danny helped me roll him over. The wound on the front of Burt's shoulder was bleeding worse. Danny removed his shirt and applied pressure while I continued to apply pressure to his back. He winced with pain at our touch, then gritted his teeth and endured it.

Danny gave Burt's body a quick once over as he held the makeshift bandage in place. He patted him on his good shoulder. "Well, the bullet went all the way through . . . which is a good thing," he said and then turned to a strange man watching nearby.

"Scooter, run and get the doc. Tell him to bring his bag and come quick," Danny ordered. The man continued to stare, dumbfounded.

"Now!" Danny barked, like a drill sergeant.

The man snapped out of his shock-induced trance then turned and sprinted through the woods on the other side of the mess hall. He passed the cook who was running towards us carrying towels and several bottles of water.

We washed the wound and kept pressure on it until the doctor arrived a few minutes later. The doctor was a man I saw leaving the mess hall earlier, his name was Dr. Frank Acosta.

After examining Burt for several moments, he pulled back the towel covering his back and examined the wound. Shaking his head, he said, "Move him to a mess hall table. We need to get him off this nasty ground."

I grabbed Burt under the shoulders and Danny took his legs. With one strong heave, we lifted him in the air and carried him to the mess hall. Burt screamed in pain the whole way until we set him on one of the old wooden tabletops.

"Get me some gunpowder and a match!"

Danny stared with a vacant expression at his twin pistols for a moment. He shoved one back in his chest holster and then popped the cartridge out of the other. He flicked two bullets out with his thumb and knelt down beside the doctor. He began to twist the casing back and forth at the point it met the bullet. After several moments of intense effort, the bullet and casing separated as a few drops of gunpowder leaked out. Danny handed the casing to the doctor and then stuck out his hand to Barbara. "Lighter!" he demanded.

Barbara seemed uncharacteristically sheepish as she turned three shades of red. She stared at her feet and didn't move.

"Come on, come on," he said with impatience. "I saw you smoking down by the lake last night before we left to get your husband."

I understood the reason for her embarrassment. Barbara quit smoking three years ago. I was proud of her for showing the will and fortitude to stop the disgusting habit. It seemed she had fallen back into it again. At any other time, I would be upset and voice my disapproval of the habit. Now was not the time. She glanced at me, and then slid her hand in her pocket. She produced the cheap, pink Bic, and handed it to Danny.

They gently rolled Burt over and the doctor tore the shirt away from his wound. He picked up an oak twig nearby and asked Burt to bite down on it.

"I am going to cauterize the wound . . . on the count of three," Dr. Acosta said.

Burt clamped down on the stick.

"One . . ." he poured the gunpowder on the wound.

"Two . . ." he held the lighter at the ready.

"Three!" he clicked the lighter and held it to the powder. There was a bright flash followed by a muffled scream from Burt. The doctor withdrew his hand in one swift motion, shaking it as if trying to douse a fire. He had singed his fingertips.

Burt grunted and panted as the doctor cleaned the cauterized area with one of the water bottles. After a minute or two of cleaning and observing the back of Burt's shoulder, the doctor seemed satisfied.

"Lay him down on this towel," he said, as the cook spread out a fresh towel underneath my wounded friend.

As soon as Burt was settled in place, he examined the wound on the front of his shoulder. After a few moments, he said, "Burt, I would like to cauterize this wound as well. Even though the bleeding has almost stopped, I think cauterization would help sterilize the area."

Burt spat the stick out of his mouth. "What about disinfectants?" he pleaded.

"Don't have any," the doctor said. "Even if I did, the only thing preferable would be hydrogen peroxide or iodine . . . alcohol would burn worse and longer than cauterization."

Burt laid his head back and closed his eyes. His face was ashen from the blood loss and pain. He took a deep breath and uttered a single word. "Stick."

The good news was Burt would survive. He would be out of action for a while, but the doctor said the bullet passed through cleanly. As long as infection did not set in, he should make a full recovery.

When we carried him back to his cabin, I thought Sally was going to have a heart attack. After we assured her that Burt would be okay, she calmed down. Sally started fussing over him, rubbing his feet and legs then dabbing his forehead with a cool damp cloth. Satisfaction bloomed on Burt's face. Seeing he was in good hands, we left and returned to the mess hall.

The motivation of our two shooters was more disturbing than Burt's injury. We sat and listened to the radio with heavy hearts and growing fear. I think my heart was heavier than everyone else's because my father was on the radio.

"Yes, we think so," General Garrison told the unnamed host. "As hard as it is to believe, my worst fears are confirmed."

"What fears are those?" the host asked.

"I always said these Impals are abominations and now we have definitive proof."

"What sort of proof?" the host asked.

"There has been a unanimous declaration from the religious community. Not just Christian leaders, but Jewish and Islamic are in agreement on this. The Impals are in fact demons."

"Demons?" the host asked with respectful incredulity.

"Yes sir," the general said with arrogant conviction. "Several verses of scripture backup this conclusion."

"Can you cite one?" the host asked.

"Several," he said. "We can start with Matthew 12, verses 43 to 45."

He cleared his throat and spoke.

"*When the unclean spirit is gone out of a man, he walketh through dry places, seeking rest, and findeth none.*

Then he saith, I will return into my house from whence I came out; and when he is come, he findeth it empty, swept, and garnished.

Then goeth he, and taketh with himself seven other spirits more wicked than himself, and they enter in and dwell there: and the last state of that man is worse than the first. Even so shall it be also unto this wicked generation."

"Very interesting," the host said, sounding impressed. "Any quotes from the Torah?"

"I'll be an honest. I am not an educated man in Judaism, so no; I cannot give you a specific quote. However, I can tell you what a rabbi shared with me yesterday. He assures me that everyone else in the faith is of the same mind." General Garrison said then cleared his throat again.

"He said in Jewish belief, demonic powers constitute an unholy parody of the sacred realms against which they are in constant battle. They compare the "Other Side," the domain of the evil powers, to a vicious dog held by its owner on a long leash. The dog, though it appears to enjoy independent power, is pulled back whenever it is in danger of getting out of control."

"So he is saying the Impals are these vicious dogs or demons who have strayed into our realm or existence? And will be pulled back when they get out of control?" the host asked.

"Yes, I think that sums it up," Garrison said.

"When will God pull them back?" the host asked.

"He is doing it now," General Garrison said. "He has used me and this great country as an instrument to do his will. We are sending them back now, jerking their chain so to speak." He said with a humorless laugh.

"How?" the host asked.

"It's classified, I'm afraid," he replied. "Rest assured, your government and military will protect you to the last man from these Pythonians. These are the things everyone has been referring to as Impals."

"Pythonians?" the host asked. "What is that?"

"It's the name our religious leaders agreed on. Pytho is the demon of lies and deceit. There is not a better description for the worldwide deceit perpetuated by these abominations."

"So what is the final word you would like to leave everyone with this morning, general?" the host asked.

"We are calling on every red-blooded American to turn in these evil beings. Remember, anything made of iron can restrain them. We are also offering a bounty of five hundred dollars a head for each Pythonian turned in. Godspeed, and good luck!"

"That was an interview recorded with General Ott Garrison earlier this morning. We will be welcoming Father Harold Dawson in the next hour who will back up the general's claims. Good day and enjoy some patriotic music while we prepare for the next broadcast."

There was a static buzz then a moving rendition of 'The Star Spangled Banner' began to play. We all sat and stared at one another for several moments, nobody spoke. As the song faded out and morphed into 'America the Beautiful', Danny stood up and patted my shoulder. After all, we just listened to my crazy father. Our jobs were now much harder.

"Burt's down, so it's you and me on the run tomorrow night, Garrison . . . you up to it?" Danny asked.

"I'll be ready," I said.

"Nineteen hundred hours tomorrow, meet me here," he said, then left the room.

I put my head in my hands trying to process everything. If we had two redneck bounty hunters this soon, it was probable more would follow. Five hundred dollars a head, why not? We harbored about sixty-thousand dollars sitting in the mineshaft. Who cares if they took down a couple of us fleshers in the process? That's more souls to turn in. Dread filled my guts like molten metal as I pictured murders now occurring for nothing more than to collect on the bounty. I bolted from the room to find my girls.

CHAPTER 9

THE RUNAWAY

"Ooh, she's a little runaway."
~Jon Bon Jovi

I KNEW MY FATHER WAS CRAZY AND A ZEALOT. In some ways I guess that is what made him such a good soldier and elevated him through the ranks. However, you don't get to the position of the president's chief military adviser on pure piss and vinegar. Charisma is a must. You had to make people believe in you even in the times where there is nothing to believe in. True charisma makes the public believe you to be a hero for doing your job, even when you should be court-martialed. My father had been able to do this to both the president and Congress. He convinced them that his brutality in Panama was necessary for the national security of the United States. He was now doing it on a grander scale.

His charismatic deceit began with his ghastly ability to make a child believe each sickness was a punishment for some evil. I don't know how many times I lay in my bed with my mother tending to me as I racked my brain trying to figure out why I was being punished. He treated my mother the same way.

I knew his unfounded condemnations broke my mother's heart. I still believe that is what she died of two days before my twelfth birthday. Abigail Garrison was a strong, loving woman. She was the only reason I made it through childhood with a modicum of sanity intact. I was proud to name our first daughter after her. I wish she was there when I got in the nest of snakes at church camp because all I could do was lie in bed and wonder what I did wrong. It must have been pretty bad to invoke the wrath of Satan's slithering envoys.

To my knowledge, my mother did not remain after she died, and now I was thankful. There was no doubt my father would not hesitate to throw her into the Shredder. He would say she was nothing more than an abomination.

As I stumbled through the woods calling for Abbs and Steff, I wondered how my father had been able to convince so many people in such a short time. All the major religion's leaders were now behind his twisted cause. I guess in a time of fear and uncertainties, even the most faithful among us seek answers and leadership. Fear can be a powerful motivating force as well as a blinding one. I couldn't blame people for being afraid, not even my father. However, I could blame *him* for exploiting their fear.

After a few minutes of shouting, I heard Abbs calling back to me from somewhere ahead. A second later, she emerged through the trees in front of me.

"Dad, what's wrong? Is everyone okay?" she asked with wide eyes. She could see the fear and panic etched all over my face.

"Where's your sister?" I blurted.

She blinked; tears of panic beginning to well in her eyes.

"I-I don't know," she stammered. "She said she was going to take a walk by the lake after breakfast this morning."

"You haven't seen her since?" I asked as Barbara caught up to us on the trail. Her face was beet red and she panted in loud gasps. I wondered if it was from the cigarettes.

"Lake . . . come," Barbara panted, motioning for us to follow her.

I took Abbs by the hand and we ran towards the glistening water in the distance. A few moments later, we stood a few feet from the bank at a large inlet from the lake. I believed my fear for the safety of my daughter would take the place of everything else I felt. I was wrong. The cove bore a striking resemblance to the one where I encountered the water moccasins so many years ago.

"Abbs, you go that way," Barbara said, motioning to the right. "We'll go this way and keep going until we meet or we find her."

"Yes, mom," Abbs said and started to walk away.

"No!" I shouted in a harsh tone. Both women jumped.

I grabbed Abbs hand and pulled her back.

"We stay together!" I insisted.

We did stay together and covered the entire perimeter of the lake. There was no sign of Steff. Taylor and Andrews joined the search after securing the Impal prisoners. They put them in a side chamber of the mine where Sergeant Beeson now resided. With their help, we were able to make another perimeter search in twenty minutes. Still, there was no sign of Steff.

Barbara, Abbs and I were beginning to boil over with panic when we started our third search. The worst-case scenarios ran through my mind from drowning or snake bite to being taken prisoner by bounty hunters. We passed under a group of large sycamore trees when I noticed a few leaves falling, accompanied by some bark and twigs. I squinted up into the foliage. It was difficult to see now because the sun was almost directly overhead. I could just make out two red tennis shoes through the leaves. I remembered buying those for Steff on our last family outing a couple of months ago. It seemed like an eternity now.

"Steff!" I called, gazing up into the tree.

One of the shoes moved a little. Barbara and Abbs stopped and followed my gaze into the treetop. Both of their jaws tightened with anger when they saw the same thing I did. This was our third time to pass this location.

"Steff!" Abbs snapped. "We've been worried sick about you!"

Still no response; one of the shoes moved a little.

"We see you up there, you little brat!" Abbs prodded. "Come down or I'll pelt you down!" She said picking up a rock and throwing it into the water to make her point.

"Steff, honey, please come down," Barbara said with remarkable calm in her voice. I was glad one of us was cool; if Abbs and I jumped in the lake, we most certainly would bring the water to the boiling point.

Still, there was no response from the tree.

Abbs picked up a piece of granite about the size of a silver dollar and began to aim her shot when I held up my hand to stop her. There would be time for harsh words and punishment later, the important thing was to get Steff back with us; to keep her safe. I decided we needed to be honest.

"Steff, Mr. Golden was shot outside the mess hall a short time ago. There are some crazy people lurking about and we need to get you back and keep you safe. Please come down."

There were several long moments of silence before I heard a faint reply.

"Did he die?"

"No, but you're going to!" Abbs promised.

I held up my hand to silence her and mouthed the words, "*Let me do the talking.*"

"Come on Steff, let's all go back home," I pleaded.

"That's not home!" she snapped. "I don't want to go back in that nasty place . . . I want to go to our REAL home!"

I whispered to Abbs to head back and let Taylor and Andrews know we found her. I could see them a short distance away; otherwise, I would not have let her out of my sight. She reluctantly agreed and began to walk away. Abbs continued to glance over her shoulder to catch a better view of her sister sitting in the treetops.

It took another twenty minutes of coaxing before we finally got her out of the tree. Barbara and I each grabbed a hand. We led her around the lake and back to the camp. I decided that any discussions of irresponsibility or punishment would wait until we got back to the cabin. Steff decided she was now in a talking mood.

"Why can't we go home?" she prodded. "Did you do something wrong?"

I tried to ignore her question, but Barbara intervened. She gave an answer I hoped to avoid.

"No, your father did nothing wrong! It's your grandfather!" she spat. I could tell by her face she instantly wished she could take it back.

No matter how Barbara and I, or the rest of the world felt about my father, we would try not to show it in front of the girls. Abbs was old enough to form a somewhat informed opinion. However, Steff was only twelve and immature for a preteen. Her response did not surprise me.

"Grandpa is the nicest man I know," she said, glaring at me. Her expression suggested that I was included in her not so nice list. "It's not his fault!"

I tried to wrap my arm around her shoulders, but she pulled away and put a couple more feet of distance between us. She folded her arms across her chest and scowled straight ahead.

"It's nobody's fault," I lied. "There are some crazy people out there trying to take advantage of the situation. Did you hear the gunshots this morning?"

She didn't reply for a long time. Not breaking her mood and demeanor, she finally asked, "Is Mr. Golden okay?"

"Yes, he'll be fine. He will need to rest for a few days. I don't want you and Abbs wandering off in case any more of those crazy people come around."

She didn't break stride or her scowl.

"Am I clear, Steff?" I asked.

She shrugged her shoulders as if to say *whatever*. Her arms and face were still locked in a defiant stance. A few moments later, we arrived at the cabin. Steff went in ahead of us, slamming the door in our faces with one final temperamental gesture. Part of me wanted to hug her neck and part of me wanted to strangle it. I was a patient man, but my limits were stretched to the maximum. I didn't blame her for being upset with our situation. The one thing I did blame her for was the way she was handling it. I turned and looked at Barbara before she went inside. She could tell I needed to remove myself from the situation. She kissed me on the cheek.

"I'm sorry," she whispered. "I love you."

I smiled despite the tears of frustration I felt beginning to well in my eyes.

"I'll go get the cleaning stuff they showed us this morning. Maybe she'll feel different once the place is cleaned up a little."

"I'll go help," Barbara offered.

"No, stay here with her and keep an eye on her. I don't want either one of the girls to get out of our sight again until this thing is over."

As I made my way back to the mess hall, I met Abbs walking back toward our cabin with Taylor. I thanked him for his help and asked where Andrews went. He shook his head and said, "He . . . uh, he had something to do."

"Yeah, he had to go off and cuss Steff," Abbs said. "He's a little bit presumptuous considering he doesn't know us. I really can't say I disagree with him though."

"Sam Andrews has got a temper," Taylor said. "I've learned to take everything he says with a grain of salt and give him a wide berth."

I was glad that I ran into them, especially after I saw the cleaning supplies. It was more than I could manage in one trip. I was surprised when Taylor offered to help carry everything. However, I was downright shocked when he offered to stay and help clean. The shock only lasted until I saw the way Abbs and Taylor looked at each other. It reminded me of the way Barbara and I looked at each other when we first started dating. It would seem I had one more thing to worry about.

"Hands off, cradle robber," I almost said. I wasn't sure how old Taylor was; he was one of those people who enjoy a mature youthful appearance. He could be anywhere from eighteen to thirty-five. The only thing I am certain of is that he is older than Abbs.

Barbara, Abbs, Taylor, and I spent a couple of hours cleaning the cabin. Steff sat outside under a tree drawing in the dirt with a stick. When we finished there was a noticeable improvement. The ancient cabin no longer resembled a roach-infested crap hole. It was more like a well-scrubbed, roach-infested crap hole. In any case, I found it tolerable. Judging by Steff's grimace when she reentered, I don't think she agreed with my assessment. She sat on the edge of her cot and glowered at me.

"I think it's great, Dad," Abbs whispered in my ear. "And I don't care what anybody else says," she proclaimed, raising her voice to a hoarse shout. She then gave Steff a contemptuous scowl.

We returned to the mess hall early in the afternoon. We enjoyed another fine helping of Vienna sausages, Saltine crackers and bottled water. I made a mental note to check for a grocery store when we went for our pickup tomorrow; although I wasn't quite sure what good it would do me. I never carried cash and neither did Barbara. Our debit cards were our preferred medium of exchange. I'm almost certain they had been frozen or were being tracked right now, so our monetary options were limited.

We decided that when we departed for our pickup, we would be taking the two SUV's. The first one would be for Danny and me while the follow vehicle would hold Sam and Charlotte. There were to be no civilians in this party. A fact I did not notice at the time. It proved to be a wise decision on Danny's part, considering our target destination.

"I'll keep an eye on your wife and daughters," Taylor promised. His Winchester rifle hung on his back with a nylon sling. He reached back and patted the butt of his weapon for reassurance.

I liked Taylor, yet I wasn't certain how confident I was by this promise. It would be hard enough letting the girls out of my sight. Leaving them in the hands of a total stranger, especially knowing the stranger is attracted to my oldest daughter is disquieting. There was little choice, not if I was going to do anything more than cower in a hole with my family until the storm passed. I had to trust in the people around me because I did trust we were doing the right thing.

The night was a little more restful than the previous one. A clean and familiar environment worked wonders. The next day was uneventful. Steff's mood did not improve so I spent most of the day visiting Burt. He was in good spirits even though he said his shoulder hurt like a "*sumbitch.*"

We left camp a little after seven in the evening and, according to Danny, we had about an hour and a half drive ahead of us. This meant we would be getting to our destination right at dusk. We were just out of sight of the mess hall when Danny finally revealed our mission.

"We are going to DC to pick up another load of Impals," Danny said. "We will have about fifteen refugees waiting on us."

I felt as if my heart dropped into my boots. We would be going to Washington, into the lion's den. I was about to question the sanity of this plan when Danny spoke again.

"I know it sounds crazy, but this is our last trip there. According to our source in the city, this is the last group of refugees. All the others are either captured or evacuated."

"Who is your source?" I asked.

Danny gave me a wink, "That's classified, only not for much longer. They'll be meeting with us tonight."

"Impal or flesher?" I asked.

"Both fleshers," he said. "I'm sure you'll recognize them."

We arrived at the main parking area of Arlington National Cemetery at little after eight o'clock. The sun had just set in the distance. The waning glow, coupled with the ultraviolet quality of the night gave our surroundings an appearance of surreal reverence. The somber grounds seemed to magnify this to breathtaking proportions tonight. In the past seven weeks since this storm came along, I don't think I ever witnessed a scene so awe-inspiring. I noticed the parking area was vacant aside from a mid-size tour bus in the distance and a black limousine. The limo was almost obscured from view as it sat between the bus and a large hedgerow. The shadow of the bus threw the limo's parking area into almost complete darkness.

We pulled up behind the tour bus and parked. I noticed the sign on the side advertised The Monuments at Night Tour.

"Are we taking a tour while in town?" I mumbled.

Danny got out first. He left his door open, bathing me in the bright overhead light. I felt completely exposed. He stepped in front of the vehicle and behind the limousine with his hands raised in the air. My heart began to thunder in my chest. Were we caught? Seconds later, the back door to the limo opened and two men emerged. They stood in the dark so I couldn't make out their features other than each man wore a suit. I heard Danny speaking with them in muffled tones. After a few very long moments, he turned and motioned for me, and our two companions in the other SUV, to join him.

We got out and walked to Danny's side, flanking him, and preparing for any trouble.

"Cecil Garrison, Charlotte McVey, Sam Andrews . . ." Danny said pointing to each of us in turn. "I would like you to meet Dr. Ray Winder, the president's science adviser."

I met Dr. Winder once before when he spoke at an Army confer-

ence at the Pentagon. His speech was about scientific advances ben-
efiting the military. I remembered him as a slender and graying man.
In the three years since our encounter, he seemed as if he aged twenty
years. His hair was almost completely gray and his haggard face and
slumped shoulders bore the weight of the world.

"Nice to meet you and thank you for your service to our country,"
he said as he shook each of our hands.

He stepped back in the shadows and waited as Danny introduced
the doctor's counterpart.

"Our next ally needs no introduction," Danny said as he held out
his hand in welcome for the other person to step forward.

A collective gasp went up from everyone and I found myself frozen
in disbelief as the other figure stepped forward. We all recognized him,
how could we not recognize our own Commander in Chief . . . the
President of the United States.

CHAPTER 10

THE SHREDDER REVEALED

"Do not tell secrets to those whose faith and silence you have not already tested."
~Elizabeth I

AN EERIE, AWESTRUCK SILENCE FELL OVER THE GROUP as we stared in disbelief. Danny watched us for a few moments before he spoke.

"Mr. President, this is Charlotte McVey, Sam Andrews and Cecil Garrison," he said, pointing to each of us in turn.

The president waited as Danny pointed each of us out, and then he stepped forward and extended his hand to me.

"Major Garrison, I know this must be hard for you. I want you to know how much I appreciate your loyalty to your country," the president said, shaking my hand.

I could have said thank you, or my pleasure, or just doing my duty, sir . . . or I could have said screw you, you coward. I didn't say anything at all, I was still in too much shock to get my tongue and brain to coalesce and make a lucid statement. I wasn't star struck. I met the president before. It was about a year ago during a White House dinner at the invitation of my father. I believed this man was our enemy, in league with my father and other cronies in the government. However, here he was in a deserted parking lot offering his help. According to Danny, he had been helping for a while.

Andrews broke the silence. His unpredictable temper boiled over at the sight of the president. He stepped forward with malice as he spoke.

"You son of a bitch!" he raged. "Do you know what the hell you are doing? Do you have any idea? Maybe we ought to turn you into one of them so you'll understand!"

Andrews reached behind him to retrieve the pistol tucked in his waistband. As he brought his arm back, I instinctively lunged at him, hitting him square on the chest. My larger frame won out as he sprawled backwards, landing hard on his back as the pistol discharged. Danny was on top of him before I could move again. He disarmed and pinned him before I could straighten up. Charlotte watched with her hands over her mouth, her eyes as big as saucers.

Dr. Winder ushered the President back to the car, keeping his body between Andrews and the Commander in Chief. I kept expecting Secret Service to emerge from the bushes or the car at any moment.

Danny sat on Andrews's chest with his knees pinning his arms to the pavement. He bent low, his face inches from the would-be presidential assassin. He let loose with a string of obscenities as Danny stared at him with contempt. After a long couple of minutes, Danny got up and helped Andrews to his feet. On Danny's orders, he walked over and climbed on the tour bus, the metal door slamming shut behind him.

Danny walked back to the limo and leaned inside. After a couple of moments of conversation, he beckoned Charlotte and me to come over. The president leaned out and spoke.

"Major Garrison, as I was saying, I want you to know how much I appreciate your courage. I'm sorry I haven't been able to do more to help. My hands are somewhat tied trying to take care of my own family."

He confirmed what I already suspected, the president wasn't pulling the strings, and my father was. In some kind of bizarre coup d'état, he and the military controlled the government. Not by removal and replacement, it was accomplished through control by intimidation. If he was able to do it with the president, I'm sure the Supreme Court was a piece of cake.

"I'm sorry, Mr. President," I said, which was all I could muster.

"I am too, Major Garrison," he said. "It's more my blame than anyone. I trusted him and appointed him. I had no idea he was capable of this."

I shook my head.

"Don't call me major, please . . . just Cecil. I gave up the title when I joined the resistance."

The president regarded at me for several long moments; I could see tears welling in his eyes.

"It is men like you who make this country great, major. And as long as I am Commander in Chief, you will always be a major."

"Thank you, Mr. President," I said. He then turned his attention to Charlotte.

"Thank you for being a patriot and a decent human being, Charlotte," he said. "I'm proud of you."

Charlotte blushed and shook his hand. She muttered something unintelligible before stepping back behind me.

"Well Colonel Bradley," the president said. "This is your last run to DC. I wish you Godspeed in your mission." He paused for a moment before asking, "Is there anything else I can do for either one of you?"

Without hesitation Danny said, "Could Dr. Winder please explain the Tesla Gate to Major Garrison? Winder explained it to me a while back and I'm still not sure I completely understood it." He glanced at his watch and said, "Besides, our pickup is in about fifteen minutes and we really don't need four people."

The President and Dr. Winder gazed at each other for a long moment, and then Dr. Winder shrugged. "That's fine by me, Mr. President," he said. "Do you have the time?"

"I think so, as long as there is not a national emergency it should be several hours before the Secret Service notices I am missing."

I wasn't sure how the president could get out of the White House without the Secret Service noticing. That wasn't the question I wanted answered. I wanted to know about the Tesla Gates.

"Would you mind sitting inside, Major Garrison?" Dr. Winder asked.

"Are you sure you don't need me?" I said to Danny before slipping inside the massive car.

"Nope, we got it covered," he said, and then glanced at his watch. "We should be back in a half hour. We are going in to pick up a load in the bus . . . much more inconspicuous."

"There should be a few more crates of batteries on the bus," Dr. Winder said. "I figured you could use more."

We collected a good stockpile in the mine back at Brentwood Springs, but the more the better.

"Thanks, we'll be back shortly," Danny said and shut the door, leaving the President, Dr. Winder and me in relative darkness.

Dr. Winder activated an overhead light, illuminating all our faces and casting the interior into eerie relief. I felt as if I was in an interrogation room or perhaps gathered around a campfire about to tell ghost stories. I guess, in a sense, that was what we were about to do.

"Well, if you gentlemen will excuse me, I am going to go up front with Kingston and make a call. My wife is in California today and she will be expecting a call from me in a few minutes," the president said.

"Kingston is our driver," Dr. Winder offered. "He is an ex-Marine and Secret Service agent. There is no one I would trust more when we are travelling covertly like this."

The president pressed a button by his head.

"Kingston, I am coming up front for a while . . . passenger side door."

"Yes sir," responded a deep voice on the speaker. He sounded like Boris Karloff's narration of The Grinch.

The president slid out the passenger side and closed the door. I caught a brief glimpse of the taillights of the tour bus as they pulled away. A moment later, we heard the front door of the limo slam shut.

"Is he all right?" I asked.

"Oh yes, like I said there is no one I would trust more," Dr. Winder said.

"Why the hell did he not at least get out of the car when Andrews threatened the President?" I thought to myself.

"So you want to know about the Tesla Gate?" Dr. Winder asked.

"Yes, I do."

"There are very few people who even know of its existence," Dr. Winder began. "A handful of people in the upper levels of the government and on a few military bases have any knowledge. I take it you knew about it on your base?"

"Enough to know it was there and what it was being used for. I find it hard to believe that the government could come up with something like this so fast, even if Einstein agreed to help them."

Winder grimaced as if I struck a nerve with my mention of Einstein. "Yes . . . well, I don't think he would. He seemed to be one of the few people who had enough foresight to see what was happening after this storm hit. Besides, the Gates were around long before this event."

"Where is Einstein?" I asked.

Dr. Winder and Albert Einstein made several radio appearances together. When the storm first started, they speculated about the cause and consequences of the phenomenon.

"I don't know," Winder said, sadness in his voice. "He disappeared a couple of weeks ago. I'm not sure if he got away or if he was taken away." I could tell he was choosing his words carefully, because if he were taken away, my father would be to blame.

"I'm sorry," I said.

Dr. Winder shook his head as if warding off a pesky fly.

"Well . . . anyway. They were created a few years ago with a completely different purpose in mind."

He put a finger to his lips for a moment.

"Have you ever heard of the Philadelphia Experiment?" Winder asked.

Indeed, I had. I remembered it as a science-fiction movie from when I was a kid. Since then, there have been a number of documentaries and conspiracy theories trying to either prove or debunk its legitimacy.

"The Philadelphia Experiment was a military experiment alleged to have been carried out at the naval shipyard in Pennsylvania," Dr. Winder explained.

I had the feeling it would soon be no longer alleged.

"I forget the exact date," Winder continued, "it was sometime around October of 1943. The United States Navy destroyer escort *USS Eldridge* was reported to be rendered invisible, or "cloaked" to both the naked eye and to tracking devices. This disappearance was due to an experiment based on an aspect of the unified field theory, a term coined by none other than Einstein."

The fact he did not say 'allegedly' based on Einstein's theory was not lost on me.

"The Unified Field Theory," Winder continued after taking a deep breath, "aims to describe mathematically and physically the interrelated nature of forces that comprise electromagnetic radiation and gravity. In other words, this unites electromagnetism and gravity into one field. Consequently, if light were bent, then space-time would be bent, effectively creating an invisible time machine."

I had heard all this before and, while interesting, I was not certain how this pertained to the Tesla Gates. I wanted the layman's answer and I hoped Dr. Winder would get to the point soon.

"According to the accounts, unspecified 'researchers' theorized that some version of this Unified Field Theory would enable a person to use large electrical generators to bend light around an object so that the object became completely invisible. The Navy would have regarded this as being of obvious military value, and by the accounts, it sponsored the experiment."

Dr. Winder paused to remove his glasses and pinched the bridge of his nose as if trying to fight back a headache

"I will skip all of the conspiracy theories out there and stick to the subjects I know to be fact. Besides, the important event, which pertains to the Tesla Gates, happened on October 28, 1943. This time, the *Eldridge* not only became invisible, she vanished from the area in a flash of blue light and teleported to Norfolk, Virginia, over two hundred miles away. The claim is that the *Eldridge* sat for some time in full view of men aboard the ship *SS Andrew Furuseth*. A short time later the *Eldridge* vanished from Norfolk and then reappeared in Philadelphia at the same site from which she vanished."

I had heard that story as well, however I had always believed it to be nothing more than a conspiracy theorist's dreams or Hollywood chimera. "You mean it is true?" I asked in disbelief.

"One-hundred percent," he said. "I personally saw the documentation and testimony from several scientists who worked on the project, including Einstein himself."

"So . . . you are telling me the Tesla Gates are a version of the Philadelphia Experiment?" I asked.

"In a way. The experiments were abandoned after the war ended. Data was hidden or destroyed so it would not fall into Communist hands. It was almost lost to history until revived by a grandson of one of the original scientists. He sold his late grandfather's journals and schematics to the government. He got a very hefty paycheck and then disappeared to Europe to live off his newfound wealth."

"I'm still confused over what this has to do with Impals," I admitted.

"Well." Winder began. "The military's goal with this technology was to develop a teleportation device to send equipment, tanks or men anywhere instantly, the ultimate surprise attack."

"Did it work?" I asked.

"Sometimes," Winder admitted. "With equipment anyway."

"Did any people go through it?"

"Yes, one was burned alive in the electrical current and the other . . . well they still don't know where he is."

"So somebody got the idea that this thing would shred Impals?" I asked as my temper started to flare. The human capacity for ignorance and cruelty was beyond my comprehension.

"Not exactly . . . it was kind of an accidental discovery, you know like how the microwave oven was invented." Winder said, trying to muster a small smile that never materialized. I would have questioned his sincerity if it had.

I heard this story as well. Microwave emitters powered Allied radar in World War II. The leap from detecting Nazis to nuking nachos came in 1946, after a magnetron melted a candy bar in Raytheon engineer Percy Spencer's pocket.

"How?" I pressed.

"As coincidence would have it, they ran another human test at the facility in Arizona minutes after the cosmic storm arrived. The volunteer, if successful, was supposed to rematerialize about a mile away at a designated location on the base. Instead, he was thrown backwards by the electric current as if he hit a brick wall. He died on the spot, burned to a crisp. His spirit, his Impal part remained. It was probably due to disorientation, but the man's soul, his Impal, ran at the current and vanished without a trace."

I swallowed hard, having a good idea what happened next.

"So my father got wind of it and seized the opportunity?" I half stated and half asked.

Dr. Winder ducked his head and stared at his lap, avoiding eye contact. He shook his head as he spoke.

"No, major . . . he took it as more of a sign, a sign from God on how he was supposed to eradicate these unholy abominations. He got everyone riled up into a frenzy of fear so fast no one took time to stop and question it before it was too late."

"Jesus," I muttered.

"Yes son, He is who we must look to right now," Dr. Winder said.

I was about to ask how many Tesla Gates or 'Shredders' existed when a loud crack sent my heart leaping into my throat. The sound of gunfire erupted outside the car.

CHAPTER 11

THE BACK SEAT

"Tell mother, tell mother, I died for my
country ... useless ... useless."
~John Wilkes Booth

PANIC GRIPPED DR. WINDER. He pressed back into his seat almost as if he believed he were an Impal and could somehow pass through the padded leather into the safety of the trunk. I pulled my pistol out of my pocket and doused the overhead light. Total darkness engulfed us as a muffled yell and another gunshot rang out. My heart jumped into my throat.

I peered through the dark windows, trying to catch a glimpse of one of the shooters. There was only eerie silence. I could hear the rapid breathing of Dr. Winder close by in the blackness. He emitted a pathetic whimper with each exhalation; the man was terrified. And why shouldn't he be? I was scared as hell too, and I trained for situations like this.

I jumped in surprise as something heavy and metallic smashed against the top of the car. Whirling in the direction of the sound, my heart almost stopped as a bright light blinded me. I first thought they shot out the window. Unless they used a tank, that would be impossible on a presidential limo. My second thought was an explosion, but this theory was dispelled when I saw the source of the light. My jaw became unhinged as I watched the shimmering luminescence of an Impal almost land in my lap. This Impal just passed through rear passenger door. He lay there dazed on his back staring up at me with horrified eyes. This was not just any Impal; this Impal was the President of the United States.

"My God . . ." he muttered in the tinny sounding Impal timbre. The sound, coupled with the gruesome surreal circumstances, made hackles stand up on my neck.

I jumped again as the heavy-metal object slammed against the side of the car, this time on the opposite side.

"Kingston . . . shot . . . got chains . . . captured," the president stammered as he continued to stare at me with wild-eyed panic.

I got the impression that Kingston was killed, and then captured. The president, by either a calm presence of mind or stupid dumb luck, had stumbled back here before he could be caught. Judging by his expression, I would say it was the latter.

"Who are they?" I hissed as a fist pounded on my window. I could hear unintelligible muffled voices.

The president shook his head. He appeared as if all hope had left him.

"It was a bunch of street punks. I opened the door for some fresh air and they . . ." he said, trailing off.

I finished the sentence for him.

"Shot you?"

He stared at his glowing, luminescent hands as if he had never seen them before. I guess he hadn't, not like that anyway.

In the glowing ambience of the president, I could see Dr. Winder staring into space. His expression was as vacant as an empty glass. I wondered for a few moments if he were still alive until I saw him take a shuddering breath.

"Doctor!" I snapped. "Doctor . . . is there any way they can get in here?"

He didn't respond at first then his eyes turned toward my face. He reminded me of one of those creepy funhouse portraits with the eyes that follow you. All factors considered, I hadn't been this frightened and creeped out since my encounter with the nest of snakes as a boy.

"No," he said, emptiness in his voice, and then returned his gaze to the unseen spot in the air.

I sank to my knees in the floor and cradled my gun skywards as I listened to the noises outside. One thing kept running through my head. How the hell could this have happened to the President of the United States. A bunch of street punks? I guess if the President has no security detail and exercises poor judgment, he's as vulnerable as the rest of us.

I felt a strong desire for a cell phone or walkie-talkie to get in touch with my friends on the tour bus. I wasn't sure when they would be back and I didn't want them to be ambushed as well.

Muffled voices and banging on the roof seemed to engulf the car from all sides. The blows vibrated the roof and windows like a violent thunderstorm. Dr. Winder remained vegetative while the president sat up and tried to compose himself. The man was a war hero and a tough politician, not to mention a brave advocate for the Impals. I would imagine that this was the most incredible and disturbing experience he ever endured.

My heart sank as I watched him try to regain composure. I'm sure Andrews will be pleased to see the president in this state. It broke my heart. I felt like I deserved some amount of the blame for this because, after all, this was my father's, my flesh-and-blood's fault. As the pounding ceased and the muffled voices faded away, I sat my gun on the seat beside me and buried my head in my hands . . . I was ashamed.

"What am I going to do?" the president asked, trying to sound more like a world leader asking for strategic advice than a scared, lost child. He succeeded, although not completely. How could anyone totally compose themselves in a situation like this?

"When Danny and the others get back, you'll come with us, Mr. President," I said, glancing at Dr. Winder. The scientific adviser was still a statue of fear.

"I-I can't," he stammered. "I have my duties . . . I can still perform them."

"Mr. President," I said. "Do you think General Garrison is going to treat you different from any other Impal? He will declare you an abomination that has infiltrated the highest level of government. He will then ship you off to the nearest Shredder."

"My wife, my children," the president said in the saddest voice I have ever heard.

I shook my head. "We can try to get them to you," I said. "It won't be easy."

He paused, his face twitching as if considering something unpleasant. When he spoke, he sounded as if he were about to wretch. "And . . . my body?"

I had no idea. I would discuss that subject with Danny when they returned and it was a decision that needed careful consideration.

"We'll work it out Mr. President. We'll do the best thing."

The next several minutes passed in uncomfortable silence. I listened for the return of our friends, the return of our attackers or worse . . . the approach of police cars. If the police arrived on the scene, we were screwed. Inside the car, there were two dead bodies. One was the President of the United States and the other a Secret Service agent. Add a wanted rogue major, a catatonic science adviser, and an Impal. An Impal my father would claim is impersonating the President of the United States. Yep, there was no way we weren't going to jail.

Finally, after what seemed like an eternity, I heard the familiar rumble of the tour bus as it pulled up beside us. I picked up my gun, aiming it at the door, and then slowly opened it. Bus exhaust fumes wafted inside and I coughed and squinted my eyes. My two companions seemed unaffected for very different reasons.

"Cecil! Are you in there?" Danny shouted from the far side of the bus.

"Yes, I'm okay . . . I think they left!" I called.

My heart leapt as a shriek ripped through the heavy, humid air. Charlotte had seen one or both of the bodies.

"Shut up!" Andrews hissed from somewhere to my right. "Do you want every cop within ten miles on top of us?"

I eased out of the back seat then turned and gave the president a reassuring salute before closing the door. Danny and Andrews eased into sight around opposite ends of the bus, their guns at the ready. We all crept towards the front seat of the limo.

"Dear God," Danny muttered as he peered in the driver's side window, which was rolled about halfway down.

A large, bald black man wearing a dark suit slumped over the steering wheel. His well-groomed and professional appearance suggested he was a Secret Service agent. A dime sized hole trickling blood above his left temple offered little doubt about the cause of death.

I eased to the other side and opened the passenger door to find the president's body lying sideways across the seat. One foot was in the floorboard while the other hung out the open door, which he opened for 'fresh air'. The tassels on his brown calfskin loafers blew in the breeze like a macabre wind chime. I shuddered and backed away when I saw blood dripping from the seat and pooling in the floorboard beneath him.

"I think we saw a group of men taking him into the metro station," Andrews said, pointing at Kingston.

"Where?" I said, not comprehending.

Andrews turned and pointed. In the distance, I could just make out the black pole brandishing an 'M' for metro. It marked the entrance to the Arlington Cemetery Metro train station.

"Why the hell would they take him there?" I asked.

"Convenience," Charlotte muttered, stepping into sight from the other side of the bus. "The Federal Triangle Metro station is under the Reagan Building. That's where they are holding Impals until they can be shipped off to bases with Shredders."

I visited this building several times. Not because I had business there, it was because it was the closest Metro station to the Smithsonian's American History Museum. The entrance to this station is in the dead center of an enormous courtyard, which the Reagan building encompasses. There are three or four narrow passageways leading out of the courtyard to the surrounding streets. They are narrow enough to be easily blocked and guarded by a minimal amount of soldiers. It was the perfect Impal-holding center with the convenience of rail transportation beneath it.

"We can worry about Impal detention centers later!" Danny

snapped. "We have a bigger issue to deal with at the moment!" He pointed at the bodies in the limo and put his hands on his hips as he shook his head. "How the shit did you let this happen, Cecil?"

I didn't appreciate the accusatory tone in his voice.

"I was getting briefed in the back seat like you told me to!" I snapped. "The president stepped up front to make a call and get some fresh air! What in the devil was I supposed to do? Say, no Mr. President, sit your ass down?"

Danny glared at me for several long moments until finally Andrews spoke up. He said exactly what I expected him to.

"Son of a bitch got what he deserved," he muttered.

"In the bus, NOW!" Danny growled, turning on him. Andrews started to protest before Danny cut him short. "Both of you get back on the bus and reassure our guests!"

Charlotte complied, but Andrews stood fast. He and Danny eyed each other like two dogs about to fight over territory. The stalemate was finally broken when Danny brought his gun forward. He still aimed at the ground, grasped tight with both hands. There was no doubt that he could bring it up and fire in a split second.

"Now . . . unless you want to be an Impal too, you need to fall in line. We don't have time for this hot-headed bullshit, understand?"

Andrews glanced at the gun and then stared in Danny's eyes as if he wanted to gouge them out with a dull knife. Keeping his gaze planted on Danny, unblinking, he joined Charlotte on the bus.

"Where are Winder and the other half of the president?" Danny asked, relief washing over his face as he slid his gun back in his waistband. It dawned on me that this was more than a temperamental dispute. I think Danny believed he might have to shoot Andrews. This troubled me on many different levels.

"In the back," I said, motioning with my head.

He followed me around to the rear passenger door and I opened it. Dr. Winder was still unmoving. He could have been a terrified mannequin as he sat there, staring into space. The president seemed to have composed himself. "I didn't feel comfortable in my own skin," he said with a laugh.

Danny began to chuckle in spite of himself. As it turned out, laughter was contagious as we all shared a laugh. Dr. Winder did not. I was starting to worry about him. It felt good to break the tension for a moment, even though we still faced a long and dangerous night.

"Mr. President, I need you to take these," Danny said, reaching into his pocket and producing a couple of D cell batteries.

The president reached out and took the batteries. The instant they touched his hand, his luminescent glow faded and he appeared to be flesh and blood. For the first time I realized he was not in his typical suit and tie. The President was wearing blue jeans and a button down Oxford shirt; just one of the guys.

"Mr. President, you and Dr. Winder will ride back to camp in the SUV's with Andrews, Charlotte and our Impal refugees," Danny said.

"What about this car and . . ." he stopped, glancing toward the front of the car.

"Cecil and I will take care of it, don't worry."

"They can track the car," the president said. "There is a GPS transponder under the dash."

"I know," Danny said. "We'll take care of it."

I wasn't sure if he knew or not or even how to take care of it. I hoped to God he did.

In a few minutes, the group of fifteen Impals, which now included the President of the United States, packed into the two SUV's. They each received their own pair of batteries so they could blend in. Charlotte drove one while Andrews drove the other. We carried Dr. Winder like a rag doll and strapped him into the seat next to Charlotte. He was going to be a challenge for Dr. Acosta when we got back to camp.

As soon as the vehicles were out of sight, Danny and I went about our unpleasant task. First, we moved the bodies from the front seat to the back. Miraculously, we were able to move both men with only getting a minimum amount of blood on us. Kingston was a large man and required a considerable amount of effort to move. We laid out both men with great respect, shoulder to shoulder in the back floorboard. I would like to say they appeared to be sleeping. I cannot. Their gaping bullet wounds and bloodstains suggested otherwise.

Before the others left, Danny retrieved a couple of blankets from the back of one of the SUV's. These we draped over the bloodstained seats while flipping the floor mats to conceal and cover the pooled blood in the floorboard. It reminded me of a scene from the movie *Pulp Fiction*. The two main characters tried to camouflage the inside of a blood soaked car.

Danny produced a large pocketknife and then leaned up underneath the dashboard. After a couple of minutes of poking and prying, he produced a small black box and sat it in the seat.

"We'll dispose of this when the time is right," he said.

Danny got behind the wheel and I carefully sat down on the passenger side. I hoped the wool blankets and inverted floor mats would be enough to contain the gruesome fluid.

A few moments later, we pulled out, headed for home; hoping God and dumb luck would be on our side. We faced a long drive, in a very noticeable automobile. Not to mention, the corpse of the President of the United States was in the back seat.

CHAPTER 12

THE SILENT SALUTE

"Soldier, rest! Thy warfare o'er."
~Sir Walter Scott

DURING HIS FIRST PRESIDENTIAL CAMPAIGN, the president took a lot of heat from health nuts for his contradictory lifestyle. He was an avid runner and swimmer and kept in good physical condition, especially for a man in his late fifties. Nevertheless, he also held an affinity for fast food, more specifically, Martian Burgers fast food.

It was not a national chain. Most of its restaurants existed east of the Mississippi river with a few springing up in Europe. It was known from coast to coast because of the president's paparazzi shots. He could be seen on a newscast or in a newspaper almost every week enjoying an Out of this World Saucer Burger with a side of Martian Finger Fries. Always washed down with a Take Me to Your 'Liter' sized soft drink.

We left the tour bus behind. Danny said it would be morning before it is discovered. When we left the lot and turned onto the parkway, Danny spoke in a mischievous voice. "Where is the nearest Martian Burgers?" he asked.

I could not believe that he could be hungry. Then as his sly grin registered, I understood.

"You want to leave the GPS tracker there?"

"I know we are in a damned morbid situation right now, and I can't think of a better reason to enjoy a little laugh. It keeps the arteries clear and the blood pressure low."

"Won't we be spotted?" I asked. "It's not like the presidential limo can pull into the Martian Burgers' parking lot without being noticed."

I realized Danny was trying to soften the mood. God knows driving a blood soaked makeshift hearse requires a lot of mood softening. It was a risk. Most of these restaurants are located in high population areas. I am sure the great majority, if not all; of them have surveillance cameras inside and in the parking lot. I wasn't sure how we would be able to pull a limo through there unnoticed. However, Danny wanted to be noticed.

"After they discover where the tracker is, they will review the footage of the parking lot. When they see the limo pull through and then leave, they will know the president has been kidnapped. They'll have an APB out on the car, but they'll never find it."

"Why not?" I asked.

"The lake at our base, it used to be an old soapstone quarry, it's pretty damned deep."

"So you're gonna dump the car in there? It still doesn't change the fact that every cop and all the military personnel in five states will be searching. Won't it increase our risk of being discovered?"

Danny shook his head. "It would if we were staying put. After we make the delivery to the Chesapeake, we are going to break camp and relocate."

"Where?" I asked.

"You'll know when you are there," Danny said.

I knew he wasn't going to tell me, so I didn't push it. It was probably better I didn't know.

Ten minutes later we spotted the distant flying saucer shaped sign of Martian Burgers. We approached with caution, watching for police cars. We didn't think anyone would be aware of the president missing yet. The one thing in our favor is, strangely enough, the car. Limousines were almost as common as taxicabs around the Washington D.C. area.

Washington Police officers have a tendency to look the other way if one of these behemoths is speeding or running a red light. The reason being, one never knows who the important, powerful individual is behind the tinted glass. Writing a ticket was not nearly as important to them as their job. A limo with government plates, like this one, gave us an extra layer of immunity to the police. At least, until the president is reported missing. Then all bets are off.

Danny produced a leather glove from his pocket and slid it onto his right hand. Kingston's blazer was lying folded on the dashboard. He removed it when he and the president sat idle enjoying the fresh air of Arlington Cemetery. He reached out and grabbed it then said, "Here, take the wheel."

I steered down the four-lane road, which was light on traffic tonight, as Danny slid into the dead man's jacket. It was a bit big on him, yet manageable.

"If they see the driver's arm coming out the car window, they will assume it is Kingston since I am wearing his jacket. My skin color is concealed," he said, holding up the gloved hand.

My mouth hung open. I was convinced that Danny received a blow to the head sometime tonight. There was some logic with what he was saying. Most insane people possess some sort of method to their madness. I didn't think Danny was insane, however I did think we were going out of our way for a joke.

We pulled into the parking lot, drawing curious stares from bystanders. Danny drove up to the large trash can before the drive-up speaker. It was an alien with his mouth opened wide to greedily accept each patron's trash. A silly, lolling tongue and crossed eyes gave it a comical appearance.

Danny grabbed the black box and stuffed it down the alien's throat before driving away. I half expected him to pull up to the window and order dinner. The prospect didn't sound half-bad, considering our culinary choices at camp. We didn't press our luck. Once we were safely away from the restaurant, Danny asked me to take the wheel again. I did as he shed the coat and tossed it in the floorboard.

An hour later, we pulled up to the mess hall at camp. The limousine did not traverse the old dirt road as smoothly as the SUVs. The knots on the top of my head were evidence of that. The SUVs were parked nearby and the Impals already escorted to the safety of the mine. Barbara and Abbs ran out to greet us joined by Taylor and Charlotte. Sam Andrews was nowhere in sight. Did he take the president away somewhere, torturing him with iron bars and chains . . . knowing he had an hour or two before Danny got back? I didn't dwell on the question long because I was soon wrapped in the warm embrace of my family.

"Thank God you're back!" Barbara exclaimed. "We heard what happened."

Even in the purple luminescent glow of the night, I could see Danny's face turn three shades of red. It was his place to come back and inform everyone, not for Andrews to come back and start a panic.

"Where is he?" Danny growled.

Everyone seemed confused except for Taylor and me. Taylor jerked his head toward the mine. Without a word, Danny turned and hurried in that direction. My stomach knotted when I saw him pull out one of his pistols and inspect the chamber before passing into the total darkness of the woods.

"What's wrong?" Barbara asked.

"Nothing," I said and ushered them back inside the mess hall.

There are few words I have uttered in my life that made me feel more ridiculous. Nothing? What we endured was far from nothing. Nevertheless, it was the only answer I could manage right now. To Barbara's credit, she did not question further.

Abbs answered my question before I could ask.

"Steff is asleep. We couldn't wake her. I guess she had a long day," she said with a smirk.

I received a pleasant surprise when we got to the mess hall. There was a slight improvement in our menu choices. Instead of Vienna sausages, I was treated to a can of name brand tuna, not the cheap watery value brands. I also enjoyed a side of Ritz crackers and a canned soda to wash it all down. The soda was warm, but it still tasted wonderful. To top it all off, I relished a Twinkie for dessert.

I remembered the greasy goodness of an Out of this World Saucer Burger and an ice-cold Take Me to Your Liter sized soft drink. Oh well, those luxuries were just pipe dreams for a person on the run with no cash. They would have to wait until this phenomenon has passed. Deep down, I feared it would probably be a long time, if ever.

We retired for the night with the promise from the cook of a hot shower before breakfast. He rigged up a makeshift privacy fence using scrap lumber from some of the surrounding cabins. A metal bucket hung on a rope and pulley would serve as the showerhead. I appreciated his ingenuity and I was sure my own olfactory system would appreciate it as well. I was starting to smell my own ripeness and after tonight's activities, I felt beyond filthy.

We would need a good shower after Danny and I buried the bodies of the two men in the back of the car. We debated on the way back what type of funeral it should be. We both agreed the president deserved a funeral with full military honors, especially since he was a veteran. The problem is, the traditional twenty-one rifle salute would have to be eliminated. A single gun firing in the valley would attract attention, let alone seven of them firing three times. We couldn't risk it.

The next morning, at sunrise, we located a secluded thicket on the far side of the lake. It was a beautiful location surrounded by towering pines and a peppering of dogwoods. Danny and I each dug a grave then gathered rock from the shoreline around the lake. There was enough width between the trees for us to drive the limo around to the thicket. We removed each body from the car and, with great care and respect, placed them in a grave and then covered them with a blanket. After filling the graves in and stacking them with rocks, we pushed the limo into the lake.

At first, I didn't think it was going to sink when it stopped a few yards out, with water just up to the windows. After a couple of minutes it began to slide forward and then turned nose down as it eased beneath the black water. I pictured the sheer cliff of the rock quarry as the car slid into the silence, coming to rest more than a hundred feet below the surface in its own cold, dark, and watery grave. A shiver ran up my spine as I turned away from the ring of bubbles left by the sinking car.

Danny and I went back to the mess hall and took turns showering. It wasn't the Ramada Inn, but I definitely felt better afterwards. We went inside and helped the cook start breakfast. Barbara and the girls showed up as we were frying up a side of bacon. The cook drove one of the SUV's last night to an all-night grocery and restocked some nonperishables. He also brought us a treat of bacon, eggs and donuts for breakfast.

The girls finished their showers as we cracked the first eggs in the iron skillet on the propane cook stove. It dawned on me that we would soon need more propane since we were now using a propane tank to heat water for the shower. Danny said we were moving eventually. I did not know when.

Soon the whole camp arrived and those not partaking of our fabulous breakfast were showering. After a while, it occurred to me that everyone was here except for Andrews and Burt. I planned to go and see Burt after breakfast. I was sure he was taking it easy this morning, especially since Sally was here and seemed in a chipper mood. She fixed Burt a plate and left after she finished breakfast.

"I'll be up shortly," I said. "Before the service . . ."

Danny hadn't said anything about last night when he went after Andrews and I didn't ask. I hoped he didn't have to shoot him. Almost in answer to my question, Andrews showed up in the doorway wearing a scowl on his bruised and scraped face. I was sure the man sitting across the table from me did it.

"Crazy prick," I heard Danny mutter under his breath.

If looks were lasers, Danny would now be a pile of ashes. The hatred on Andrews's face was palpable. He walked through the mess hall and out to the shower. I didn't see him again until the funeral.

"What the hell did you get yourself into last night?" Burt asked, sitting up in bed and hoisting his legs over the side. He let out an involuntary cry of pain as he shifted his shoulder the wrong way.

"I've been wondering the same thing all night," I said. "I woke up this morning thinking I had a very bizarre dream until Danny came by and . . ."

"Roped you into shovel duty?" Burt asked. His question was a bit crass even though it was accurate. Burt sometimes possessed a knack for blunt speech.

I shrugged and then wrinkled my nose. "You're getting a shower before the service, right?" I asked.

"What shower?" Burt asked, incredulous. "Are we checking in to Motel 6?"

He reached for his plate beside his cot and took the final bite of a donut now saturated in cold egg yolk. Sally strode over from the window she just finished cleaning and took his plate.

"Why don't we go get one together?" she said, stroking his hair.

Burt grinned and slapped her on the rear. "You'll have to excuse me," he said. "Duty calls."

I didn't know whether to laugh or to grimace. That mental image was going to take me a while to lose. The shower was very close to the mess hall. For the sake of myself and all the other residents of our camp, I hoped they reserved their amorous intentions for the privacy of their cabin.

At noon, we gathered in the thicket to pay our respects to Kingston and our fallen Commander in Chief. The whole camp was there, including Andrews, although he kept his distance from the rest of us. When it came time for the honor guard, seven men stepped forward. They were a mixture of military and civilian, one of which being Taylor. They stood together in straight line next to the graves. Instead of firing rounds, they held their rifles skywards with their left hand and saluted with their right. They stood in place for exactly twenty-one seconds.

There are several theories and stories about the origins of the twenty-one rifle salute. Given the current circumstances on the planet, one particular story came to mind. I heard one time as a child that the three volleys fired at a funeral are not a salute. Instead, they are a funeral custom. It started a long time ago when they believed the shots would scare evil spirits away from the grave. Come to think of it, I believe I heard it from my father.

The irony was not lost on me because we could now see spirits and I have not encountered any I deemed to be evil. A childish idea followed my childhood memory. "What if we still couldn't see evil spirits, but they were there all the same, like the Impals before the storm?"

"Preposterous," I answered the voice in my head, turning my attention back to the service as Danny said a few last words.

In the distance, on the other side of the lake, I caught a faint glimpse of something shimmering among the trees. I first thought it was a reflection from the surface of the black, placid water until I saw it move. I screwed up my eyes to see what it was then, all at once, recognition dawned on me. It was the president.

A knotted dull ache started in my gut. I was embarrassed. He wasn't supposed to see this; he shouldn't see this. I could only imagine the disquieting feeling of watching one's own funeral. My own embarrassment was soon replaced by aggravation when I realized what a risk he was taking. Impals were not supposed to be outside of the mine without batteries.

I stepped back a little from the group, staring directly at him. He didn't notice me at first; his gaze was fixed on the two mounds of soil and rocks in the center of the thicket. After a few moments, he turned his head toward me. I was too far away to see his expression; however his posture suggested he felt guilty. He fidgeted for a few seconds then turned and strode away through the woods. My heart jumped into my throat when I saw he was not heading in the direction of the mine. I hoped the service would be over very soon.

CHAPTER 13

PRESIDENTIAL INTRODUCTIONS

"I think 'Hail to the Chief' has a nice ring to it."
~John F. Kennedy

As SOON AS THE SERVICE ENDED and everyone dispersed, I pulled Danny aside and told him what I saw.

"For God's sake, maybe Andrews did knock him senseless with that iron bar last night," Danny spat.

"Andrews attacked the president?" I asked. I already suspected it.

"Like a damned piñata," Danny muttered as we turned to walk in the direction where I last saw the president. "I had to kick his ass to get him to stop."

"Where did he do it?" I asked, hoping none of my family saw or heard Andrews's brutality.

"Inside the two barriers at the entrance to the mine," Danny said, holding his hands a couple of feet apart.

I remembered the tarps that Burt took me through on my first night in camp. It was so completely dark in the area between the tarps; I had no real concept of the size of the space. There were about five paces between them, which is not much room to conduct a flogging.

"Jesus," I said. "Did any of the Impals inside know what was going on?"

"I don't know how they couldn't," Danny said. "I could hear the commotion when I was still a good distance away."

"They were probably too frightened to intervene," I said.

"Yeah, I guess they thought your daddy showed up with his storm troopers," Danny quipped.

The remark cut, even though every word of it was true and Danny immediately regretted it.

"Sorry," he muttered, "It's been one hell of a last twenty-four hours."

"Tell me about it," I said.

We walked in silence for a while. When we reached the place the president stood, we headed north. Did he run away? The question troubled me. If he did, we must find him immediately, for his sake and ours.

We walked about ten minutes when we spotted the president sitting on a large rock in the middle of a patch of ferns. Danny and I froze in place when we got a little closer. The president's head rested in his hands and appeared to be weeping.

A bizarre image suddenly popped into my head. I recalled a scene from the novel I did my sixth-grade book report on, *Tom Sawyer*. Tom and Huck's raft had been run over by a steamboat in the Mississippi River and they were presumed dead. The town mourned their loss all the while Tom and Huck were camping on an island in the river. The boys happened to stumble into town on the day of their funeral, oblivious to the fact they were proclaimed dead. They wandered into the back of the church and began to weep for the two boys being eulogized. They didn't realize they were crying for themselves. Was that what the President was doing . . . mourning himself at his own funeral? I found that hard to believe. Nevertheless, there he was, luminescent tears disappearing into the rock like shimmering ethereal rain.

The president glanced up and saw us watching. He composed himself and got to his feet.

"Lovely service, gentlemen. Although I never pictured myself being put to rest in a mining camp next to a rock quarry. That has to be a first for presidents," he said with an uneasy laugh.

"You shouldn't have come, Mr. President," Danny said with respect. "I warned you it would be unsettling."

He blinked as if not comprehending. "Oh . . . this?" he said point-ing to his eyes. "I must admit, it was an odd experience." He paused as if searching for the right words. "No, I was mourning my family. I don't know if they are okay or if I will ever see them again."

His voice quivered as he finished. The emotional vibration to his Impal voice reminded me of a Theremin instrument from one of those old science-fiction movies. I think it was the most pitiful noise I have ever heard.

"It's all my fault . . . this whole damn thing is my fault. If I hadn't been so weak, so vulnerable . . ." his voice trailed off as more silvery tears streamed down his face.

My heart went out to him. Not because this was uncharacteristic behavior for the leader of the free world, but because I knew it was genuine. He gained a reputation for wearing his heart on his sleeve during the campaign. He shed tears during one of the debates as he professed his love for his country and the brave men and women who serve it. His critics called it a stunt. I didn't believe that. I think it is the mark of a man who cares. Most Americans agreed with me. He took a sizable lead in the polls after that debate and ran away with the election.

"It's not your fault, Mr. President," I said. "It's my father's. He fooled us . . . he fooled us all."

The president got up and strode over to me. He put his hand on my shoulder; the cold of his touch was unsettling, yet appreciated.

"You're a good man, major," he said. "I do not hold your father's actions against you. In some strange way he believes he is doing the right thing."

"So did Hitler," I said. Like an involuntary belch, it was out of my mouth before I knew it.

He considered me through narrowed eyes for several moments. Soon, a wry smile creased his shimmering face. "No, Hitler didn't have an honorable son," he said and then turned back in the direction of the mine.

"Okay, colonel . . . I'm going back to time-out now," he proclaimed as we started to walk with him. The president turned to Danny with a smirk on his face. "And do me a favor please. Don't get me those cheapo batteries anymore, they make me itch," he said as he pretended to scratch his arms. "Get me some Duracells or Energizers or something!" he snapped.

Danny took his request very seriously and promised to requisition a case for him at once. I, on the other hand, never heard of an Impal getting an itch from generic batteries. I suspected this was the president's attempt at humor. He confirmed this a few moments later when he turned and winked at me. Danny continued to yammer on how every Impal would get only name brand batteries from here on. I liked this man and was sorry to see him in this state, especially being separated from his family. I made a silent vow to do whatever I could to reunite him with his family or at the very least find out how they are doing.

I knew deep down my options were limited. We were secluded and his family is monitored day and night. The biggest problem was the president would be leaving the country with the other Impals. It would happen in the near future and that gave me no time.

When we reached the mine, Danny and I entered under the tarp with the president. I noticed his unease as we walked across the barrier between the tarps. This was understandable since he had just gotten the crap beaten out of him in here last night.

When we entered the mine, my breath escaped me again. The surreal atmosphere of the low lantern light and the ethereal shimmer of the Impals astounded me. I spotted Chief Powhatan and President Abraham Lincoln sitting side by side in a couple of folding chairs. The two men seemed to be having an intense conversation. The chief spotted me and raised his right hand in greeting. I returned the gesture as Lincoln got up and walked over to us.

"Are you all right, Mr. President?" Lincoln asked, addressing the president.

"Fine, fine . . . I have never felt better," the president said. "Thanks again for coming to my rescue last night."

I raised an eyebrow at Danny. I was under the impression that *he* had come to the President's defense.

"Well . . . I finished him off," Danny said.

"That you did, sir! That you did!" Lincoln said with jubilation. "I only hit him a few times with one of those squench buckets," he said, suppressing a laugh.

I guess it would explain the crusty appearance of Andrews's hair this morning and his determination to get a shower.

I knew Lincoln met Thomas Pendleton and his son, Seth, because Thomas told me. "Did you get the term from Thomas and Seth?" I asked.

Lincoln's face changed as if someone threw cold water on him. "Well I'll be darned . . . you know them? Where are they . . . are they here? They disappeared several weeks ago in the city and I haven't seen them since. Please tell me they are okay."

My somber expression and a single shake of my head was all the answer the former president required. "The accursed Gate?" he exploded.

I didn't answer.

"Damn that man, damn that man to Hell!" Lincoln snapped. "I watched that vile man for a long time in the White House, even before he could watch me back. I always knew there was something sinister about him!" He paused for a moment as if something suddenly popped into his head. "How did Thomas. . . ?" he asked, trailing off as if he already knew the ghastly answer.

"He was trying to save Seth," I said.

"Damn that sadistic son of a whore!" Lincoln continued in an uncharacteristic rage. "How he ever became a general is beyond me. If he were on my watch I would bust him down so far, he could kiss his own ankles without bending over!"

As soon as the words left his mouth, Lincoln realized he put his proverbial foot in it. Regret etched his noble face. "I'm sorry, Mr. President," Lincoln said. "I know what the circumstances were like for you . . . I didn't mean anything by what I said. You are a good and honorable man and a good president."

"No, you are absolutely right Mr. President; I should have done more," he said.

The two men stood in uncomfortable silence for several moments. Finally, Lincoln broke the tension. He turned to me and extended his hand.

"I don't think we have been properly introduced, I'm Abe Lincoln. You can call me Abe."

I grasped his hand and flinched a little from the extreme cold of his touch.

"I'm Cecil, Cecil Major," I said. I wasn't about to tell him my real name and let him put two and two together. The president cut his eyes at me, however he said nothing.

The president's heart was in the right place. He insisted that Danny and I keep our ranks. Unfortunately, he made one of the stupidest statements I have ever heard.

"He is a major in the Army too," the president said. "I guess he's like the character from *Catch-22*, Major Major."

Lincoln did not understand the reference. That book was not published until almost a century after Lincoln was assassinated.

"We need to be getting back, Cecil," Danny said. "We need to go over our evacuation plan."

"I'm still not too keen on leaving the country," the current president said. "Not when so much is going on."

Lincoln was in complete agreement. He didn't want to run away.

"Mr. Presidents," Danny said, addressing both of them. "We've been over this, you can't stay. It is far too dangerous."

Danny stopped short of telling both men that they were irrelevant. Neither one of them wielded power anymore. President or not, they were now Impals . . . public enemy number one. There was nothing they could accomplish by staying, however, Danny did a very kind and decent thing. He gave both of them a purpose.

"The Impals we are evacuating will need guidance and leadership in their new home. I believe the two of you are the best ones to provide it for them."

They agreed somewhat reluctantly. We excused ourselves to go back to the mess hall.

"I need you to do me a favor," Danny said as we walked through the woods.

"What?"

"We are going to need all hands on deck when we evacuate the Impals. We also need to have some people left here to guard the camp."

"Agreed," I said.

"I want you to help me keep an eye on Andrews. We need him, but we also don't need his hot head getting the best of him." I nodded as Danny continued. "And I sure as Hell don't trust leaving him here at camp unsupervised."

"Definitely not with our families here," I said.

Danny took a deep breath before he made his final request. "I want you to promise me the first time you see him getting even a little out of line, you'll put him down. Put him down and then put the irons on his sorry soul."

CHAPTER 14

I TIMOTHY 4:1

"Integrity is the lifeblood of democracy. Deceit is a poison in its veins."
~Edward Kennedy

I BLINKED, UNSURE IF I UNDERSTOOD.

"You want me to kill him?"

Danny glanced at the other side of the trail as if he heard something. After a few moments, he faced forward and spoke in a voice just above a whisper. "You didn't see him last night . . . the rage in his eye. There was no remorse, no shred of any compassion; it was if he was filled to the brim with pure hatred." He paused to wipe the sweat off his brow and then whispered, "He scared the crap out of me, Cecil, and you know I don't admit that lightly."

My heart skipped a beat. Danny was one of the toughest and most fearless men I have ever known. Even when we experienced combat together in Iraq, I never knew him to display an ounce of fear. The fact that a punk kid like Sam Andrews scared him was enough to throw up a dozen red flags in my head.

"Jesus . . . to think we have enough to worry about with my father and the rest of the government," I said.

"Yep, and then we've got a ticking time bomb in our midst," he said.

"So why the hell do you need him?" I asked, a little ticked off.

Danny sighed. "Because we need all the eyes and ears we can get for this venture and," he shrugged his shoulders, "because Andrews's brother owns the boats we need to evacuate the Impals."

I felt my chest constrict. I forgot Andrews's brother owned the boats. So, until the Impals were away; we needed Andrews, temperamental or not.

Danny stopped and grabbed my arm. "I always knew Andrews was a hothead. That's one reason why he has been a lieutenant for years," he paused and took a deep breath. "What I did not know until a few days ago is Sam Andrews is an alcoholic, a pretty bad one according to Burt."

No further explanation was needed. We had a tough enough time providing decent food for the camp. Keeping a supply of alcohol was not only impractical, it was also impossible. I was certain that an alcoholic cutoff from the outside world would be going crazy about now. That, coupled with a short temper, presented a very dangerous combination.

"How long has it been since he had a drink?"

Danny shrugged. "I don't know, he's been here at least a week."

Before I could reply, Derek Vandeputte emerged from the woods a short distance in front of us. The same hunting rifle he used in our makeshift funeral this morning hung over his shoulder.

"How goes patrol?" Danny called to him.

"Taylor and I ran off a couple of hillbillies up on the north ridge. I think they are running a still somewhere up there," he chuckled.

"Do you think they were suspicious?" Danny asked.

"Maybe a little. We told them this was now a government controlled area and they needed to keep their distance," Derek said.

"Do you think it worked?" I asked.

"Maybe not. That's why I added the woods are littered with land mines. You should have seen their faces."

Danny and I couldn't help laughing at the mental image of a couple of slack-jawed hillbillies tiptoeing out of the woods.

"Derek, I'm going to need you and Taylor to be on guard duty next month when we take the Impals out," Danny said.

You could see the frustration on Derek's face. He wanted to be part of the action. I think my disappointment was every bit as obvious. We would be here until next month.

"It's an important job," I assured him. "There will be lots of family members here, including my own. I would be honored if you watched over them."

In all honesty, I would feel more comfortable with Derek keeping an eye on my family. I liked Taylor, but his attraction to my daughter made me uncomfortable, as a father, and as a leader. We just couldn't afford any distractions right now.

"I'll take care of them," he said with a boyish grin.

It suddenly struck me how young he was. That didn't help my confidence. Nevertheless, Danny and I continued back to the mess hall.

"Next month?" I prodded. "When next month?"

He shrugged.

"Not sure . . . haven't got that ironed out yet. Sometime in the first couple of weeks of October."

Only a little over two weeks, I guess it wasn't quite as bad as it sounded. Still . . . I was hoping it would be sometime in the next couple of days.

When we reached the mess hall, I was surprised to find Steff sitting on an old wooden bench outside the door. Her elbows were on her knees and her chin rested on clinched fists. She wore a disgusted scowl on her face.

"I'm sick of this crappy food!" she huffed. "Will you PLEASE take me to Martian Burgers? I know I saw one on the way in here!"

She was right; I noticed it last night on our way back from DC. There was a Martian Burger in a small town a few miles away. It seemed out of place because the only other things in this town were a gas station and a tiny Post Office. It sounded like a good idea to me, even though I knew we couldn't. I had no cash, I'm sure my debit, and credit cards had been frozen or were being monitored.

"I'm sorry, honey," I said. "We can't risk using my cards. It's too dangerous."

Danny, who paused to listen to our conversation, reached into his pocket and retrieved a wad of folded bills. He peeled a single bill out of the wad and held it out.

"Here's twenty bucks," he said, "Take your daughter to lunch."

"I-I can't," I stammered.

"Why not?" Danny asked.

"Well it wouldn't be fair," I said, pointing to the mess hall. The sounds of conversation and the smell of some type of fried meat wafted through the door.

"I won't tell if you won't," Danny said as he pitched me the keys to one of the SUV's then turned and went inside.

I was left standing dumbfounded with twenty dollars and car keys in hand and an expectant twelve year old staring at me.

"Let's go!" she said and began to lope towards the SUV's parked across the road from the mess hall.

Like a man in a dazed stupor, I began to follow her.

It only took ten minutes to reach the small hamlet with a Martian Burgers resting at the crossroads of two state highways. Steff was silent the whole way there, staring out the window. I knew she was just ignoring me. I remembered when she was little, which was only a few years ago, we couldn't go anywhere without her talking my ear off. A tear slid down my cheek and I quickly wiped it away. Where had my little girl gone? I believed she was still there underneath all the preteen hormones and attitude. Underneath her anger at me, I believed she was still there. I needed to figure a way to coax her back out.

"Do you remember when we went to Disney World?" I asked as we descended the mountain into the small town.

She shrugged and kept her gaze fixed out the window. Our trip to Disney World was our best family trip ever, according to Steff, and I don't think I have ever seen her happier. When we got off the ride 'It's a Small World', she turned and wrapped her arms around my waist and squeezed as hard as she could.

"Thank you, Daddy for bringing us here! I love you!" she beamed.

I will always cherish that memory.

"Well . . . maybe we can go back again when this is all over," I said.

This time it did not even warrant a shrug; she continued to stare out the window. After what seemed like an eternity she spoke, her back still too me, addressing my reflection in the glass.

"Can Grandpa come?" she asked.

I felt like something slimy slithered down my throat. I knew why she asked the question, she has always been a grandpa's girl. The absurdity of it caught me off guard. Even if this storm ended today and things went back to normal, my father and I would no longer have a relationship. In good conscience, I couldn't let Steff have one with him either.

"Maybe," I lied.

I knew things would never go back to normal. How could they? Countless relationships were destroyed. Multitudes of bridges were burned. Not to mention mankind's beliefs had been turned on their head. No, *normal* would have a new definition when this storm was over, *if* it ever was.

We got to Martian Burgers without another word between us. As we pulled into the parking lot, it occurred to me that I did not told Barbara and Abbs where we were going. I'm sure Danny would tell them.

"Where were your mother and Abbs? Did they know we were leaving?"

She seemed a little more talkative once she smelled the aroma of grilling hamburgers drifting from the restaurant.

"In the 'messy' hall having a fine meal of fried Spam, I'm sure," she said with condescension dripping from her voice.

I felt my frustration with her rear its ugly head inside me. I managed to tamp it down before it escaped into a regrettable outburst. Barbara and Abbs should be with us as well and I felt very peeved that I brought little miss attitude instead. She didn't deserve any special treatment. I had to keep in mind that she was just a kid. She didn't understand everything.

We went inside, ordered, and then took a seat by the large front window. Painted on the glass was a green, comical alien with a long red lolling tongue. I kept having the strange sensation as if he was trying to lick me. I slid the coin change across the table to Steff, which was our custom whenever we ate out. It started out as candy money, until her monetary earmarks evolved as she got older. We have been doing it since she was three years old. I guess old habits are hard to break. She snatched the coins, like a cat snagging a mouse, and slid them into her pocket. There was almost a dollar there. I didn't think Danny would mind. Besides, I wasn't going to ask for them back, not when I was trying to get on Steff's good side.

It wasn't long before I found myself lost in a world of ecstasy. After I took the first bite of my Flying Saucer Burger, I realized this burger truly was Out of this World. As I relished my meal, a strange idea occurred to me.

The irony of the situation began to sink in as I studied our fellow diners, everything appeared, well . . . normal. Aside from the lavender sky and yellowish clouds outside, one would never know that anything else was going on in the world.

People talked and carried on like always. Traffic flowed by as normal. The trash man emptied a dumpster across the street. A group of bicyclists cruised by wearing their spandex bike pants and matching color coordinated helmets. Across the highway, a man mowed his lawn. A noisy bunch of peewee football players came in to celebrate a victory. A police car waited behind a large hedge next door with a speed trap. Life went on as usual.

How could this be? Did these people not realize what was happening in the world? The title of an Edgar Allan Poe poem floated into my mind, *A Dream Within a Dream*. Though it was not completely fitting, it was more like these people were living a dream within a nightmare.

I felt my appetite slipping away. I put down my burger, took a sip of my 'Take Me to Your Liter' sized soft drink then pushed back from the table. I wanted to get up, to slap them awake, and to tell them to care. I knew it would be fruitless. People rarely pay attention to things they don't believe affect them. I couldn't convince them otherwise. My father has a lot bigger pulpit than I do, and he was being broadcast loud and clear over the restaurants radio speakers.

"The president is under the weather right now," he told the female interviewer. "We expect him to be up and around very soon."

"Not unless you accept Impals," I mumbled.

"He has asked me to give the American people and the world the assurance that everything is under control. He will be present at the United Nations conference in a few weeks to discuss the growing concerns over the Impal issue," my father said, venom dripping from his voice when he mentioned the word 'Impal'.

"Why isn't the vice president making this announcement?" the interviewer asked.

"He has more pressing matters to attend to with our current situation and the president on the sidelines. He asked me to fill in." Garrison said as smooth as a snake's tongue.

"There have been rumors, General Garrison, that the Impals here in our own country are not being rounded up for population issues. It has been said they are being exterminated instead. What do you say to those claims General?" the interviewer asked.

"Ridiculous!" he spat. "Why would we even consider something like that?"

"Well . . ." the interviewer began. "For one thing, you were very vocal a few days ago about the evil origins of Impals. Wouldn't that be reason enough?"

With the smooth finesse of a snake stalking it prey, he countered in the most innocent voice. He sounded so convincing that I damn near believed him. "Yes my dear, I did say it and I still believe it. Let me make one thing perfectly clear. This is the United States of America, the greatest and most humane country on the entire planet. We do not treat anyone in a cruel or unfair manner. Never have, never will."

A group of blue-collar workers in the back erupted into misplaced patriotic applause for my father's statement. I don't think anyone else in the restaurant even noticed. One person did notice. I turned to see Steff listening with rapt attention, a huge smile on her face.

"Grandpa sounds good on the radio, doesn't he?" she said proudly.

I didn't say anything. I felt horrified, like my child discovered a piece of pornography that they proudly proclaimed as fine art. I knew I couldn't say anything against my father to her and if I did, it would make things worse between us. Instead, I continued to listen to the verbal sewage coming over the airwaves.

"You mentioned a couple of days ago that there was a unanimous declaration from the religious community, not only from Christian leaders, but Jewish and Islamic leaders as well. They are agreeing these things, these Impals, are in fact demons. Assuming they are correct, why wouldn't you exterminate them?" the host asked.

"1 Timothy 4:1," my father said in a cold tone. "Now the Spirit speaketh expressly, that in the latter times some shall depart from the faith, giving heed to seducing spirits, and doctrines of devils."

Before the interviewer could respond, he continued.

"And let's not forget Matthew 7:1," he said. "Judge not, that ye be not judged."

"Okay, so what do those verses have to do with getting rid of demons?" the interviewer asked.

General Garrison cleared his throat and spoke in a very condescending tone.

"That should be obvious, my dear. We should not judge these Impals. If we do, we will be lowering ourselves to their level, giving heed to these seducing spirits. God is the only one who can judge their fate."

"So you are rounding them up for God?" the interviewer asked, returning a little of the condescension.

"Yes," my father said without emotion, "and to protect the rights of our citizens."

I swallowed hard. I appreciated the journalistic integrity of the interviewer. She was the first one I heard really challenge him. I hoped this wouldn't be her last broadcast. I also hoped this wouldn't be her last day before meeting a bullet and then the Tesla Gate.

The downright filthy hypocrisy and deceit made me feel a sudden wave of nausea. I excused myself to the restroom where I purged the first decent meal in days. After splashing cold water on my face, I returned to the table.

My heart stopped when I saw a police officer sitting at the table with Steff.

CHAPTER 15

CASUAL DETOUR

*"Propaganda does not deceive people; it merely helps
them to deceive themselves."*
~Eric Hoffer

"ARE YOU MR. GARRISON?" the chubby, middle age officer asked as I approached the table.

I stopped in my tracks and swallowed hard. I glanced at Steff and saw she was sitting there staring out the window. I guessed there wasn't any point lying since Steff had probably already told him the truth.

"Yes . . . can I help you officer?" I asked, trying to remain as calm and collected as possible.

The police officer narrowed his eyes, and then reached in his pocket. He retrieved a small steno pad and an ink pen. He looked me up and down for a moment then looked back at Steff. She was still staring out the window.

"What happened?" he asked, pointing to his own nose.

It took a minute for the meaning of his question to sink in. Then it dawned on me that he was referring to my swollen and broken nose. A lie flew into my head so fast it surprised me. It then spilled out of my mouth without hesitation.

"Softball," I said, touching the fingertips of both my hands together to demonstrate the dimensions of a softball. How could I have been so stupid to come out in public like this?

He grunted. "I used to play, wasn't too bad back in the day."

Judging by the officer's physique, I couldn't imagine him participating in any sports besides donut ring toss.

"What can I do for you, officer?" I asked in as helpful a tone as I could muster.

"I was going through the restaurant talking to folks and then I came across your daughter. Do you know what she told me?"

I thought my heart would take flight out of my chest it was hammering so hard. I glanced out the window. My first impulse was to grab Steff and run. That idea vanished when I looked outside. Another police officer stood in the parking lot talking to an elderly couple. There was no way we could make it out of the parking lot and even if we could what would we do, lead a police chase back to the camp? We were screwed. All I could do was answer the officer's question.

"What?" I asked, watching Steff, hoping to glean some iota of what she told the police. She was unreadable.

"She told me," he said, glancing back at Steff, "that you would be more than happy to make a donation to the Fraternal Order of Police association."

"I what?" I said in a defensive tone, as if he just accused me of harboring Impals. I was sure I hadn't understood.

"Well, she said you would be willing to make a donation to the Fraternal Order of Police. It's a good cause, we're just asking folks to donate whatever they can afford."

I stared at him for several moments before the truth sank in. Fumbling in my pocket, I pulled out the nine dollars in change left over from our lunch and handed it to him. He took it with an appreciative smile and counted the bills. When he finished, he produced a bank bag resting in his lap and inserted the cash. He set it down in front of him and picked up the pad and pen again.

"Would you like a receipt, Mr. Garrison?" he asked; ready to scribble on the pad.

"No, no . . . that's fine," I said as my senses started to come back to me. "I wish I could do more. That's all the cash and I don't have my checkbook with me."

"Thank you, sir," he said shaking my hand, "it is very much appreciated." The officer paused for a moment. "You folks aren't from around here, are you?" he said.

"No, Winchester," I lied.

He seemed satisfied. "Well, let me warn you, there's an Impal rights rally coming through here today. Things could get ugly."

"Impal rights?" I asked, trying to sound as innocent as possible. He didn't realize he was speaking to one of the biggest proponents of Impal rights east of the Mississippi.

"Yeah, it's this crazy fringe group who still believes those things have rights, can you believe it?"

I shook my head, pretending to play along.

"Well, so far they have been peaceful. There was a demonstration that got out of hand in Los Angeles the other day. Six people were 'killed," he said making quotation marks with his fingers.

I faked a puzzled expression. After hearing my father speak, I knew what he was saying.

"Yep, six demons appeared imitating the people who died. The LAPD put them in iron so fast they didn't have time to say boo," he said with pride. He then explained that his pride wasn't only because of police unity. "My cousin is on the LAPD. He said the city is now almost completely demon free."

"That's great," I said with a fake smile through gritted teeth.

I felt as if I was going to be sick again. To my relief, he got up and went to the next table.

"Stay off the main highway and watch out for those Pythonians," he said. Then he turned and began to solicit money from the elderly couple seated next to us.

There was that word again, the one I heard my father use on the radio the day Burt was shot.

"Oh . . . by the way," the officer said, turning on his heels and reaching into his shirt pocket. He produced a crumpled piece of paper, which he unfolded and held up for them to see. Crudely sketched on the paper in black ink was the Myriad symbol. "If you see anyone carrying or wearing this symbol, stay clear of them. They are Impal supporters and very dangerous."

"I guess I will have to stay away from my oldest daughter since she is wearing one around her neck." I thought.

"Thank you for the heads-up, officer" I said.

He gave me a satisfied smirk and then crumpled the drawing back in his pocket as he went to the next table.

As disturbed as I was by the officer's flippant attitude, I was also encouraged by what I heard. More people were involved with the resistance than we knew. While unorganized and unfunded these people are trying to make a difference, to stand up for what is right. They may or may not be harboring and protecting Impals, but their support was heartening. I liked these Pythonians.

Steff stared at me with a blank expression.

"Are you ready to go?" I asked.

She said nothing as she stood up, glanced at the police officer who was now across the room, then strode out the door.

I discarded our trash in the nearest Martian Head receptacle and followed her outside. She waited by the passenger door with a smirk on her face and her arms folded.

"Thanks for lunch," she said. It sounded more like a statement of obligation than appreciation. I took it as progress.

"You're welcome," I said then unlocked the doors.

The same silence returned as before while she continued to stare out the window. Maybe I had made progress today, however small. I hoped so because I love Steff more than anything and it killed me to see her like this, unhappy and miserable. Of course, we were all unhappy and miserable. Steff did not have the maturity to deal with it. As much as I wanted to yell and shake her in frustration, I knew it would make things worse. I needed to continue to be patient and supportive.

"When can we go home?" Steff asked as we started to climb the hill going out of town.

"Soon, I hope. Very soon," I lied.

I knew it would be a long time; if ever, before we could return home. Even if we did, I knew nothing would ever be the same again. I saw a smile begin to curve on the edge of her lips. I both felt encouraged and guilty. She was becoming a little more receptive, yet I lied to illicit a reaction.

I was about to attempt to engage her in conversation again when terror paralyzed me. The road to the mining camp was a long, winding, rut-filled trail winding through the woods. About fifty yards in and out of sight of the road, was a barricade and no trespassing sign, which we moved and replaced on every trip in and out. Directly across the highway from the "abandoned" road sat a small mom-and-pop grocery store and gas station. A Virginia State Trooper patrol car sat in its parking lot, its nose pointed toward the road. The single occupant watched us pass through mirrored sunglasses.

I tried to keep my cool as much as possible and continued down the road, passing by the entrance to the mining camp.

"Where are we going?" Steff asked, breaking her self-imposed silence.

"A little detour," I fibbed again. "I'm going to see if there is another entrance on the other side of the valley."

I felt terrible; my falsehoods were starting to come more frequently and with disturbing ease. I hated not being truthful with Steff, but what was I supposed to say? *I didn't want the cop to see us turn in there and get suspicious*? It would either alarm her or add fuel to her fire of distrust and anger towards me right now.

She stared at me with deep skepticism for a few moments. Then, to my surprise, she seemed to accept my excuse. Steff sighed and then turned her attention back to the window.

We drove close to five miles before I turned in to a small clearing, claiming the existence of the road must not be accurate. I then headed back towards the entrance across from the gas station, hoping the cop had decided to move on.

"So, the road coming in by the gas station is the only one?" Steff asked shortly after I turned us around.

"Looks that way," I said.

She pursed her lips for a few seconds and then turned back to the window.

I breathed a huge sigh of relief when we rounded a bend in the road and the gas station came into view. The cop was gone. An old man with a long white beard, wearing overalls with an orange hunting cap leaned against the sidewall. He was engaged in deep conversation with someone on a pay phone.

"They still make those?" I said aloud. I knew the nostalgia would be lost on Steff since she was a product of the smart phones and laptops generation. I noticed her watching the man as if she was trying to figure out a puzzle.

"Is that a phone?" she asked in disbelief.

I couldn't help grinning.

"Yep, that's how I asked your mother out for the first time," I said, turning onto the road to the camp.

Steff gave a disgusted grimace. "You didn't have a phone at home . . . a landlubber?" she asked.

It took everything to suppress a laugh. I could tell by her serious tone that this was not a time for jokes, especially not at her expense.

"Yes, we had a land*line* at home," I said, subtly correcting her mistake. "I was at boot camp when I asked her out; all we had were pay phones."

She considered this for several moments. After she processed the information, Steff returned to her window gazing.

We bounced and jolted down the old trail until finally descending into the camp. As I rubbed a knot on my head from bouncing into the ceiling, I wondered how we ever drove a limousine down this road. My mind drifted, causing me to lose focus on the trail.

Less than a hundred yards away from the mess hall, two rifle-toting men sprang out of the bushes. My heart almost took flight from my chest as I moved to cover Steff with my body. I felt foolish when I realized it was Taylor and another man I did not know. They quickly lowered their weapons and raised their hands in an apologetic wave. I sat up and waved, trying to recover some dignity. Steff looked at me as if to say, "*Oh please, Dad . . . really?*"

After parking near the mess hall, Steff hopped out of the vehicle without a word. She made a beeline through the woods towards our cabin. I felt a weird mixture of frustration and encouragement from our quality time together. In all honesty, I wasn't sure how to feel. At least I had gotten her out of her rueful existence in the camp, if only for an hour. Perhaps it would help her attitude. I wasn't going to hold my breath.

Danny stepped out of the mess hall and summoned me inside. When I entered, it surprised me to find the room completely empty except for Vandeputte and Andrews. They sat side by side at a table. Andrews wore a scowl, though it didn't seem to be a hateful one, maybe one of frustration. He seemed a little better than last time I saw him. To my great surprise, he spoke to me.

"Major," he said curtly.

"Andrews," I said.

Andrews was calm, civil and fidgety. He was in deep alcohol withdrawal.

Danny sat down beside me with the portable radio under his arm. It was something we would have called a 'boom box' or a 'ghetto blaster' back in the day. He set it in the middle of the table and turned on the power.

"Thank God we've got a good supply of batteries," he said, pointing to the assorted cases of AA, AAA and 9 volts in the corner.

When he found the station, he sat back with a grim frown. "I want y'all to hear this," he said.

It was a different station than the one playing at Martian Burgers. The only difference between radio stations anymore were the hosts. The message was all the same; government good, Impals bad. That was why I was surprised by what we heard; the radio station was actually hosting a debate. A couple of members of the Impal Citizens Empowerment, or ICE, debated a couple of members of the newly formed Impal Relocation Services, or IRS. I appreciated the irony that IRS was one acronym that could not seem to escape negative connotations. As the rest of the interview unfolded, my appreciation vanished.

"Why do you think the Impals should be given the same rights as everyone?" the male host with a deep baritone voice asked the members of ICE. A young woman spoke up, at least she sounded young on the radio.

"Because they are the very essence of what we are and what we will become," she said quite calmly. "The only difference between them and us is this."

Her example may have projected a more profound effect if on television. Nevertheless, even over the radio there was no mistaking the sound of a hand smacking flesh.

"Why should having a solid body make any difference?" a male member spoke up. "Isn't it what is inside that makes us special? Isn't our body just wrapping paper to be discarded by the hands of mortality?"

The kid's clever metaphors were impressive, but drowned out as one of the IRS members responded.

"This is assuming these things in fact are what you claim them to be. I think the general consensus now is quite the opposite," he snapped.

"General consensus sucks!" the ICE girl retorted.

It suddenly occurred to me why they invited these two on here for the debate. There was no desire for an open and equal forum. It was an ambush to discredit ICE and they were off to a good start.

"Sucks?" the IRS man chuckled. "My dear, consensus is what built this great country. How can you say it sucks?"

"She's saying your claim about consensus is bullshit," the ICE man retorted.

"Well, I will not repeat your inappropriate language on the radio. Let's just say I have a signed statement from the head of every major religion in this country. A statement that says our claim about consensus is not bovine excrement," he said with heavy sarcasm. "These, these things not only don't have rights, they are also a threat. The population increase and the threat of these devils is dire. This makes it more urgent than ever for the government to continue acting on the people's behalf."

"Devils?" the ICE girl chided. "What proof do you have they are devils?"

I agreed with their point of view. However, this young woman and young man were digging themselves an impossible hole. They played right into the agenda. It was like watching a train wreck in slow motion and there was nothing I could do.

"What say you on?" the host asked the IRS people with an obvious smile in his voice.

Another one spoke up this time. He had a strong Southern accent. "Well, let me ask one question. What one material are these things vulnerable to?"

"Iron," the host replied with rehearsed enthusiasm.

"E-x-a-ctly," the southern IRS man replied. "Can I give you a little history of iron?" he asked.

"Please do," the host beamed.

"Well, as you may know, iron has been the subject of a lot of superstitions and myths throughout history. There are a lot of legends that have their basis in fact and this very thing, iron, is on the top of the list."

The two ICE kids remained silent as this human incarnation of Foghorn Leghorn rambled on.

"Wrought iron is the key. It has been asserted over the centuries to repel, contain, or harm ghosts, fairies, witches, or other malevolent supernatural creatures. This belief continued into later superstitions in a number of forms."

"Such as?" the host asked, bubbling over with rehearsed fascination.

"Nailing an iron horseshoe to a door was said to repel evil spirits or later, to bring good luck. Surrounding a cemetery with an iron fence was believed to contain the souls of the dead. People used to go so far as burying an iron knife under the entrance to one's home, which was alleged to keep witches from entering."

"That's the most stupid thing I ever heard!" the girl shouted. "Where's your proof?"

"My proof is that iron shackles are used to restrain these things when no other material known to man will work. Where's *your* proof honey?" the Southern IRS man said, as if talking to a three-year old child.

The debate was over because neither ICE person offered a response outside of shouting platitudes. Danny reached up and switched off the radio as the ICE girl called Foghorn Leghorn an ignorant hillbilly.

"I wanted all of you to hear that so you will know what else is going on out there," Danny said, turning down the volume. "We are not alone, however our comrades aren't well organized, in any case . . ." he continued, "That was not the important thing."

"What is the important thing?" Derek asked.

"This is the third time they have played this debate this morning; I guess the government is trying to get a lot of mileage out of it. The important thing is that it goes on for another several minutes of back and forth. Then, near the end, the girl announces a 'Save the Impals' rally on the day after tomorrow. It's in Lunnington."

"Just a short drive away," Andrews said.

"Yep. The day after tomorrow we are picking up another load of Impals down near Lynchburg," Danny said. "Lunnington is gonna be crawling with police and military. We will pass straight through there, and then come back with about fifteen plus Impals in tow."

CHAPTER 16

THE VOICE FROM THE GRAVE

"The boundaries which divide Life from Death are at best shadowy and vague. Who shall say where the one ends, and where the other begins?"
~Edgar Allan Poe

"I THOUGHT WE WERE DONE WITH PICKUPS?" Andrews said as anger flared in his red cheeks. "We're barely going to have enough room as it is on the boats with the ones we have!"

Danny shrugged like it was no big deal and rage begin to bloom on Andrews's face.

"Is there not another route?" I said, trying to break the tension.

Danny shook his head.

"No, not unless you want to go down a fifteen-mile logging road and it hasn't been used in years . . . I doubt if it's even passable."

"We could take one of the SUV's down it tomorrow and check it out," Derek offered.

"We need all hands on deck to move the Impals. We can't afford to get a vehicle out there and get it stuck!" Andrews spat, still glaring at Danny.

"That's true," Danny agreed. "We have some help coming. When it's time to move all the Impals out, our two vehicles aren't enough. Not to move them in one trip anyway."

"Who's coming to help?" I asked.

"Well, I would be a little more secretive and tell you that you will find out when they get here. This is too important not to plan ahead," he said and then continued, "this is not to go past this room . . . understood?"

We all leaned in a little closer, as if our bodies would be able to contain the secret Danny was about to impart.

"Cecil, you remember . . ." Danny started then stopped abruptly when a voice boomed from the doorway.

"You boys aren't scheming without me?" Burt said as he walked toward the table.

He was in pretty good shape for someone who had recently been shot. He just showered and wore a clean pair of jeans, hiking boots, and Harley-Davidson T-shirt. Aside from the white makeshift sling holding the arm, a person would have no idea of his recent brush with death.

"You look pretty damn good," I remarked. "Dr. Acosta did a good job with you."

"Sally has taken good care of me," he said with a wink.

"The doc left this morning," Danny said. "We're only going to be here another couple of weeks. He returned to his practice before he raised suspicion. He's not on the government shit list like we are."

He smiled and motioned for Burt to sit. "Sorry, Burt. You should have been invited too. I thought you were out of commission," Danny said reaching over and shaking Burt's hand.

"So, what I think Danny is trying to say is don't get sick, don't break your leg, and don't get shot, or you're screwed," Burt said.

Everybody laughed, even Andrews.

"Where's Charlotte?" Andrews asked.

A black cloud descended over Danny's face. "She is not feeling well," he said. "She won't be joining us on this. I'm sorry."

All of us had the same question burning our tongue, yet Danny's tone was clear. Questions were not welcome on the subject.

"What were you saying when we were so rudely interrupted?" I asked, elbowing Burt in the ribs. I immediately realized my mistake. It was too late because he howled in pain.

"Sorry!" I exclaimed.

Everybody glared at me as if I was the most stupid person on the planet. At that moment, I felt like it. Burt huffed and puffed, closed his eyes and insinuated my mother was canine along with a few other choice expletives. After several long and arduous moments, the pain finally subsided.

"Don't ever do that again," he muttered. There was no malice in his tone, yet he meant what he said.

"Sorry," I muttered again as we all leaned back in to listen to Danny, all except Burt; he wasn't moving again for a while.

After all the interruptions, Danny finally told us that a friend of his was bringing a truck. It was not just any truck; it was an eighteen-wheeler.

"We could almost fit the whole lot in there," Derek said. "We might not even need the SUV's."

"Oh yes we will," Andrews said. We were all puzzled until he pointed out the simple fact that should have been obvious to everyone. "How the hell do you plan on getting an eighteen wheeler in here?" he asked.

"We'll have to take them out one carload at a time," Burt said through gritted teeth. He was still in pain.

"To where?" I asked. A narrow highway ran past the mine road with not much room to pull over, especially not for a large truck.

"There's a place up the road big enough," Danny said. Judging by the direction he pointed, it could have been where Steff and I turned around.

"How secluded is it?" Derek asked.

"The nearest house is about two miles. We'll start loading at dusk so we'll have cover of darkness and can spot headlights coming," Danny said. "We are expected at our rendezvous point about midnight, so if we don't experience any delays, we should make it."

I could think of plenty of delays, all the way from being caught and arrested to engine trouble. So many things had to go right, I doubt any of us would be getting much sleep until this is over and two weeks was a long time to go without sleep.

The meeting broke a few minutes later and everyone headed for the door.

"Hold on a second you two," Danny said, holding his hand up to Burt and me. "I need to discuss something with you."

When the room was clear, Danny turned his chair to face us.

"One thing I didn't share in the meeting is the news report on the president. I was listening to it when you and Steff pulled up earlier," he said. "I think it would have been a little too awkward with Andrews sitting there."

I very much agreed. "Are they admitting he is dead?" I asked.

"Yes, and you're not going to like the reason they are giving."

Somehow, I knew what he was going to say. It was my biggest fear since the president's spirit landed in my lap.

"I will skip the bloody details, which are all made up crap anyway. They are saying he was attacked by a group of Impals in the Oval Office," Danny said.

I couldn't do anything other than shake my head. I expected something like this although not quite this blatant and ridiculous.

"And where are they saying his spirit is?" Burt asked.

"That's the part that would make me bust a gut laughing," Danny said. "If it wasn't so damn scary."

Danny stretched his arms out on the table in front of him and began to tap his fingers in a nervous drumming. He took a deep breath. A strange mixture of amusement, sadness, and disgust swam in his eyes.

"They said the president had no Impal. They said the damned demons knew better than to try and impersonate such a good, decent and God-fearing man."

Little did we know that our meeting with the president was going to give my father's regime another gallon of gasoline to throw on their righteous fire. Regime . . . that's what I should call it now, there was little doubt that my father was in total control. He would probably be sitting with his feet propped up on the Resolute Desk in the Oval Office right now if it wouldn't appear too obvious. This was the slickest coup d'état in the history of the world. It was accomplished in a little less than two months with not a single shot fired. At least not a public shot.

"When's the funeral?" I asked.

"Tomorrow . . . full honors and all that jazz," Danny said.

"No lying in state under the Capitol Rotunda?" Burt asked.

"No, I'm sure they want to get their rock filled casket buried as soon as possible. You know, in case someone wants to peek under the lid," Danny said trying to force a smile.

"What about his wife and children?" I asked.

Danny shrugged. "Who knows? I imagine they're being fed some line of crap like the rest of us."

The next week passed without incident. The Impal pickup in Lynchburg was cancelled because it was too risky. Danny reassigned the task to the North Carolina camp. We didn't hear anything until about three days later, but their mission was a success.

In the time leading up to our mission, we lived on pins and needles. We feared more bounty hunters would stumble across us, or even worse, the military. Perhaps people would show up searching for the two dead bounty hunters. Aside from the hillbillies with a still who were now frightened away, our small camp was quiet.

Besides pins and needles, we also lived on what seemed to be an unlimited supply of potted meat and Spam. We received no more treats and no one was allowed to venture out of the camp. I wasn't certain if it was due to security concerns or if Danny ran out of cash.

Our limited menu choices didn't help my relationship with Steff. I felt as if we made some progress the day we travelled to Martian Burgers. Since then, she had not said two words to me. She became more introverted and sullen, refusing to interact with Barbara and Abbs. Her social decline worried me more than any bounty hunters. I had no idea how to deal with her and neither did Barbara. The only person she would speak to was Derek and that was only because he always seemed to be the one on duty when she tried to go on one of her walks. Nobody was to be alone after what happened to Burt.

The Impals of the two rednecks who shot Burt had a change in spirit in more ways than one. They were provided up close and personal proof that Impals are not Pythos. They wanted to become a contributing member to our camp. After much discussion and deliberation, Danny allowed them to leave their small alcove in the mine. Lincoln promised to take full responsibility for their supervision and of Sergeant Beeson. He was the man who beat me. I almost forgot about him until his name was brought up in the rednecks' parole discussions.

The past two weeks seemed as far away as two decades to me, especially now that the soreness from my beating was nearly gone. My nose was healed enough I could almost breathe normally again. I found that I thoroughly enjoyed the smell of the surrounding pines as the subtle hints of autumn air blew through them. It was the first scent I was able to enjoy since my face met the tarmac.

It turned out to be three weeks instead of the promised two before we were able to carry out our plan. Danny and Andrews stayed in touch with Andrews's brother. In less than three days before our anticipated Impal extraction, the plan was finalized. Danny was the only one who knew all the disturbing details, which he did not share with us until the last minute. Andrews was still grouchy, but he was at least tolerable for the past few weeks. Either his alcoholic withdrawals passed or he found the hillbillies' still. I didn't care which it was as long as I didn't have to shoot him. I still found it hard to believe that Danny ordered me to do it if the need arose. I guess I did see his point. Andrews could be a huge risk if his temper got the best of him.

Danny, Burt, Andrews and I were all having lunch together in the mess two days before our mission when our monotony was shattered like a broken window. Taylor came bursting through the door with a tall slender man, one of the few people in the camp I did not know. Both men's faces contorted with pure horror and their skin was ashen white. They both panted with their hands on their knees.

"Get . . . shovels . . . come," Taylor managed in between labored breaths.

"Someone is buried alive on the south ridge!" the other man shouted with a wheeze, and then he leaned back against the doorframe for support.

"Who?" Danny asked.

Taylor shrugged and shook his head as he continued to gasp. "Dunno, heard a voice under the ground, it was . . ." he said then trailed off.

"It was in an overgrown cemetery," the other man finished for him. "It was coming from one of the old graves."

"Burt, you stay here!" Danny ordered.

Burt protested until Danny reminded him of his injury. We couldn't afford for him to get hurt worse because we needed him. My injured friend reluctantly agreed. "Fine, at least I don't have to run up the hill!" he snapped.

"Andrews and Derek, you stay here as well," Danny ordered.

Before they could protest, Danny explained.

"We only have four shovels anyway. We need to leave a couple of people here guarding the camp. We can't all go gallivanting off through the woods."

A feeling of fascinated horror rushed through me as I bolted out the door. This was a mystery, to be sure, one right out of the pages of an Edgar Allan Poe tale. We each grabbed a shovel and a gun then followed Taylor and the other man. Danny referred to him as Travis. It ended up being a very long run-walk through the woods and up the steep southern ridge of the valley. After twenty minutes of trudging uphill, jumping roots, fallen trees and ducking under low hanging limbs, we were all exhausted.

When we finally cleared the hill, we found ourselves on an old trail. It was like a slow healing scar in the forest. The ancient trail was still passable, but it seemed as if the woods could reclaim it at any second.

"What were you guys doing up here?" I asked as I wiped sweat off my forehead.

"Patrol," Taylor said. "Trying to make sure we don't have any more uninvited hillbillies."

We were in such dense foliage and so far from the camp, someone could light all the cabins and mess hall on fire and we wouldn't be able to see them. As we sank deeper into hopeless vegetation, we stumbled on a wrought-iron fence about waist high. It was intertwined with vines and brambles making it almost indiscernible as a man-made structure.

Peering over the fence, I could see a number of objects. On first glance, I thought they were large rocks. After further scrutiny, I saw names and dates etched on their weathered surfaces. They were gravestones. As the rectangular boundary of iron fencing took form, I could see at least twelve gravestones in this small overgrown area no larger than an economy sized house.

"Shhhh . . . listen!" Taylor whispered.

We all froze like statues, not daring to breathe as we listened. At first, there was nothing other than the sound of the breeze blowing through the trees, the distant sound of an airplane and the faint rumble of traffic on the highway a good distance away. Then, as we were about to start breathing again . . . we heard it.

A faint muffled noise could be heard coming from somewhere inside the overgrown cemetery. It was indiscernible as a voice at first, more like a dull rumbling in the ground. As we listened, our eyes widened in unison. I could barely make out a faint pleading for help. It sounded as if it was coming from a hazy dream. My heart sank when I recognized it as the diminished cry of a terrified child.

"Jesus!" Danny said as he vaulted over the fence, and then cursed as he found himself entangled in a web of briars. He used his shovel to hack himself loose then began to crawl on his hands and knees, listening for the source of the small voice.

Taylor and Travis climbed over a deadfall of branches as they went to the other side of the small plot. I was about to climb in behind Danny when I saw something out of the corner of my eye. With one leg draped over the small fence, I slowly turned my head toward the movement. I knew what it was even before my eyes confirmed it. A very large snake was making its way through the undergrowth of the cemetery, slithering on a direct path to me.

Every hair on my body stood up like hackles, my breathing became slow and shallow. My heart beat against my ribs like a caged bird when I saw the distinctive markings on the serpent. The triangular head and the distinguishing feature on the end of its tail left no doubt. It was a timber rattlesnake.

My voice came out in a hoarse rasp.

"Danny, don't move!"

He wasn't in any immediate danger. He was several feet away and the snake was moving towards me. Nevertheless, it seemed the right thing to say at the moment.

Danny turned and saw the movement in the brush. Before he could get up, I brought my shovel down hard behind the snake's head, severing it from the rest of its slimy body. My skin crawled as I watched its jaws snapping and its body twisting like a demonic worm. I brought my leg down and looked around, searching for more unwanted visitors.

Danny stood up quickly and turned to Taylor and Travis. They stood paralyzed with bewildered expressions.

"Everyone, get your shovels out and let's clear this place!" he ordered. "I don't need anybody getting bitten, especially now that the doctor has gone home."

Twenty minutes later, the graveyard was clear. It could still use a good once-over by a weed eater, but at least we were certain it was free of any more snakes.

Taylor sat down in front of a small tombstone to rest when a moment later he jumped to his feet. "It's here, they're right here!" he said, pointing at the ground in front of the headstone. "I can feel the vibration!"

Chester Henry, born May 9, 1906, departed this life August 16, 1918.

As we stared at the small forgotten gravestone, reality shook us with a vengeance when we heard a voice calling from beneath.

"Help me! Please help me!"

Like a call to arms, we all started to dig at a separate corner of where a grave should be. It was slow going, hacking through a number of roots. After a lot of combined effort, we uncovered a coffin sized metallic box. This casket wasn't made of just any metal, it was made of iron.

Danny and I dropped down in the hole and began to work feverishly with the blades of our shovels to pry the lid open. Lucky for us, the casket was in the ground for a century. The iron hinges were eaten through by rust, making them easy to crack. A few moments later, we popped the crumbling lid up and then fell back in horror at what we saw.

CHAPTER 17

CHESTER HENRY

"Buried alive here inside a nightmare, living a life where you're gone. There is no light here, It will be light-years until my mind's clear."
~Jhene Aiko

I DON'T KNOW WHAT WE EXPECTED TO FIND. In my mind, it was not this. Perhaps a person lost in a collapsed hillside cave. Maybe even something as farfetched as some kind of hidden electronic device. What I saw horrified and shocked me. Considering the circumstances in the world, I guess I should have expected anything.

An Impal lay in the corroded iron box. His panic and terror ridden face was from a nightmare. The worst was his appearance. His ghastly manifestation froze my soul. He was a young boy and, assuming this was indeed his gravestone, he was only twelve years old when he died. The boy wore typical clothing of his time, brown trousers, blue shirt and a nice pair of Nettleton shoes. As normal as his appearance seemed, what lay beneath the surface of his luminescent 'skin' was beyond frightening. The poor child's skeleton was visible. It made him appear like a demonic apparition with four arms. Two bony hands rested over his breastbone and two luminescent hands lay frozen at his sides. His skull grinned from beneath his luminescent face. I reached down to help him out, but he recoiled from my extended arm as if it was a loaded gun.

Danny spoke in a soothing, fatherly tone, "It's all right son. You're safe now. Let us help you."

The boy's eyes darted to each of us. He behaved like a wild animal trying to determine who posed the greatest threat.

After several moments of long silence, the poor boy finally spoke.

"Help me," he muttered in a pitiful whimper. His cry was even more disturbing now that hundreds of pounds of dirt and an iron lid did not muffle it.

"We will, son," Danny said, sitting down on the edge of the grave. "We'll all help you."

Danny glanced up at the rest of us as if soliciting backup for his statement. We all obliged and took a less threatening posture by sitting at the edge of the grave.

"Can you sit up?" Danny asked in a soft voice.

The boy frowned. His face contorted as he considered if sitting was a possibility. After several moments, he managed enough determination to attempt it. As he slowly rose, the skeletal features dissipated until they were all gone, except from the waist down. The waist up remains were now visible, resting behind him, unmoved in the hundred years since laid to rest.

I stuck out my hand since I was sitting right in front of him. He reached out and took it with a little hesitation. I tried hard to seem reassuring even as I felt the frigid cold of his touch. As I started to pull him forward, his hand slipped through mine and he fell back into the casket. The boy gave me an untrusting frown as if I just played some cruel prank on him.

"It's okay, son. Focus on grasping my hand. It'll be all right. I'll do the rest," Danny said stretching his arm out to the boy.

The boy glanced at me, then turned to Danny, who seemed to have developed a real rapport with the kid. He stretched out his hand and grasped Danny's arm. After a few moments of focusing on his grip, he began to pull himself up. He took a seat by Danny with his back turned to the open grave.

The boy's eyes darted about with a wild vacancy. He seemed to be trying to take in as much of the scenery as possible. For a moment there, I was sure he was going to get up and run away. Soon, his demeanor began to calm.

"Is that me?" he asked, giving a quick glance back over his shoulder at the grave.

"This is you," Danny said taking his hand and patting him on top of the head. "This is what matters."

"Why . . ." he began, and then broke into sobs as silvery tears rained off his cheeks.

Danny leaned down and whispered gently to the boy "Is your name Chester?"

Chester nodded as he continued to cry.

"Well Chester, why don't you come home with us and you can have a nice meal and meet some other kids your age. Aren't you hungry?"

Chester continued to weep as he looked up at Danny with bewilderment expression. "Yes," he said. He *was* hungry and he didn't understand why. Nobody else understood it either. The Impal's desire for food was an accepted way of life.

We all got to our feet without a sound. Chester followed by grasping Danny's hand. He continued to stare at his feet while venting a century of frustrations and terror through his ethereal tears.

"Chester, will you wait right here for a minute? I need to step right over there and I will be right back," Danny said.

Chester didn't want to let go until Danny whispered a few comforting words to him. He released his grip with a great deal of reluctance. As the boy stood with his back turned to us and sobbing into the palms of his hands, Danny huddled with us on the far side of the grave.

"Jesus, what . . ." Taylor began before Danny held up his hand for silence. There would be time for questions later.

"Taylor and Travis, I need you to rebury this poor kid once we get him out of here. Cecil, you come with me . . . I need your help to assimilate this child into the group. God only knows what this has done to him."

Danny then gave a quick jerk of his head to indicate it was time to move out. I followed him back to Chester. As I passed by the open grave, I couldn't help taking a final peek inside. The iron casket was lined with some sort of red fabric, which was all gone now except for a few tattered shreds. There was nothing left of Chester outside of his skeleton and a couple of tufts of blonde hair on his head. His clothing was completely gone except for a few indiscernible pieces of fabric hanging from his rib cage. If he was buried in shoes, they were gone as well. Many times back in the day, they buried people without shoes because it was considered a terrible waste.

I immediately regretted my morbid curiosity as I turned my head away with a shudder. I knew the morbid image was going to be burned into my memory for the rest of my life. What made it worse was Chester existed there for almost a century. I could not imagine it. The poor kid was going to require a lot of attention.

We soon made it back to camp, thankful the return trip was downhill. We decided to approach from around the far side of the lake. It was a more direct route to the mine and avoided the mess hall along with most of the cabins. We didn't need any questions or distractions until we got our new resident accustomed to his surroundings.

Upon reaching the entrance to the mine, Danny motioned for me to go on inside. I pulled back the first tarp to slip inside and Danny sniffed the air. "Mmmmm, smells like it is dinner time!" he proclaimed as he patted Chester on the head. "Cecil, why don't you go on in and tell President Lincoln to prepare another seat at the table!"

Chester was dumbfounded. "President Lincoln?" he squeaked.

"Yep, and a whole lot of other folks I think you will like," Danny said as he squatted down to be eye level with Chester.

Chester didn't look happy yet, although he seemed like he might be willing to entertain the idea of being happy.

I disappeared into the tent and soon found Lincoln and a few other Impals. I explained the situation and they all agreed to help. In less than five minutes, the word spread to every Impal in the mine. They began to rearrange the interior furnishings. Several tables and crates were lined up to form a very long table. The cots were lined up alongside like bench seats.

A group of nineteenth-century women broke out the food and placed it on the table. Unfortunately, the Impals' menu was not any better than ours. All they had was potted meat, crackers and a few loaves of bread. Lincoln prepared a seat of honor for Chester at the head of the table and everyone else took their seat on the cots. Seeing a group of Native Americans and Colonial people seated in such close proximity made me think of Thanksgiving. When I was satisfied that everything was complete, I went back out and brought Danny and Chester inside.

Chester's face lit up with wide-eyed astonishment when Lincoln walked over and introduced himself.

"Good evening, Chester," he said. "Would you care to accompany me to dinner?"

The boy's mouth dropped open. It was as if a hundred years of torment and misery suddenly melted away. He almost floated to the table then took a seat with pride beside the former president.

He looked about with gleeful excitement as Mrs. Fiddler sat down on the other side of him. She gave me a knowing wink. I knew little Chester would be safe. Danny and I slipped back out through the tarp. I started to speak, but Danny cut me off. "Hold your questions for the meeting," he said as we started out through the woods.

It was late afternoon and the canopy of trees made it seem as if it was almost dusk. I did think it was a bit odd for Danny to call a meeting right now. I guess our earlier one was interrupted. In addition, we now have something else to talk about, something both wondrous and disturbing. I was sure Chester was going to be our primary topic though.

Our dinner would not be served for another hour, so Danny said he would grab a private table in the mess hall if I would go and get Burt.

"Derek and Andrews should be patrolling near the road right now. I think Taylor and Travis will be back here any minute. Would you run over to Burt's cabin and get him?"

I set off through the woods and returned with Burt five minutes later. I found Taylor and Travis sitting at a small table in the corner furthest from the stove. The cook was already there frying up something that smelled like garlic and Spam. The instant we sat down, Burt exploded with questions.

"Okay, Cecil wouldn't tell me anything on the way over here . . . so where the hell did you guys go? What's this crap about somebody buried alive?"

Danny told the whole story to Burt as I watched his expression shift from annoyance, to curiosity, then to excitement and finally utter horror.

"Oh, God . . . to think the poor kid . . . oh, Jesus," was all Burt could manage.

"How the hell did it happen?" I asked.

"The flu," Travis said as if he was a thousand miles away.

"The flu?" we repeated in unison.

"Yes, did you see the date on his headstone?" Travis said. "His date of death was right in the middle of the great flu pandemic between 1918 and 1920. It infected five-hundred-million people worldwide and killed about seventy-five-million of those. This outbreak wiped out about five percent of the world's population."

"You figured out his cause of death by his headstone?" Burt asked. "How the hell do you know all that anyway?"

We all turned to Travis, a man I had not met until today. He sounded trustworthy.

"I'm a history teacher," he said. "One of my students won the National History Day competition in D.C. last year. They did an incredible paper on the social and economic effects the pandemic inflicted on the world and the United States."

"That's all well and good," Burt said. "It still doesn't explain how you know this boy's cause of death . . . for all anyone knows he could have been kicked in the head by a horse."

"It's the casket, isn't it?" I asked.

I read a little about the pandemic after the swine flu scare a few years back. I remembered something about iron caskets.

"Yes, they were expensive so only the wealthier families could afford them," Travis said. "The caskets were believed to be the next-best thing to prevent spread of the disease from the dead. Cremation was the preferred method."

"Maybe the Henrys were a wealthy family who lived nearby," Taylor said. "After you guys left we found an old sign that read 'Henry Cemetery'. We also found the rotten remains of a house a short distance away."

"His last name was Henry, wasn't it?" I asked, recalling the engraving on the headstone.

"Yep, Chester Henry," Travis said. "Born May 9, 1906, departed this life August 16, 1918. He . . ." Danny suddenly cut him off.

"Does it matter *how* the boy died?" Danny snapped. "The question is how the hell was he trapped in there. We know the soul leaves the body immediately upon death, we have seen it a hundred times over the last several weeks. His soul should be long gone before he was stuck in that Godforsaken metal box and buried."

"Well . . ." Travis began. "I think the first thing we must assume is that iron had the same effect on Impals before the storm as it does now. There is only one plausible explanation."

My heart sank to the pit of my stomach as the realization sank in. Several pale faces surrounded me, stricken at the revelation.

"Oh Jesus . . ." Burt croaked. "The poor kid was buried alive."

Travis wiped a tear from his eye. "Medical technology was not as advanced back then. It was not uncommon for someone to be pronounced dead when they were still alive, undetectable to the ear of the physician. It . . ." he shuddered as if he was going to be sick. Travis remained silent for the rest of our meeting.

We tried to focus on our upcoming mission; however, none of us was in a talkative mood. We agreed to reconvene the following evening at Danny's cabin.

I left the meeting feeling numb, unable to process all the emotions swirling about inside me. I felt terrible for little Chester. The poor child had endured so much over the last century; I didn't know how he would ever be all right again. One thing I heard about Impals was that, prior to the storm, the passage of time was different for them. A hundred years might have seemed like a couple of days from Chester's perspective.

Still, I couldn't imagine spending two days in those horrific conditions. I wondered how many other premature burials now lay trapped and screaming for help around the world. I reasoned this away by the justification that it would only be those in iron caskets, which were rare, and they had to be buried while still alive. Given that combination, the odds decreased dramatically. Yet I knew the Law of Averages suggested there has to be a few out there.

I was also excited and a little scared about our upcoming mission, hoping Murphy's Law would decide to take the night off for once. What can go wrong will go wrong seemed to be the story of my life as of late. It was the story of all our lives.

I was also angry. The sudden arrival by Chester strengthened my resolve that we were doing the right thing. My father says Impals are demons here to deceive us. What would a demon be doing in a situation like that? Buried alive seemed more like a torment dealt by evil than one endured by it.

I didn't think I could hate my father any worse than I did the day I found out he was using the Tesla Gates. He succeeded at proving me wrong on almost a daily basis. This anger and hatred always led to an overwhelming feeling of sadness; I had lost my father. I pushed it deep down, in the darkest recesses of my soul. Even there, the sorrow still managed to reach out and pierce my heart. I was struck by the overwhelming desire to be with my family, so I headed for our cabin.

CHAPTER 18

WINDER'S REPORT

"Recovery begins from the darkest moment."
~John Major

I DECIDED I WOULD NOT DISCUSS little Chester Henry with my family, not even Barbara. The topic would be too upsetting to everyone and would serve no purpose. As far as they were concerned, Chester was just another Impal refugee in the mine. I didn't keep much from Barbara, but this was something she simply didn't need to know. I would live with the horrible images myself.

Barbara and Abbs sat on our cot playing a game of Gin Rummy. Steff sat on the other side of the room flipping through the pages of some teenage girl magazine. She at least glanced up and gave me a half smile; I felt that was more progress. Barbara and Abbs invited me over to join them in their game; I happily agreed.

After several rounds of getting my tail kicked, we went to the mess hall for dinner. Steff refused to eat her fried Spam and only ate a few crackers with peanut butter. I choked my Spam down. I hoped this would be over soon and we could start living again with some degree of normality. A real shower, air-conditioning and trips to Martian Burgers were luxuries I would never take for granted again. At present, it seemed like an empty hope, yet it was something to hold on to all the same.

When we returned to the cabin, I added another hope to my list, one of privacy. Barbara and I had not been alone in weeks and as we lay there petting each other in the dark, the hope burned like fire. We kissed and caressed in silence. Nevertheless, in a fifteen-by-fifteen-foot room with our daughters a few feet away, it was all we dared. Besides, maneuvering on two cots pushed together was not an easy task.

"When is this happening?" Barbara whispered as I stroked her hair.

"Day after tomorrow," I said.

"Can you talk about it?" she asked.

"Not now, after," I promised.

"I want to come with you," she said, moving her lips inches from my ear.

"You can't . . . you have to stay here with the girls. They need you to watch over them."

She sighed, knowing I was right and it was too dangerous to take the girls with us. Besides, space was at a premium and we couldn't afford to take any more than we must, not if we wanted to get all the Impals out in one trip.

"How long will it take?" she asked, her mind full of worry.

"I'm not sure; it's at least a two-hour drive where we are going."

"You can't tell me where?"

"Not now, later." I said.

The truth is, I only knew the general area where we were going. That is to say, somewhere near the Atlantic Ocean.

"Do you know what Steff asked me tonight?" she asked in a cheerful voice, which was very refreshing considering she was talking about Steff.

"What?"

"She wanted to know how a payphone works, of all things."

I gave a small chuckle, and then explained how we saw the man on the payphone the afternoon of our Martian Burgers trip.

"It's been so long since I used one I almost forgot how," Barbara giggled. "Do you remember—"

"The first time I asked you out?" I interrupted.

She didn't say anything as she leaned over and kissed me on the lips. It was deep and passionate and after a few moments, we knew we had to stop. That was the hardest thing I have done lately, which is saying a lot.

We fell asleep with our arms draped over each other, our bodies as close as the joined cots would allow. Sleep was good and restful. Little did I know, it would be the last peaceful night I would enjoy for a while.

The next day was also one of the best I in a long time. We had now entered the month of October and Mother Nature decided to give us our first preview of fall. The highs would be in the mid-seventies and almost nonexistent humidity. I think everyone in camp lamented the absence of air-conditioning over the last few weeks.

I sat in an old wooden chair by the front door of our cabin soaking in the autumn like air. I admired the bizarre beauty of the lavender sky speckled with yellowish clouds. On a calm and peaceful day like this, it was hard to comprehend that the planet was still engulfed in a cosmic storm. This storm never felt like a storm to me, not in the traditional sense anyway. Actually, the ultraviolet nights, with lavender and yellow days were a nice change of pace to me.

There was nothing traditional about this storm. No matter how beautiful I deemed it to be, it was still a storm. The winds of hatred and prejudice blew harder than any hurricane ever has, and the rain of tyranny was as oppressive as any monsoon. Fear struck without discrimination in the hearts of everyone like lightning. Traditional or not, we had a storm all the same.

The news as of late was slanted towards social and political objectives. Very little, if anything, was mentioned about the storm anymore. I guess why would you mention something if it is old news? In a news cycle, two months is ancient. Besides, if the government didn't want it reported, it was not going to be reported.

I sat absent-minded, staring at a large yellow cloud as it drifted by through the branches overhead. In a strange way, it reminded me of a horse with a tail way too long for its body. Soon cloud gazing became the furthest thing from my mind. I started to wonder again about the composition and origins of the storm. I guess like with everything in life, when we get used to something it loses its mystery. Its distinctiveness becomes routine and blasé. While I had not lost sight of the storm's side effects, the Impals, I was as guilty as the rest of the world of forgetting about the storm itself.

Have scientists discovered the origins, the composition, the long-term benefits or liabilities? Did anyone know the who, what, when, where and how? If and when this storm is going to end? As I pondered this, a pungent odor hit my nose. Five years ago, I might not have even noticed this smell. The smell of cigarette smoke reminded me of a time when my resolve was as tainted as my yellowed teeth and fingers. The irony was it made me want one again.

I searched for the source of the smell and spotted Dr. Winder standing a short distance down the hill. He leaned against a tree with a cigarette between his fingers, staring out over the shimmering surface of the lake. The cool morning breeze wisped the smoke on a direct path to our front door. I got up and made a wide arc around the path of the smoke as I descended the hill to talk to the doctor. It dawned on me that the last time I saw him; he was frozen with shock in the back of the presidential limo.

"Good morning, doctor," I said as I emerged from behind a pine tree to his left.

He jumped as if he received a shock. For a moment, it seemed as if the poor man would stumble into the lake. As I was about to move to grab him, he regained his balance by grasping a low hanging limb. The cigarette dropped into a pile of pine needles and he quickly kicked the smoldering stack into the water.

"Jesus, major . . . you scared the hell out of me," he said, embarrassed.

I almost wouldn't have recognized him if it weren't for his distinctive eyeglasses. He traded in his suit for blue jeans and a T-shirt, which I could only assume came from Danny since the two men are about the same size.

"Sorry, doctor," I said. "How are you this morning?"

"I guess I'm doing as well as expected. I can't imagine how difficult this would be if I had any family out there now."

"No one?" I asked.

Winder shook his head.

"Nope, grandparents died when I was young, parents were killed in a plane crash when I was in junior high. I'm divorced and I couldn't give two shits for what my ex-wife is doing. Thank God we didn't have any children."

"Did . . .?" I began, but Dr. Winder anticipated my question.

"Did my grandparents or parents hang around? Not that I know of and God, I sure hope they didn't."

I tried to think of a way to get our conversation back on positive footing. Dr. Winder beat me to it. "How's your family?" he asked.

"Fine," I said, nodding back towards the cabin. "All sleeping in this morning."

He smiled and pulled a pack of cigarettes out of his pants pocket. Sliding one out of the pack, he offered it to me. Out of old habit, I almost accepted. For a moment there, I wanted to accept. I recalled the pleasurable experience of enjoying a cigarette on a cool fall morning. Besides, hadn't Barbara lit up a time or two since in camp? I never mentioned it to her because we had way too many other things to worry about than my wife falling back into a nasty habit. So what would it hurt if I lit one up? I very well might have accepted his offer, considering the stress I was feeling. However, my hand was stayed as one of my stressors made an appearance.

We both glanced up at the sound of the cabin door slamming. Steff stood on the front porch stretching and yawning. Her eyes fell on me and my heart lifted as she gave me a little wave. It seemed obligatory. Of course, a few days ago, I wouldn't have even warranted an acknowledgement. Her eyes then narrowed into pure contempt as Dr. Winder fired up another cigarette. She stormed off through the woods in the direction of the women's latrine. My stomach knotted with a feeling of guilt even though I knew I had no reason to feel guilty. I was sure to get an earful when Steff reported me to Barbara and Abbs. So, I figured it would be best to nip it in the bud and tell her what happened as soon as she got up.

I watched Dr. Winder for several long moments as he puffed on his cigarette and gazed at an invisible point across the water. I wondered how such an intelligent man could have taken up such an idiotic habit. If anybody should know better it would be the National Science Adviser. Still, my family doctor smoked like a chimney when I was a kid, even in the clinic in front of patients. If the three of us served as any indication, intelligence and good judgment do not always go hand in hand. At least I finally developed the good judgment to quit.

As I followed his gaze, I realized it wasn't such an invisible point after all. He was staring at Kingston and the president's graves.

"You know, it could have been me over there," he said in a distant voice. "It should have been me over there."

The doctor was heading down a mental road where I did not want to follow this morning. It was too damn nice a day to lament about the morbidity and cruelty of life.

"Dr. Winder, has anything else been learned about the storm since it arrived?" I asked.

He blinked at me as if he did not comprehend what I said, and then a dark cloud seemed to dim his features.

"Well, according to your father, it came from the devil himself," he said.

The remark was uncalled for yet not completely out of line because it was true. I decided to ignore any personal jabs, whether intentional or not, and continued with my questions.

"Where do you think it is from?" I asked.

"Deep space, some form of energy we have never seen before. I am not a religious man so I will not proclaim it is a sign from God, Satan, Buddha or Bozo the Clown."

I smiled a little at his remark, but I also felt a little sad. I never could comprehend how anyone could be an atheist or an agnostic. Especially in times like now. I guess my father brought me up right in that respect. Thank God I didn't inherit his fringe interpretations.

"Is the energy dangerous?" I asked.

Dr. Winder shook his head. "In a physical sense, no. Socially, morally, politically and religiously, hell yes. There is the proof," he said, pointing with the lit end of his smoldering cancer stick at the distant graves.

I was beginning to realize that engaging Winder in conversation this morning might not have been the best idea in the world. He was jaded and angry, but who could blame him? It was a constant battle for me not to fall into his rut. I decided to attempt one more question.

"When do you think it will end?" I asked.

Dr. Winder shrugged.

"To sum it up, major . . . here is all we know, which is not much," he paused to take a drag off his cigarette before continuing. "This storm, this energy cloud, this anomaly from space has a definite size even though it was almost impossible to measure since we have never seen this energy before. NASA and most scientists right now feel about as ignorant as a Neanderthal trying to explain the dynamics of nuclear fusion. Since it has a defined size, it will end one day. Whether it is one day or a thousand years no one can say for sure. There is something else I think people need to be worried about with this storm."

"What?" I asked, fearing I was not going to like the answer.

He took another puff off his cigarette then flicked the smoldering butt into the water. He yawned and for the first time I could see his teeth were as yellow as the clouds.

"Even though we don't know what the hell this storm is made of . . . we can still differentiate it from other energy. This storm is not unlike polar lows, tornadoes or hurricanes here on Earth. We were able to detect a distinguishable 'eye' in the center of it. This eye is very different. It is not a calm center; it is a different form of energy. This cosmic storm hit Earth head on, so this eye will pass over us sometime in the future."

"When?" I asked.

Dr. Winder sighed. "Again . . . it could be one day or a thousand years; there is no way to predict. And before you ask, nobody has any idea what energy the eye is made of or what effect it will have."

I didn't know whether to be glad or not about my talk with to the doctor. It seemed now I had more questions than before. I decided to end our conversation there and before I could stop myself, I extended an invitation.

"Well, doctor . . . would you care to join me and my family for breakfast this morning?"

The dark cloud on his face seemed to part in an instant as he beamed at me. My eyes were drawn to his yellowed teeth. He was a professional, clean-cut man until he smiled.

"I'd love to!" he said. "What time?"

"Give me about thirty minutes," I said. "I'll round my group up and meet you by that tree on the trail," I said pointing up the hill at a gargantuan pine tree. "Just try not to burn the woods down in the meantime," I said, pointing at his cigarette, which had burned down millimeters from his fingers.

He pulled his pack of smokes back out and retrieved another one. I turned and walked up the hill, feeling a little frustrated at Dr. Winder's lack of answers and disturbing new revelations. I also felt frustrated from the fact that I really wanted a cigarette right now.

I told Barbara about my conversation with the doctor and Steff's appearance on the front porch. She grabbed my hands with a playfully and sniffed my fingertips.

"What are you doing?" I asked.

"Just double checking," she said with mock suspicion, and then kissed me.

"You guys need to get a room," Abbs said as she sat on the side of her cot and stretched.

"We do," Barbara said. "The problem is that you and your sister are in it."

"Ewwww!" she said as she walked to the door.

"Are you going to the latrine?" I asked.

"Dad!" she snapped, flushing red as if I asked her what her bra size was.

"I want you to find your sister. I saw her heading that way a few minutes ago," I said, starting to turn a little red myself.

She shrugged, rolled her eyes, and then went out the door. Our sudden alone time was tempting. We didn't want to scar the girls for life, so we got dressed and walked down to meet Dr. Winder by the large pine tree.

He was there early so we slowly walked to the mess hall in hopes the girls would catch-up to us. Abbs caught up as we reached the door. To our surprise, we found Steff sitting by herself at a table, poking at a slice of fried Spam with her fork as she munched on a red apple. The resourcefulness of the cook never ceased to amaze me given his shoestring budget and little or no access to a supermarket. A nice juicy apple sounded good this morning.

As we dined and talked, it became evident Dr. Winder was desperate for companionship. His mood was much more chipper than it was earlier and it seemed that even Steff warmed up to him a little. She did have a fascination with science and unlike most kids her age; she knew who Dr. Ray Winder was.

Spending much time in close quarters with Danny was enough to grate on anybody's nerves. I believed Danny was a good person and a great friend, however his personality could be considered gruff. Even when in a good mood, his conversation style left a lot to be desired.

Before we got up from the table, Dr. Winder leaned over and whispered to me.

"Can I see the president?" he asked.

"You bet!" I said. "We can go now if you like."

He looked skeptical.

"It's okay," I chuckled. "We're all friends here."

Dr. Winder approached his longtime friend with apprehension. It was like the same fettered and uncomfortable caution many people exhibit at a funeral or wake as they approach the open casket for the first time. It didn't take long for him to realize there was not much different about the president other than the obvious distinctions between Impals and fleshers. They engaged in conversation while I took this opportunity to speak with Abraham Lincoln again. Mrs. Fiddler joined us along with another man. Judging by his clothes, he was from her same era. His name was Jim Valentine and was a cricket player from Liverpool, England.

"How did you wind up here in the States?" I asked him.

"My wife and I were here on holiday to see the sights. I think we perished in a train crash. I am not completely sure. At least *she* had the good sense to move on," he said with a rueful smirk.

I did not know what to say because as far as I was aware, Mrs. Manners hasn't released a revised book on etiquette for Impals. There was no addendum yet containing a section titled: *How to be tactful when speaking to a deceased person when their deceased spouse has moved on.*

"Well, you're going to be almost back home," I said. "You will all be going to an island in the English Channel."

"Hopefully," a voice said behind me. I knew without turning around that it was Danny.

I turned to see him standing with his arms behind his back and Burt standing beside him, his one good arm behind his back. Danny made a subtle motion for me to come.

Excusing myself, I turned to follow as he led us into a deserted corner of the mine, which was well out of earshot of everyone.

"What do you mean, hopefully?" I asked.

Danny didn't answer at first, so Burt jumped right in.

"It seems Europe has been doing some back door dealing with our government. They publicly denounce the rumors of the existence of the Tesla Gates. On the other hand, they seem desperate enough to start sending their Impals over here, gate or no they will turn a blind eye."

"Is it that bad?" I asked.

"Well you have to take into consideration that even with Native Americans; Europe has boasted a higher population for many more years. No telling how many they have who stayed throughout the centuries. Then couple it with everyone who has died in the last few months. Well, I'm sure they do have a problem."

"You agree with them?" I snapped.

"Of course not!" Burt spat, showing a rare glimpse of his temper. "That is what is happening whether we like it or not!"

"The bottom line," Danny interjected, "is that we could be sending them over there to be rounded up and sent right back."

"Is that the way it will be?" I asked.

"Admiral Dyson assured me that the Island of Guernsey is secluded enough that no one will notice or care," Danny said then sighed and rubbed his eyes. "Besides, this is Europe we are talking about; England does not share the same view . . . at least not yet." He shook his head and held out his hands in supplication. "I guess we don't have a choice, do we?"

It was the truth. We could do nothing and be caught or we could send them out tomorrow night as planned. At least by going through with our plan we would be giving them some degree of hope.

"Where's Chester?" Danny asked, peering over my shoulder.

It didn't take long to spot him sitting on a cot and playing a quiet game with Mrs. Fiddler's daughter. We started to walk that way, but Mrs. Fiddler met us halfway.

"He's doing fine," she said. "He had a few rough moments last night. I rubbed his head till he fell asleep."

"How did the dinner go?" I asked.

"It was great. That was such a good idea; I think it helped him to assimilate better. He was quite taken with President Lincoln."

Before we knew it, there was movement among us. Chester stood in our midst, beaming up at Danny. "What was your name, Mister?" he asked.

"Danny."

"Thank you, Mr. Danny," he said.

"No, just Danny," the colonel insisted, but Chester shook his head.

"No, my folks said all grown-ups are Mister or Misses. Can I call you Mr. Danny?"

"Sure you can, son."

After formal introductions were made, we would now be known as Mr. Danny, Mr. Cecil and Mr. Burt. I felt encouraged that Chester seemed to be doing well, yet there was still something amiss. He harbored an almost imperceptible feral look in his eye. I was thankful that Mrs. Fiddler was there to nurture him.

"I'm going to stay here for a little while. I'll see you guys tonight," Danny said as Burt and I turned to leave.

"Can you at least give us a little hint about what this plan is all about?" Burt asked.

I wished Burt had kept his mouth shut because my stomach churned at Danny's response.

"You boys aren't afraid of the ocean at nighttime, are you?"

CHAPTER 19

LINCOLN AND STEFF

*"No problem can be solved from the same level of
consciousness that created it."*
~Albert Einstein

As is usual for Danny, his answers were vague and frustrating. Burt and I were not sure whether he was trying to keep as much of the information as possible classified or if he was having fun making us sweat. I guess it was a little of both. All we could get out of him was we would be in very tiny boats.

Burt and I left after saying goodbye to Dr. Winder. He barely acknowledged us because he seemed to be having a splendid time with a group of Impals, which included the president. Much to our surprise, Lincoln asked to join us.

"I'll grab a couple of them batteries over there," he said, pointing at a box of batteries stacked near the entrance to the mine. "No one will ever know the difference."

"Nothing could be further from the truth," I thought to myself. One of the most recognizable faces in the history of the United States, if not the world . . . yeah, nobody would notice. Nevertheless, he was who he was and far be it for me to tell the sixteenth President of the

United States no. Besides, it was not as if he would be parading down a street in the middle of Washington.

Danny seemed exasperated as Lincoln dug into the box to retrieve his batteries. I shrugged. Danny shook his head as he walked over to Chief Powhatan. Impals were not supposed to leave the mine unless there was a very good reason. Danny didn't regard Lincoln's desire for some fresh air a good reason.

With batteries in hand, Lincoln stepped out of the tarps into the bright sunny day. He reveled in the moment like a man sealed in a dark hole for years. The batteries masked his ethereal presence, however he seemed to emit a glow all the same as he basked in the sunlight.

"Oh, that feels good!" he said as he walked between Burt and me, clasping our shoulders.

"Would you like to meet my family, Mr. Lincoln?" I asked.

"It would be my pleasure!" he said, "And please, call me Abe."

I found Barbara and the girls back at the cabin. Barbara made a fuss about the condition of the cabin as if she was receiving a visit from the former president at home. It is one of the things I love about her. She takes pride wherever she goes.

Abbs was star struck, as if she had received a personal visit from one of these modern singing groups.

I was shocked at Lincoln's reaction to Steff.

"Well hello, young lady!" Lincoln said. "I did not know this great fellow was your father!"

"You know each other?" I asked in shock.

It would seem that Steff's long disappearances were not only for a solitary walk in the woods to vent her frustrations. Steff had been visiting the mine as well.

"Absolutely, we've had several conversations about her grandfather. She's a lucky young lady to have such a grandpa," he said with a jovial wink.

I could feel my insides sink into my shoes. What in the hell had she told him?

"You have?" I said, my voice quivering with nervousness. "What has she told you?"

Lincoln stroked his beard for a few moments as if he was trying to recall every detail of their conversations.

"Well, she said what a good man he is. He always tries to do the right thing even when people criticize him. She also said she misses him very much."

"Is that all?" I asked, probably a little too strong.

The last thing I needed or wanted right now was for the Impals to find out who my father was, not when we were twenty-four hours from evacuating them. I didn't need to feel the shame I already felt pressed down on me by the distrustful gaze of each Impal.

"Pretty much," he said, with a frown. "Why, did I miss something?"

"No," I lied. "Nothing at all."

I was glad Burt came in with us because he broke the tension.

"Mr. President, would you like to accompany me to my cabin, I know my wife would love to meet you," he said.

"It would be a pleasure," Lincoln said as he followed Burt to the door.

He turned and gave farewell pleasantries to everyone in the room, bowed, and then turned to follow Burt. It struck me what a kind and decent man Lincoln is. I must continue to fight the tendency to say 'was' in his case. Since the storm arrived, 'was' and 'is' have developed interchangeable meanings. An unexpected jolt of anger surged through me when I considered how Lincoln met his demise. I found myself cursing John Wilkes Booth because I could not comprehend how anyone could shoot this man in the head. He did it in front of his wife and then celebrated on the stage of Ford's Theater. "Sic semper tyrannis!" he shouted. *Thus always to tyrants.*

An image passed through my mind's eye of a soldier standing over my father's bullet ridden body as he shouted the same proclamation. This brief vision scared the hell out of me. It didn't frighten me because of its horrifying imagery, but because it gave me a feeling of relief and satisfaction. I added my father to my silent curses. I cursed him for what he was doing and because of what he forced me to become. I was now a jaded son who might take some pleasure in his own father's death.

I only dwelled on this for a few moments because I had my own fatherly duties to address.

"Why have you been going to the mine without permission?" I asked, turning to face Steff.

"I wasn't aware I need permission," she said with a flippant shrug.

I considered the motion belligerent and disrespectful. The frustration I managed to maintain over the last few weeks finally bubbled over.

"Listen young lady, you knew damn good and well you weren't supposed to go out there without permission or a chaperone!" I hissed.

Everyone's eyes widened. Temperamental outbursts were a rarity for me. When they came, everyone understood I meant business.

Steff stared at me, fear and resentment mixed in her eyes producing a deluge of tears.

"Do you understand?" I boomed.

She gave an almost imperceptible nod, never taking her eyes off me. Her gaze began to grow more defiant by the second as tears sheeted down her cheeks.

"Why the hell did you go down there?" I shouted.

"Were you just curious, honey?" Barbara interjected, trying to ease the tension.

Mothers have a way of being sweet and buddy-buddy to get what they want out of their child. However, if a child is approached too often with this technique, the parent is perceived as soft. Parental respect goes right out the window. This was not the time for a mother's coddling.

"I asked her a question, Barbara, and she needs to answer it!" I snapped. "No pussyfooting around!"

Barbara stepped back and gave me a scowl only I could see. She turned and stomped out the door, causing a rain of dust as it slammed shut in its rickety frame. Abbs sat down on her cot with her back to us. I know I saw a little satisfaction on her face. Sisters can be vindictive, especially when one of them has carried such a bad attitude.

I never stopped to consider why I was so upset. Was it the fact she could have put herself in a dangerous situation? No, Impals are not dangerous, at least the ones I met anyway. The transition from flesh to Impal seems to have a calming effect on even those who possessed some violent propensities.

No, there was only one real reason I was mad. It was because of her flagrant disobedience. That was why I was chastising her. The embarrassment and loss of trust I would endure with the Impals if the identity of my father were revealed was secondary.

"Why did you go down there?" I repeated, a little louder.

"I don't know!" she screamed, "to get away from you?"

She turned and bolted out the door, almost knocking Barbara down where she stood on the porch.

"Steff!" I shouted as she disappeared down the trail. It was too late; she was gone.

To Barbara's credit, she remained silent even though both of us knew I was wrong. Should Steff be held accountable for her actions? Yes.

Should I have yelled and screamed at her?

I wanted to say yes because she had it coming for her attitude the past couple of weeks. Deep down, I knew the answer to that question was and always shall be . . . no.

"I'm sorry," I said to Barbara.

"I'm not the one you should be apologizing to, am I?" she said.

Part of me felt like Steff got exactly what she deserved and perhaps she did. However, as a father, I handled the situation poorly. I set out through the woods in search of my rebellious daughter. I did not get far when I met Danny.

"Come by my cabin tonight about seven o'clock. We are going to go over our final plan for tomorrow," he said.

"I didn't realize there was an initial plan," I said. "Other than we are heading out tomorrow evening and would be near the ocean."

"It's going to be me, you, Burt and Andrews at this meeting, oh yeah, and as the Impal liaison, Lincoln, will be joining us as well." Danny said, not acknowledging my comment. He seemed to believe he was imparting some exclusive grand idea. It was only natural we should include at least one Impal in our plans, since it did affect them even more than us.

"Great," I said. "I'll see you then. In the meantime, there is a little personal issue I need to address."

Danny glanced at me sideways. He was no fool. He knew I was

having issues with Steff. After all, he was the one who gave us money for Martian Burgers. He patted me on the shoulder and disappeared into the woods.

I found Steff about an hour later. She was sitting on a stump by the main road leading in to camp. As expected, she didn't acknowledge me when I approached her.

"I'm sorry for yelling at you," I said through gritted teeth.

A part of me was coming closer to winning out. I wanted to throw her over my lap and wear her fanny out. I forgot that feeling in an instant when she gazed up at me with a pitiful expression. Tears streamed from her big green eyes. Her lip quivered so hard I thought the vibration might shatter my heart.

"I wanna go home, Daddy . . . I just wanna go home!" she wailed as she stood up and buried her face in my chest.

I was as powerless as a feather in a strong wind to be mad at her anymore. I hugged her tight and kissed the top of her head.

"We will soon, sweetheart. Soon," I whispered.

"When?" she pressed, regarding me with hopeful, watery eyes.

"Soon," I repeated. "This will all be over soon."

Steff was immature, but she was not stupid. She knew what was going on in the world, at least to some degree, and she knew my promises to be as hollow as the stump she was sitting on. I don't know what she expected me to say . . . *sure honey, let's go home right now?* She was frustrated, and so was I. There wasn't a single thing we could do about it, aside from turning ourselves in. I actually entertained the idea for a brief moment, except we have come too far with too many counting on us to do something cowardly.

Steff pulled away from me and took off in a dead sprint towards our cabin. I considered chasing after her. I also considered borrowing one of the vehicles and giving my youngest child her wish. Isn't that what daddies are supposed to do? Instead, I sank down on the stump where she had been sitting. I pinched the bridge of my nose to quell the tears of frustration welling in my eyes. It was more than frustration, though.

The betrayal by my father hurt me worse than I let on. It cut deep like an old dull knife, reopening the wounds of my childhood that I believed healed long ago. Of course, my father would say I betrayed *him*. The thing that hurt so much is I think Steff believed it. After a few moments of resistance, the tears came and I did nothing to stop them. I let them run their course. At least Abbs and Barbara were supportive and I focused on that to get me through our task tomorrow.

We held our meeting at seven o'clock sharp in Danny's cabin. Danny, Burt, Andrews, Derek, Lincoln and I all attended. We assembled around a small wooden table in the center of the room. His cabin was quite a bit larger than the rat traps Burt and I lived in with our families, not to mention, quite a bit cleaner. I don't know if it was a result of Danny's cleaning skills or he called dibs on the building in the best shape. I think the most notable difference was that he had electricity. A small portable generator ran a light, a small refrigerator, a radio, and cell-phone charger off a mishmash of extension cords. While I envied his amenities, I gave him props for planning.

We were not very far into the meeting when we discovered just how dangerous and massive an undertaking this mission was going to be. Danny's friend, Chuck Connelly, would be bringing his tractor-trailer. He would park it in a field about a mile and a half down the road. We would take the Impals in SUV's to the truck and load them in the back under the cover of darkness.

"If we load the vehicles to capacity, it will take about six trips each," Danny said.

"Okay, so then what are we going to do with them?" Andrews asked.

Danny sat back in his chair with a satisfied twinkle in his eye.

"You fellows ever hear of the Chesapeake Bay Bridge-Tunnel?" he asked.

CHAPTER 20

THE PLAN REVEALED

*"A good plan violently executed now is better than a
perfect plan executed next week."*
~George S. Patton

THERE WAS SOME RECOGNITION AROUND THE TABLE. President Lincoln was
perplexed.

"They built a tunnel under the Chesapeake Bay?" he asked with
astonishment.

Indeed they did. I crossed this marvel of modern engineering
many times and each time I found it both breathtaking and terrifying.

The Bridge-Tunnel project is a four-lane twenty-mile-long vehicu-
lar toll crossing of the lower Chesapeake Bay. The facility carries US
13, the main north-south highway on Virginia's Eastern Shore, and
provides the only direct link between Virginia's Eastern Shore and
south Hampton Roads, Virginia.

The crossing consists of a series of low-level trestles interrupted by
two one-mile-long tunnels beneath the Thimble Shoals and Chesapeake navigation channels. The man-made islands, each a little over
five acres in size, bookend each end of the two tunnels. There are also
high-level bridges over two other navigation channels. I stopped at a
gift shop on one of the islands and bought a book about the history

and engineering. There was a lot of information floating around in my head, which I never in a million years considered would be put to practical use. Trivia aside, I was curious to find out how the Bridge-Tunnel would fit into our plan.

"Yes sir," I said. "It is quite a sight."

"So, we're taking the Impals across the Bridge-Tunnel?" Derek asked.

"Not exactly," Danny said. "We are going to take them to it."

"How?" Burt asked.

Danny explained that the military guarded both ends of the structure. It was impossible to get Impals across it, let alone a whole truck-load.

"They also patrol the coast as well on both sides of the bay," Danny said. "It was guarded anyway before the storm due to all the military bases in the area. Patrols have tripled as of late."

"Why?" Derek asked.

"To keep Impals from escaping and keep them from getting in," Danny said.

"In?" I asked.

"Yeah, there are a few countries dumping Impals on the shores of the United States instead of dealing with the issue themselves," Danny said.

"Some things never change," Andrews muttered.

"Okay, where does the bridge come in?" I asked. "You said something about us being in very tiny boats."

Danny's smile broadened, making me even more uncomfortable.

"Andrews's brother is going to have his ships moored by the pier at the entrance to the Thimble Shoal Tunnel. It's the southernmost tunnel closest to Hampton, about two miles off the coast."

"So . . . if we can't drive onto the bridge and we can't take boats full of hundreds of Impals past the patrols, then how are we going to get them out there?" I asked.

It was going to be much more of an undertaking than our hundred or so Impals. We had several hundred Impals coming in from various refugee camps from New Jersey to North Carolina. Considering our limited resources, the scale of this undertaking was unimaginable.

Danny sat up in his chair. He held up his right hand and then lowered it under the table where he knocked three times underneath.

"We go under the water," he said.

"Unless you managed to commandeer a submarine, I don't know how in the blazes you think we can do that!" Burt said.

Danny didn't reply, instead he turned to Lincoln. The former president's face was a mask of utter confusion.

"Mr. President," Danny began. "It is my understanding that Impals are impervious to anything except for iron, isn't that correct?"

"Yes . . . to the best of my understanding," Lincoln said in a suspicious tone.

"Any issues with water?" Danny asked.

Either Lincoln's eyes widened from fear or comprehension. It was hard to tell because he spoke with his same witty humor.

"I'm not sure since I haven't taken a bath in over one hundred-fifty years," he said.

"Would you mind conducting an experiment with me?" Danny asked.

"I reckon," Lincoln said. "As long as it doesn't take too long, I'm getting kind of hungry."

Danny stood up and walked to the door, opening it and revealing the fading sunset between the trees. He motioned for all of us to follow. Danny led us down to the edge of the lake where he stopped and turned to face Lincoln.

"Mr. Lincoln, this part of the lake doesn't get any more than twenty feet deep before it hits the drop-off for the quarry about fifty yards out. Would you mind walking in about twenty yards or so, then turn and come back out?"

Lincoln was uneasy. Nevertheless, he pushed up his sleeves and walked with forced purpose into the water. Not breaking stride, within thirty seconds his head was completely underwater, yet he was still visible. The former president's luminescent glow was as radiant as an underwater fountain light. We watched as the light stopped about twenty yards out then turned and came back toward us. Its bluish white tint cast an eerie ripple on the surface. A few seconds later, his head emerged followed by his long and lanky frame. Lincoln stepped back onto the shore with a wide grin on his face; he appeared to be completely dry.

"It kind of tickled," he said with a chuckle.

"Do you feel okay?" I asked.

"No side effects?" Burt added.

Lincoln mimicked shaking water out of his ears then shrugged.

"Nope, fit as a fiddle," he said.

Derek shook his head.

"Nope, this will never work," he said. "We are going to have hundreds of Impals travelling under the water together. You saw what he looked like under there. Can you imagine that many together? They will light up the whole bay area!"

"Derek is absolutely right," Danny said. "I already considered that," he said reaching in his pocket and retrieving a battery. He held it between his thumb and forefinger as if he was displaying a precious metal.

"Do we have that many batteries, enough to give a couple to all the Impals?" Derek asked.

"We should," Danny said. "The problem is all the Impals are going to need two pairs of batteries."

"Why two?" Burt asked.

"Well, there are a couple of reasons," Danny explained, swatting a mosquito on the back of his neck. "Why don't we get back inside and I'll explain further. I'm getting eaten alive out here."

"They're not bothering me," Lincoln chuckled.

"No, you're attracting them . . . here," Danny said, holding out the battery to Lincoln. He took it in his hand and immediately dimmed.

We walked back to the cabin, Burt and I whispering back and forth as Andrews and Derek did the same. There were still a number of questions to be answered. After returning to the table, Danny sprayed a ring of mosquito repellent around the room as if he were performing a cleansing ritual. He then sat down and did his best to address those questions.

"Well, the reason we need two pairs of batteries for each Impal," Danny began, "is because the batteries will only last about fifteen or twenty minutes in salt water before they begin to corrode and lose their effectiveness. The Impals will be starting out about three miles from the tunnel as the crow flies, or in this case, as the fish swims."

He gave a smirk, realizing his poor attempt at humor and continued.

"Given the distance, water resistance and a half-dozen other issues, I estimate it will take them at least thirty-minutes to walk there. The batteries will be dead and they'll be exposed, all one-thousand of them, give or take a few."

I felt the need to point out the obvious. "They'll be exposed when they get there. The patrol boats will be able to see them from miles away."

"That's why they can't come up at the island," Danny said. "They'll have to pass through the tunnel, underneath the water. Someone will be there to meet them as they come through; giving them new batteries, then they walk out of the tunnel and get on the boat."

"Can they do that?" Andrews asked in disbelief. "Isn't some of the tunnel structure made out of iron?"

Danny shook his head.

"No, the tunnel structure consists of prefabricated composite structural steel and reinforced concrete tube sections. They are thirty-seven feet in diameter and approximately three-hundred feet long. Each one is sunk into place in a prepared trench and covered with about ten feet of back-fill material, usually gravel and rock. The structural steel portion of the tube sections consists of a thirty-five-foot diameter steel tube supported inside a thirty-seven-foot square box section."

"Impressive," Burt said with raised eyebrows.

"I've been doing my homework," Danny replied.

"So . . . they are supposed to hit this tunnel in pitch-black darkness, one-hundred feet under the ocean?" That's crazy!" Derek said.

Danny tapped his finger on the table as if he was about to make an important point. "It's not as crazy as it might seem. Grandview Natural Preserve just outside of Hampton is a straight shot due south to the Thimble Shoal Tunnel. The tunnel itself is over fifty-five hundred feet long, so it's not exactly a tiny target."

"Yeah, but you said yourself it is covered with rock and gravel. No telling what aquatic plants and silt have settled on it over the years. It'll probably look like the rest of the seafloor," Derek argued.

"True," Danny agreed. "Each end of the tunnel has channel markers where it rises out of the water to the trestle on the north or the man-made island to the south. These lights are bright enough for ships to spot from miles away at night, so they should be visible under the water as well."

"*Should* be," Derek said with growing skepticism. "That is one hell of a risk. What if they *can't* see it and they keep walking out into the Atlantic?"

"Well . . ." Danny said. "That's where we come in."

Here it comes, the thing I have been dreading.

"The one part I forgot to mention is that aside from the truck Mr. Connelly is going to bring, he is also bringing two flat bottom aluminum boats," Danny said.

"With motors?" Andrews asked.

"No, not with motors," Danny barked, showing impatience for the first time. "We might as well putter out there with a neon sign blinking the Myriad symbol and another with 'Save the Impals.'"

Andrews sank back in his chair with a glaring scowl on his face.

"Then how are we going to get them out there . . . paddle? It'll take longer than thirty minutes, especially with the current out there," Derek asked.

Danny sat back in his chair and rubbed his fists with his eyes. He took a deep breath then turned to face Lincoln again.

"Mr. President, this is where you and one of your counterparts come in," he said.

Lincoln didn't say anything. He raised his eyebrows and waited for Danny to continue.

"The boats," Danny explained, "will be full of batteries for when you come out in the tunnel. I will be in one boat and Cecil will be in the other. We will have camouflage covering the top. If we are spotted, we'll be dismissed as nothing more than floating debris. There will be a little over one-hundred feet of rope tied to the front of the boat."

"I suppose you want me and my Impal counterpart to tow you like a horse and buggy?" Lincoln asked.

Danny nodded, and then summed up the plan. "Yes, then when you get to the tunnel, Cecil and I will tie up to the island then unload the batteries and bring them down into the tunnel. Andrews's brother's boats will be moored on the other side of the island, waiting."

"This sounds all well and good," Burt said. "And I'm going to assume you left me out of the plan because if I had to paddle, I would just be going in circles," he said as he held up his injured arm, which was still in a sling.

Everyone at the table laughed.

"What the Hell are we going to do with a thousand Impals appearing in the tunnel when traffic comes through? Someone with a cell phone could sound the alert before we handout the first battery."

Danny gave a knowing grin. "I know you all have probably lost track of the days lately. I know I would have if I hadn't been keeping a calendar. We chose tomorrow for a reason. Tomorrow is Sunday and as of late the Bridge-Tunnel has been closing on Sundays for regular maintenance," Danny said. "There shouldn't be anybody on it that time of night since maintenance is done in the daylight hours."

It all sounded like a solid plan, nevertheless I must admit to a couple of misgivings. First, I was going to be in a tiny boat on the pitch-black ocean at nighttime. An army of Impals a hundred feet or so beneath the surface would tow my boat. If that didn't sound worrisome enough, the second issue was, aside from snakes, my biggest fear from the animal kingdom is sharks. I saw *Jaws* many more times than *Snakes on a Plane* and I guess the repetitive salt-water horror sunk in over the years.

"Okay, so what time do we need to get started tomorrow?" I asked, mustering as much confidence in my voice as I could summon.

"I want everyone here to meet at the mess hall around five o'clock tomorrow afternoon. Cecil and Burt, I would like you to accompany me to the mine in the morning right after breakfast. With the assistance of Mr. Lincoln and our own president, we will conduct a briefing with the Impals to let them know what to expect."

Lincoln agreed even though unease clouded his face. He knew this was not going to be an easy sell. How could it? The water would not hurt the Impals, at least we didn't think so. Nobody knew for sure. I didn't think any Impals have conducted deep-sea dives, although there were rumors of some crew and passengers of the Titanic stumbling ashore in Newfoundland a couple of weeks ago. The pure unnatural creepiness of walking deep under the ocean in complete darkness is enough to make anyone's skin crawl, flesher or Impal.

A short time later, we adjourned and I returned to our cabin. The girls were asleep. Barbara waited patiently, reading a paperback romance novel by the glow of her flashlight.

"Are you all right?" she asked as I kissed her forehead and collapsed on my cot.

"Yes," I lied, and then rolled over.

I was not okay. My stomach was in knots thinking about tomorrow night and all the horrible things that could go wrong, a few of which probably would. I ran the plan over and over in my mind trying to picture all the details in my head. I visited the Bridge-Tunnel a number of times, but never in a tiny boat at night. At least this would be over after tomorrow. That still didn't mean we could return to a normal life no matter how much Steff wanted to . . . no matter how much we all wanted to. The worries of uncertainty denied me sleep, even though I desperately craved it. It would be a long time before I experienced restful sleep again.

CHAPTER 21

THE MEETING IN THE MINE

"When you are grateful, fear disappears and abundance
appears."
~Anthony Robbins

WE CONSUMED BREAKFAST in a bleary-eyed haze the next morning. I was thankful the cook managed to get his hands on some coffee, even if it was of the instant variety. I drank it down and relished the rush of caffeine coursing through my veins. I was a typical daily coffee drinker. To be honest I missed it the last few weeks.

As planned, Danny, Burt and I set out for the mine after breakfast. We were all nervous and fidgety and it wasn't clear whether it was due to the momentous task in front of us or from the caffeine. We entered through the double tarp of the mine entrance to find all the Impals gathered in a semicircle near the front of the mine. Lincoln, the president and Chief Powhatan stood front and center. The three men stepped forward and shook our hands then surrendered control of the meeting. Danny stepped forward and scanned the crowd of Impals in front of us.

Since I was not speaking, it gave me a chance to observe our refugees a little closer. The first thing that struck me was just how many there were. Every time I visited the mine, the Impals were scattered about. Now they assembled into a tight group resembling a small glowing army. The official head count was one hundred-ten. The small space made it seem like three times as many. The group was as eclectic as I perceived on my first visit. As they all stood together, I could fully take-in the diversity.

At least twelve Native Americans made up the group, not counting Powhatan. Twenty-four African Americans occupied the group, eleven men, seven women and six children. They spanned from early Colonial to modern day. While they wore the clothing of their time, none of them bore any sign of slavery. Why would they?

The rest of the Impals all appeared to be Caucasian, seventy-eight in all, again with a mixture of men, women and children. I wasn't sure how many of them were American. I knew there was at least one French person, according to Burt. I met a man from England on my last trip to the mine. They made the choice to remain when they died, but it made me wonder if they were given a choice on *where* to remain. I heard a few accounts of Impals showing up hundreds of miles from where they died. Perhaps there was something about the ocean keeping them from their native country. That idea sent a nervous twinge through my stomach when I considered our plan tonight. I pushed it aside and scanned the crowd to gauge the reaction. My heart sank when I saw apprehension clouding their faces.

Mrs. Fiddler and her daughter stood near the front and I could see pure terror registering on both of their faces. My heart went out to them. It didn't surprise me, not one bit. I can't imagine I would react any different if in their shoes. Being under the ocean at night, not knowing what horror lurked in the darkness mere feet away. That scenario was enough to horrify the bravest. They would be dark because they would all carry batteries and I didn't think Impals could see in the dark, not since the lanterns seemed to burn constantly in the mine. I was scared enough and I was going to be in a boat, not in the briny depths of Chesapeake Bay.

Could anything really hurt the Impals? I didn't think so, not unless a shark with iron teeth showed up. If there is one thing I have learned in my life is harm can come from other things besides physical injury. Growing up with my father taught me that lesson well.

They cherished the same hopes, fears, love and emotional needs as any flesher. Anyone who has a dash of sanity and a little bit of heart can tell in an instant.

When I thought about the thousands of Impals who had been put through the Shredder's ravenous maws, the thirty minutes these Impals would be forced to endure tonight didn't seem that bad. Of course, I wouldn't dream of sharing that belief with them. Not if I didn't want to be clouted over the head with a bucket.

When Danny finished speaking, the chamber filled with restless murmuring and harsh whispers.

"Why can't some of us ride in a boat?" a man in eighteenth-century clothing, complete with a triangle hat and knickers, shouted. He must have been the French gentleman Burt mentioned. As with Chief Powhatan, I could tell he was speaking a foreign language, yet I could understand him as if he were speaking English.

Danny sighed and glanced sideways at us. He had gone over this. I guess it bore repeating since several other Impals indicated they wanted to know too.

"Because," Danny began, "there are patrol boats surveying the shore at regular intervals. Frankly, we'll be lucky if we can get the two small boats out there without being seen."

"What if we want to take our chances in a boat . . . shouldn't it be our choice?" a woman with a 'saucer wave' hairdo from the 1930s asked. She wore a red crepe suit, making her seem both professional and glamorous. "I'm afraid of the water . . . always have been!"

"Me too," a small voice whimpered.

I turned to see it came from Mrs. Fiddler's daughter. She now buried her face on her mother's chest.

"It won't hurt you, I promise," Lincoln said with a warm smile. "I went for a dip in the lake last night myself . . . it actually kind of tickles," he said as he patted the girl on the head and gave the frightened 1930s woman a comforting wink.

"I-I am not sure, I think I drowned," a large Native American man said. "I don't know if I can do it."

"You didn't drown!" another Native American man said. "You ate yourself to death!"

There was a smattering of uneasy laughter from the crowd and I laughed along with them.

"That's why they call you Hungry Bear," another Native American added. Again, the room filled with uneasy laughter.

"How long will it take again?" a slender African American man wearing a modern pinstripe suit asked.

"No more than thirty minutes," Danny said.

The man stared with uncertainty at his feet. He then turned to an African American woman standing next to him. Her expression was as terrified as the Fiddler's.

"It's okay, baby. You can shut your eyes tight and I'll lead you," the man said, patting the woman on the hand.

A strange thought flashed through my mind. "Do Impals have eyelids to shut?"

I supposed they did, maybe not exactly like mine. Impals slept with their eyes closed.

"I ain't scared!" Chester spoke up.

He was in the back and, due to his short stature; I did not noticed him earlier. He was not the same crazed and wild-eyed person as the day of his rescue. He seemed remarkably brave and lucid.

"I love the water!" he said, "And I can't wait to run free in it. Anyone wants to shut their eyes while I lead the way, just say so."

A few hands rose in the air. Chester folded his arms in front of his chest with pride. I was glad to see he was doing much better, as much I was glad to see the tension in the room was starting to loosen somewhat.

In my mind, walking across the ocean floor at nighttime was almost as terrifying as what Chester endured . . . almost. I guess after his experience this would be a walk in the park. At least the small spark of his confidence seemed to put everybody a little more at ease, although I harbored no illusions. I knew when we carried the operation out later tonight; we would have several who would back out at the last minute. That was why Danny was bringing along several sets of iron chains. It would be necessary to tether these reluctant Impals to the ones brave enough to attempt it. He privately discussed this with Lincoln and as terrible and hypocritical as this move would be, they both agreed it was necessary. The Impals must go or they would face the Shredder, potentially a fate worse than death.

The leaders of the Impals stayed to discuss fears and concerns as Danny, Burt and I left the mine. Danny's jaw locked as if something troubled him.

"Is there going to be a problem?" Burt asked.

"Hell yes there's going to be a problem!" Danny retorted. "Do you think you can ask a group of one hundred-ten people to do something like this and there not be some resistance?"

"It shouldn't hurt them," Burt argued.

"*Shouldn't*," Danny snapped. "We know salt water is going to interfere with the batteries, how the hell do we know what it's going to do to them? Lincoln just took a dip in fresh water last night; there could be a huge difference!"

"You mean nobody has tested this with Impals?" I asked.

Danny was about to turn his frustration towards me when I held my hands up in a calming gesture. He sighed and dropped his shoulders as if all the air left him.

"I'm sorry guys; I have a lot on my plate tonight. I guess I foolishly believed we would receive a better reception to the plan."

"*We* have a lot on *our* plates tonight," I corrected. "You're not in this alone."

Danny scratched his head and said, "You're right, I should have given the two of you more information from the get-go."

I could not agree more.

"I felt if I kept it on a need to know basis, it would reduce the risk of our plan being discovered."

"What . . . did you think Cecil was going to run and tell his daddy the moment he knew the full details of your plan?" Burt snapped.

Danny shook his head and, like the cocking of a gun, I saw his jaw pull tight again.

"No I didn't!" he shouted, sending an echo through the canopy of trees. "If either one of you were captured, the information could have been forced out of you!"

I decided it was time to step in and play peacemaker before things got too far out of hand.

"You did the right thing, Danny," I said. "I know my father wouldn't hesitate to use whatever methods necessary to get information out of any of us."

Danny's eyes flashed between us as if he was trying to figure out who we were.

"It was the right thing," Burt said with hesitation in his voice. "I'm sorry, Danny."

Danny said nothing.

"Is there anything we can do between now and tonight?" I asked.

Danny spoke in a distant voice before he turned through the woods and headed towards his cabin.

"No, just get plenty of rest today. I need both of you to be a hundred percent tonight."

Without another word, he turned and headed through the woods.

"Five o'clock at the mess hall," he called over his shoulder. "Don't be late!"

Burt and I shrugged. There was nothing more to say.

I went back to our cabin and was surprised to find it empty; I guess Barbara was doing something with the girls. I hung Barbara's blanket up over the window and stretched out on my cot to take Danny's advice. I rolled over and shut my eyes, trying to will myself to sleep. Rest did not come easy. I tossed, turned, and was shaken wide-awake when the girls came back. Barbara quietly ushered them out when she saw me on the cot. She gave me a peck on the cheek before going back outside.

Sleep finally came, I'm not sure how fast it arrived or how long it remained. It was restful. My head filled with dreams of iron caskets and ocean terrors. I think I endured a few nightmares where I was trapped in an iron casket on the ocean floor. I finally slid off the cot because I couldn't take another pulse-pounding image. I felt mentally and physically exhausted.

I stood up and checked at my watch, my heart almost stopped. It was 4:40 PM; I had to be at the mess hall in twenty minutes. I ran out the door to find the girls. There was something I needed to tell them.

CHAPTER 22

THE BAY

"Heroes may not be braver than anyone else. They're just braver five minutes longer."
~Ronald Reagan

I FOUND BARBARA AND ABBS down by the lake skipping stones. They paused and greeted me with hugs, then asked if I would accompany them to dinner. I glanced at my watch and saw it was seventeen minutes to five. I opened my mouth to speak then Barbara stopped me.

"It's okay, they're serving dinner early tonight due to your mission," she said. "I was about to come wake you."

"Where's Steff?" I asked.

"She's already there. I told her to save us a seat," Abbs said.

I accompanied the women to the mess hall for what I was sure would be another helping of Vienna Sausages, Spam or some other potted meat. However, when we got inside I found a pleasant surprise. Danny took a huge risk and went into town where he brought back several bags of Martian Burgers' saucer burgers and fries. There was no 'take me to your liter' sized drinks, however there was a Styrofoam ice chest full of a variety of sodas. Steff sat at a table beside Danny, devouring a hamburger bigger than her head. Danny motioned us over.

"What's this?" I asked as he handed Barbara, Abbs and me our own personal bag of burger and fries.

"Fuel," Danny said. "Eat up."

Barbara went to the ice chest and brought each of us the soda of our choice or at least the closest approximation to it. Danny was not big on variety or name brand. I wasn't complaining; I appreciated every morsel of my meal and every sip of my drink. Only, as good as it was, I couldn't shake one nagging thought. I wondered if this would be my last supper. The fact that we all sat in a row on one side of the table resembling the famous da Vinci painting didn't help to quell my angst.

The rest of the appointed crew showed up in the meantime, and after they enjoyed their dinner, we set out for Danny's cabin. I stopped for a moment and called Barbara and Abbs to the side.

"Listen, in case anything happens, I want you to go here," I said, pulling a folded piece of notebook paper out of my pocket. I opened it to reveal a hand drawn map I hastily sketched after my nap.

"What do you mean . . . are you expecting something?" Abbs asked in a frightened voice.

"No, I'm not expecting anything," I assured her. "It's just that we are going to be gone for most of the night. There are only a handful of folks in camp tonight. I want to prepare for everything."

"Are you going to leave me a gun?" Barbara asked.

"Well . . . Taylor will be here. He said he would watch out for you," I said.

Barbara repeated her question. This time with a stern face and raised eyebrows.

"I'll make sure you get one," I said with a great deal of hesitation.

I knew Barbara could handle a gun. She went to the shooting range with me on a number of occasions. That didn't change the fact I did not like her *having* to handle one. I guess the chauvinist in me is stubborn.

I hugged both of them before leaving and even managed to get a weak one from Steff, which was just what I needed now. It was good to know that I had the support of my whole family.

We convened at Danny's cabin as planned with Lincoln, Powhatan and the president. They arrived with batteries in hand to avoid detection. We ran over the plan again. When Danny was comfortable that everyone was on the same page, he sent the three Impal leaders to the mine to begin preparing the refugees.

"Do you think we are going to have any problems tonight?" Danny asked the three men before they left.

They all seemed worried.

"There is some apprehension, which is understandable. Among the three of us, I am sure we can manage it," Lincoln said

The president and Powhatan agreed.

I felt a sinking feeling in the pit of my stomach as the three men disappeared out the door. There were going to be problems, it was almost a mathematical certainty. There were not only our one hundred-ten Impals to worry about. There were hundreds more meeting us tonight. There would be apprehension and there would be panic. Panic can draw attention, which was the last thing we needed. It was going to be hard enough getting past the shore patrols. Even assuming the majority marched into the water like good little soldiers; a few terrified souls could go berserk and cause a scene. That was why Danny requested the equipment nobody wanted to discuss, the iron chains and restraints

We took the first group of Impals at six o'clock. There were ten crammed into each SUV and I drove the second vehicle on the first trip while Danny drove in the lead. The truck was waiting as promised in the clearing beside the road. It was an inconspicuous vehicle with a solid white cab and navy-blue trailer. The truck and trailer displayed no discernible markings except for a Department of Transportation registration number.

Chuck Connelly was a middle-aged man of average height and build. His dark-brown hair, as well as his untidy goatee, was beginning to show the first signs of gray. He possessed a weathered appearance, a man's man who had spent an abundant amount of his life outdoors. As I reached out my hand to shake his, I involuntarily recoiled as I found myself grasping a steel hook. Chuck laughed.

"The crocodile got it!" he proclaimed as he let out a boisterous laugh, referring to Captain Hook.

I laughed uneasily for a few moments until he stopped with a serious expression on his face.

"No, about five years ago I was wading out in the Chesapeake Bay doing a little surf fishing. I just cast a line when the God awfullest ugly bull shark you ever saw swam up and snapped it off clean," he said holding his hook up and making a motion with his other hand like his fingers were teeth biting at the end of his stump.

I tried not to react to a shiver that went up my spine. That was the last piece of information I needed tonight. I was about to be bobbing about in a small boat in the middle of the Chesapeake Bay like a fishing cork.

The back of the truck contained two twelve-foot aluminum flat-bottomed boats, no motor. The boats were stacked on top of each other. The top one contained a number of iron chains and restraints. A couple of large black canvas tarps covered the boats. This concealed the restraints from the Impals riding back there. The tarps would also provide us a degree of cover over the boats while on the dark water.

When we got the last of the Impals loaded in the truck, it had been dark over an hour. So far, we were right on schedule. To my relief, we did not encounter a single vehicle or person during our hour and a half evacuation. No, it was more than surprising, it was eerie and it made me uncomfortable.

I leaned against the back of the truck once we shut the doors to a trailer packed tighter than a can of sardines. If stopped and searched, we were screwed. There would be no hiding any of them. In the event of something like that happening, the Impals orders were to pass through the walls and floor then run away as fast as possible. Some would be caught. The hope was at least most would get away.

As I leaned against the cool metal surface of the trailer doors, my mind was miles away. I heard the noise of Danny's voice, the sound of the cicadas in the surrounding woods saying farewell to the day and the summer. I stared in awe at the ultraviolet spectacle of the night-time. I heard and saw all of this, yet my mind didn't comprehend any of it. My thoughts dwelled on my girls. I was scared, scared much more than I believed I would be. I wanted nothing more than for this night to be over with as soon as possible. When Danny asked if anyone had questions, I shook my head 'no' like the rest of our group. The truth is, I had a ton of questions. Unfortunately, these questions Danny could not answer. No one could. The night would have to play itself out, good or bad.

Danny and Andrews in the other SUV would be leading our small convoy. The eighteen-wheeler would follow, where Derek would ride shotgun with Chuck, both in the literal and figurative sense. Burt and I would bring up the rear in the other SUV. We all pulled out at thirty-second intervals. We tried to keep each other in sight while trying to keep enough space between us. We didn't want it to appear as if we were travelling together. We would not stop again until reaching Grandview Natural Preserve, a couple of miles north of the tunnel.

The drive took almost three hours as we took a number of back roads to get there. Thankfully, there were no problems. We experienced a few tense moments when we met a military convoy. They were transporting Impals to one of the Shredder camps. They didn't even blink at us.

Shortly before midnight, we pulled into a large gravel parking lot made for vehicles towing boat trailers. A large boat ramp at the far end disappeared into the murky waters of the Chesapeake Bay like a dark path to Hell.

I got out and inhaled the cool salty breeze. I usually enjoyed that smell because it reminded me of vacations, beaches and seafood. Tonight it was no more appealing than the acrid scent of death.

The other groups had not arrived, so we took a moment to walk the perimeter of the parking lot to make sure we were alone. There didn't seem to be a soul for miles. The only sound was the occasional fire or ambulance siren and the distant drone of traffic on nearby Interstate 64. As we headed back to the vehicles, we took cover behind a garbage bin as a bright spotlight scanned the parking lot. I peeked my head out far enough to see a Navy Cyclone Class Coastal Patrol boat slowly passing our position, a few yards out from the boat ramp. It was a small boat by Navy standards. It contained a minimal crew compliment of only twenty to thirty men. It was capable of bringing down a world of hurt on us with both its armament and its ability to call in reinforcements.

As it lumbered past and disappeared around a bend in the coast, we cautiously stood up and scanned the water. A mile or two north we could see the spotlight of another patrol boat panning the shoreline. The Navy was conducting a methodical search of the coast; tonight would be tricky. It soon became evident tonight was not only going to be about stealth and a well-executed plan, it was going to require timing as well. We would have to send the Impals and the boats out in between patrols. We would have to observe the boats for a while before we knew how great of a window we might have. This night is going to be later than we planned. We went back to the SUVs to sit, wait and watch.

About ten minutes later, the patrol boat we spotted to the north came by on the same trajectory as the first boat. They also performed a perfunctory search of the shoreline and moved on. The moment we spotted another boat in the distance, bright lights from behind us flooded the parking lot. We all jumped in unison, ready to fight, until Danny held up his hand.

"It's okay, I think it's the group from the New Jersey camp," he said.

A small box truck used for furniture deliveries pulled into the lot as Danny got out to direct traffic. A single full-sized pickup truck followed them. He sent them to park on the far side of our eighteen-wheeler where they would be out of view from the water. Both trucks pulled out of sight then shut their lights and engines off. A few minutes later the next patrol boat passed on the same course, only this time there was a fifteen-minute interval.

Danny came back to the vehicle a few minutes later with a grim expression on his face.

"I just heard the convoy from North Carolina got stopped at the state line; they aren't going to make it," he said, averting his eyes from us. He stared at the boat ramp and into the darkness beyond.

He took a deep breath and glanced at us before returning his stare to the water.

"Pennsylvania should be here soon . . . God willing," he said. He sounded far away.

"How many were coming from North Carolina?" Burt asked.

Danny shook his head and spoke in a whisper.

"Enough."

Twenty minutes later another patrol boat passed. Its movements and direction were identical to the other two. So far, we could determine that patrols were coming every ten to twenty minutes. This was not a big window to carry out such an elaborate, unrehearsed operation. The third patrol boat no sooner disappeared from view when we spotted another one in the distance. We were all thankful Pennsylvania showed up then. They also drove a dark black eighteen-wheeler escorted by a Jeep and a small four-door sedan.

Danny got out and directed them to park between our truck and the water. He hoped the dark color would be less conspicuous. He came back and took a seat as we waited for another patrol boat to pass; the next one ended up being at another twenty-minute interval. We felt certain once we spotted one of these craft approaching from the north, we had about ten minutes before it reached our position. We decided to put things in place so we could get a quick start. Andrews, Danny, Derek, a slender fortysomething man from New Jersey and I quickly unloaded the boats and other materials from the back of our truck. The Impals watched us with nervous anticipation. Some asked what was happening.

"It's okay," Danny assured them. "Sit tight and we'll be ready to move soon."

I saw the man from New Jersey glancing with intense curiosity into the group of Impals. His eyes widened with recognition as we shut the door to the trailer.

"My God . . . you've got the president in there and . . . and . . ." he stammered.

"And Abraham Lincoln?" I finished for him.

He stared in astonishment as I took one end of the boat and he grasped the opposite end facing me. He walked backwards as we carried the boat to the water. I was afraid that he was so distracted, he might trip and bring the boat down on top of him. He managed to remain sure-footed until we got to the water's edge.

"I take it you don't have any celebrities in your group?" I asked.

He shrugged. "Yeah, we have one. Not the same caliber as the president or of Lincoln."

"Who?" I asked.

"Why, the very creator of the Shredder himself . . . Nikola Tesla."

CHAPTER 23

TERROR

*"No mercy, no power but its own controls it. Panting and
snorting like a mad battle steed that has lost its rider,
the masterless ocean overruns the globe."*
~Herman Melville

MY HEART JOLTED as if I received an electrical shock. Not because I
believed Nikola Tesla was the creator of the Godforsaken invention,
which now bore his name. I knew better. I was one of the few people
around who had knowledge of the origins of the Tesla Gate. The reason this excited me was Nikola Tesla was one of my heroes growing
up. This was unusual since every American schoolkid was taught since
kindergarten that Thomas Edison was the greatest inventor who ever
lived. I felt I knew better. While Edison was a shrewd businessman,
Tesla was much more selfless.

"Can I meet Lincoln?" the New Jersey man asked.

I heard someone clear their throat and I turned to see Danny
watching us, his arms folded and one eyebrow raised. After several
long moments, he shrugged.

"I suppose it will be okay, Tony," he said, addressing the New Jersey
man. "Be cautious and discreet about it," he continued, turning his
attention back to me.

I knew it was now or never so, I belted out the question eating away at me.

"Can I meet Tesla?"

Danny motioned with his thumb over his shoulder. "Make it quick. There will be another patrol along in a few minutes."

We helped cover the boats with the black tarp and then used dark colored duct tape to adhere a few limbs and branches to it. This gave it an extra layer of camouflage. If I didn't know there were a couple of boats there, I would have thought it was an old brush pile.

Danny tied a long rope to a small metal loop on the front of each boat. He took the loose end of the massive coil and stuck it up under the tarp where it would be out of sight until ready to use it. A shiver ran down my spine. I knew it was the towline extending dozens of feet under the water to the Impals. They would be leading us across the dark surface of the bay like some ghoulish kite.

Tony and I turned and began walking briskly toward the trucks. I shook my head when I realized how much we sounded like a couple of pleading children who wanted to visit the candy store.

"Oh, well," I thought to myself. "This is a once in a lifetime opportunity."

How many people can say they have met Abraham Lincoln, Chief Powhatan, the current President and Nikola Tesla all in less than a week's time? Probably not much more than those who knew the origins of the Tesla Gates.

We went to the New Jersey truck first since it was the farthest from the water and the most concealed. The next patrol boat passed a few minutes later and we waited on the far side until it passed.

Tony went to the rear of the truck and lifted the door a few feet. I could see the legs of several Impals milling about.

"Mr. Tesla!" Tony called. "Mr. Tesla, there is someone who wants to meet you!"

A few moments later, I saw a pair of shimmering wingtips walking towards us. When they reached the opening, the owner of these shoes knelt down and peered under the low hanging door. I recognized the dark hair parted in the middle and the long sharp nose above an immaculately groomed moustache. It was a young Nikola Tesla. I was glad Impals appeared as they did at a prime point in their lives. I saw photos of Tesla taken a short time before his death and he was almost unrecognizable as his younger self.

"Yes?" he said, looking from me to Tony. He didn't have as much of an Eastern European accent as I expected. It was there, faint and in the background. On first impression, most people might presume him to be from Canada.

Tony stepped back a few steps and held both hands out to me like a game-show host presenting a prize.

Tesla focused his gaze on me and raised his eyebrows with great expectation.

I felt like an eight-year-old kid meeting his baseball hero for the first time. All I could do was stand there like a deer in headlights. Finally, Tesla broke the ice. "Hello Mr. . . ." he said, addressing me.

"Major," I said, finally coming to my senses. In all fairness, Tony threw me off by his uncouth introduction. I was cautious to not let the Impals know my true name. "Cecil Major," I said. "It's an honor to meet you, Mr. Tesla."

"Call me Nikola," He said, passing through the bottom of the truck and then through the back bumper until he was a few feet in front of me.

He made no move to extend his hand in greeting and so I followed his lead. I read one time that Tesla was somewhat quirky about physical contact. No one was sure if it was because he was a germaphobe or very shy. Judging by his demeanor and his soft-spoken personality, he definitely wasn't an outgoing person.

"I didn't create the Gates you know," he said. "I find it an insult of the highest degree that they named the accursed things after me."

I happened to glance at Tony who was standing behind Tesla, silently forming words with his mouth.

"*He does this all the time*," Tony mouthed.

"I know you didn't," I said. "I talked to the scientists who worked on the project. It wrongly bares your name because the electrical current in the center of the Gate resembles one of your famous coils."

He didn't seem very reassured.

"I want you to promise me something, Mr. Garrison," he said with deep earnestness.

"Anything," I said.

"If I am not remembered for anything else, please make sure the world doesn't remember me for these horrid Gates," he pleaded.

I sensed the conversation would not go much beyond his personal concerns about his legacy and that was all right. I understood his concerns and I sympathized. I hoped history did not remember the name Garrison in the same vein as Stalin or Hitler.

"I give you my word," I promised. "It was a great pleasure to meet you, Nikola."

"Are we still going in the water?" Tesla asked, turning to Tony. It was as if he flicked a switch, no pun intended, and gone from one concern to another.

"Yes, Nikola . . . we have gone over this. It will be a short time though and then you'll be hopping a boat for your native land," Tony said with obvious impatience. He used the same tone, which I have sometimes heard caregivers speak to the elderly. A tone insinuating they were a child and a bother.

"I'm not from the English Channel, you prat!" Tesla snapped. "I am from Croatia; there's a huge difference!"

"Now, Nikola there's no need to get all riled up," Tony said with condescension. "You're going back to Europe anyway."

I didn't appreciate Tony's attitude so I jumped in.

"Mr. Tesla, I will be in one of the boats tonight. It won't take long at all," I said, pointing out towards the water. "See, there is the bridge right there."

The Chesapeake Bay Bridge Tunnel resembled an enormous glowing serpent moving in and out of the water. Due to its massive size and lighting, it appeared much closer than it was.

Tesla frowned and stared at the bridge. He then turned back to me and said two simple words in a quiet voice. "Very well."

He cut his eyes back at Tony, and then passed through the now closed door, disappearing inside.

"He's been like this since he heard about the plan," Tony snorted. "What a chickenshit."

In an instant, I felt rage rear its ugly head at Tony's ignorance. "How would you like to walk beside him tonight?" I asked, turning to face him.

He stared at me in disbelief, his jaw hanging open. I didn't care that I promised to introduce him to Lincoln. I'm sure the former president wouldn't want to meet someone with his attitude. Was I being too harsh, too sensitive? Perhaps. However, right now social graces were the last thing on my mind. My stomach was still in knots about the upcoming mission, which was now minutes away. I walked off and left Tony standing there and got back in the vehicle with Danny and the others.

We sat and watched two more patrols pass by before we put our plan into motion. We combined the Pennsylvania group and half of the New Jersey group and then the remainder of the New Jersey group with ours. We agreed it would take too long to get two groups out before another patrol passed. Therefore, Danny would take a boat and go with them. I would wait for the next patrol. As planned, each group brought several crates of batteries and a couple were handed to each Impal before they exited their respective vehicle. The rest got piled into the boats, leaving barely enough room for a man to fit on his hands and knees. As I considered the heap of Duracells and Rayovacs, I wondered if law-enforcement wasn't monitoring purchases.

As everybody pitched in to get Danny's group ready, we ran into our first problem. A young boy started to scream and grasp at a woman's leg beside him as they began their slow march toward the water. Judging by the woman's bewildered reaction, I did not believe her to be his mother or even a relative of the child. In any case, she bent down and picked him to comfort him. Like a fool, I believed it would be the last of our worries. That was until a middle-aged man, wearing Colonial gentleman's clothing, began to mutter something as he walked away from the group. I moved to confront him.

"Sir, you need to keep moving with the others," I said.

His eyes bulged with terror. "I can't," he whispered. "My wife died at sea . . . the water terrifies me!" he hissed in his tinny voice. I felt sorry for the man. Nevertheless, we could not allow any dissension tonight; it was not safe.

"Sir, I can tell you from firsthand experience, the Tesla Gates are far more terrifying than a little bit of salt water. If you stay here you will be tossed into one, it's only a matter of time."

"I-I can't," he stammered and tried to walk back toward the Pennsylvania truck.

Before I could reiterate my position, I saw a flash out of the corner of my eye. The terrified man toppled face first onto the pavement. If he had not been an Impal he would probably require several stitches and dentures. As it were, his body rested half in and half out of the pavement. As he tried to get up, I saw the flash again as something came down across his back, sending him further into the blacktop. I wheeled around to see Andrews standing there with an iron bar clutched in his hands. Pure maniacal rage blazed on his face.

"Shut the hell up and get your ass in line, you selfish prick!" Andrews bellowed.

He moved to raise the bar as the man pushed himself to his knees. Before he could bring it down again, I moved to intercept. I grabbed his arm in one fluid motion, knocking the bar free and sending him sprawling onto his butt. Danny was concerned about this and discussed it with me on the day of the president's funeral.

"Put him down if he gets out of line," Danny told me. He knew the violence of which Andrews was capable. He beat the Commander in Chief with an iron pipe . . . possibly the same one he wielded now.

Andrews turned his rage at me and was about to get up when Derek knocked him forward and pinned him from behind. He kicked, struggled, and cursed. Derek was heavier and he did not budge.

Before the beaten Impal could get back on his feet, another Impal, a tall slender man with a handle bar moustache, came over and placed iron restraints on the man's wrists. The restraints hooked to a long chain and the mustached Impal took the other end. With calm composure, he walked back to the front of the group. This man, who could have stepped right out of a speakeasy in the 1920s was the leader of this group. All the Impal leaders were briefed on drastic measures if the need should arrive. I saw Danny watching from the water's edge, standing beside his loaded boat with folded arms. I was about to walk over to him when I realized the fire had only just begun and it was about to spread.

A woman a few yards away began to whimper, a man wearing blue jeans and cowboy boots shouting with anger followed this.

"I'm not going in there!" he yelled, pointing towards the water. "I'd rather face this gate thing than to go in there!"

A rumble of discontent started to move through the crowd.

"If we don't go, they'll beat us!" one woman shouted. "They don't seem to be any better than the others! Who are we to trust?"

Again, a wave of grumbling and agreements washed through the crowd.

I don't think I could have hated anyone more than I did Andrews, except for maybe my father. Sam Andrews made an already tense situation boil over and now it was going to be hell to get things back in order. I cleared my voice and took in a deep lungful of salty, humid air.

"Ladies and Gentleman!" I shouted.

The crowd quieted a bit, but the murmuring persisted.

"Ladies and Gentlemen!" I repeated.

This time they fell into a hushed silence.

I glanced at Danny, who had not moved an inch since this all started. He watched patiently. I then glanced to the north for the patrol boats. There was no sign of one yet. I was certain that any minute I would spot one. It was about time.

"I have seen these Shredders and, believe me when I tell you; they are the last thing you want to face. It would be the last thing you ever face."

I paused and took a breath. The fear, resentment and distrust I saw on several faces was enough to shake my resolve, nevertheless, I pressed on.

"These things are nicknamed the Shredder because some believe it shreds the soul, wiping you out of existence."

"You can't destroy the soul!" one man shouted. "God would not allow it!"

The crowd erupted again into a sea of shouts, screams and lamentations. Some remained calm, in fact, the great majority did. Unfortunately, the noisy dissenters drowned out the silent majority.

In the end, we shackled five people; the man Andrews attacked, three women and a teenage boy. Two more Impals in the group stepped forward to volunteer as leaders. Carrying the chains of five people, and the rope attached to the boat, was a little much for one person to handle.

Danny positioned his boat in the surf to where it would easily glide out once all the Impals passed. Just as everyone lined up, another patrol boat appeared in the distance; we had less than ten minutes to launch.

I stood watching the group depart as I kept one eye on the approaching boat. My heart sank as the Impals began to enter the water. The three leaders dropped their batteries to provide a guiding light to the others in the murky darkness. Their tinny screams echoed along the shoreline. Others, who showed resolve until they entered the surf, joined the shrieks of these souls. They now all formed an eerie chorus. They continued to scream even as they disappeared under the waves with the rest of the group. The water made their cries of terror sound like panicked whale song, fading the deeper they descended. After a few moments, there was no sound other than the gentle lapping of the waves on the shore.

Danny positioned himself under the tarp. A minute later, his small boat was slowly skimming the surface of the Chesapeake Bay, towed by an army of spirits under the waves.

CHAPTER 24

HIT AND RUN

*"The fear of death follows from the fear of life. A man
who lives fully is prepared to die at any time."*
~Mark Twain

I FELT AS IF A COLD CLAMMY HAND reached inside me and grasped my stomach, kneading it like a ball of dough. I wanted to be sick, I was ashamed and, worst of all, I wanted to turn and run. It would be so easy, the keys in the ignition and all I had to do was jump in and go. No one would make a serious attempt to stop me. I could be back with my family.

For the mission's sake, I didn't follow through. We retreated to the vehicles once again as another patrol boat approached. My personal anxiety faded as I watched with bated breath while the boat passed. The searchlights scanned the water's edge while two enormous lights on the port side panned across the surface of the bay. My heart jumped into my throat when I saw one light freeze as if locked onto something. It remained focused on a distant point in the water for several seconds before resuming its sweeps. I could have sworn I saw a small pile of brush in the light. I couldn't be certain, not at this distance. If it was Danny, his tarp and duct taped branches were enough to disguise his boat. I felt a little better . . . just a little. As the patrol boat passed out of sight, my stomach knotted like a nest of snakes; it was now my turn.

The remaining Impals, batteries in hand, exited their respective trucks. We lined them up as straight as possible. This task was left to Burt, one of the men from New Jersey, a teenage boy from Pennsylvania, and me. Derek took a pair of restraints and locked Andrews in the back of one of our SUVs. I knew there was going to be hell to pay with his temperamental ass later.

There were a few panicked individuals in my group, but it was not as bad as Danny's bunch. We only restrained three of them. That wasn't too bad considering I had close to two-hundred in my small army. Still, several were uncomfortable with the situation.

I crammed myself into the boat, almost in a fetal position because over half of the interior was filled with cases of batteries. I considered throwing a few boxes out before I reminded myself of their purpose. We were not only supplying the Impals with batteries for this mission, but also for their trip to Guernsey Island. In the horrifying chance that their boat was stopped, at least on the surface they would be able to appear as fleshers. Well, the ones in modern clothing would in any case.

Before getting into the boat, I handed the end of the line to Lincoln, who would be walking alongside the president. Chester Henry, the boy we were afraid would be traumatized beyond repair, volunteered to take a couple of restraint chains. He talked in low, inaudible tones to the Impals he would be guiding. After a few minutes, they seemed to calm a little. Maybe it would be enough to get things under way without dissension. This only turned out to be wishful thinking.

I glanced back over my shoulder before pulling the tarp over me. Derek and a couple of others from New Jersey and Pennsylvania gave me a thumbs-up. Andrews glared at me through the back window of the SUV. My stomach twisted when I considered I would have to deal with him again once this was all over. I gave an appreciative wave to my supporters, and then knelt in the bottom of the boat. I pulled the tarp tight, leaving enough of a gap to peer out and observe my surroundings. As the Impals began to slowly move forward, I could see most of the group through my opening. I saw Mrs. Fiddler bravely clutching her daughter. I saw Chief Powhatan and his Native American counterparts walking forward with pride, and I saw Nikola Tesla following the procession. I could see fear in his eyes, but I also saw a great deal of resolve.

When it seemed everything might go as planned, the high-pitched dirges of a few Impals started. I did not want to watch as some were forced under the water, not again. I closed the flap and hunkered down in the boat, trying to block out the sounds. It did not work. The pitiful screams only seemed amplified through the metal hull of the boat. I have never seen or heard anything so bizarre. The restrained Impals were joined in their ghastly chorus by the brave and frightened who still pushed forward. I wasn't sure which ones I felt the most sorry for. I think it was extra troubling for me because I heard similar cries of horror at the mouth of the Tesla Gate.

Weren't we saving them from the Gate? That's what I kept telling myself.

As the Impals descended into the water, the cries became distorted and I once again heard the disturbing sound like panicked whale song. This time it was worse. It reverberated on the bottom of the boat like demonic nails scraping and clawing. I was so unnerved, I almost jumped through the tarp when the boat jerked forward as Lincoln pulled me slowly out to sea.

A sudden panic came over me as I have not experienced since I was a young boy. The ironic thing was I was in a boat then too. I took deep breaths and tried to focus as the unnerving chorus from the deep started to subside. I didn't know why my anxiety just hit me. I guess the perfect storm of everything tonight. The cosmic storm cast an eerie ultraviolet glow across the bay, adding an extra layer of spookiness.

I knew there were no snakes in the boat with me, not around salt water. That didn't stop my brain from telling me otherwise. I stretched my legs out a little to get more comfortable and to convince myself that I was alone. Two D cell batteries dropped out of a crate landing on my shin . . . I had been bitten, I knew it. I jumped, pulling my legs up close and forcing myself to take long, even breaths. I felt stupid and I felt foolish. After several long moments, I started to calm. When I regained control, I rose up and peered from under the tarp.

The water was black as the darkness under the tarp. The only light was the bridge in the distance and the ultraviolet night sky. It seemed more like a solid object than it did a light source; no . . . it was more like a candescent phantom.

I did wonder why we didn't get some boats and send the Impals out or have Andrews's brother meet us right here at the park. After seeing the patrol boats tonight and the massive number of Impals moving beneath the surf, the answer was clear. I realized what we were doing was the only viable option. I doubted the patrols would be concerned with the middle of the bay where we now headed as slowly as a funeral procession. The large flotilla it would have taken to move all the Impals could not have passed unnoticed.

As I leaned against the side of the boat, breathing hard, a noise caught my attention. It was a sound like a deep penetrating throb. It grew louder by the second. I couldn't see anything at first, not until I shifted my position and peeked under the tarp. At first it took me a moment to register what my eyes were telling me. When it finally sunk in, all the air left my body in one big gasp of terror.

The dark outline of a massive super tanker loomed in the distance. From my perspective, it seemed as if the behemoth ship was miles long with a massive hull extending to the sky. It was on a course not quite in my direction. It headed to where I guessed Danny should be right about now. Training my gaze in that direction, I couldn't see anything in the black gloominess. I strained my eyes and finally caught sight of a shape. I watched for several moments until the object bobbed up a few feet on a wave, passing between the bridge lights and me. There was no doubt it was Danny's boat. Turning my attention back to the tanker, I felt like an icy hand reached inside my chest. The enormous ship was indeed on a direct course with Danny's tiny craft. It would be there in a few short minutes.

I tried to call out, but it was no use. Nothing could be heard over the sound of the waves and the throb of the massive engines. The noise grew louder with each passing second. Danny must hear it; I was sure of that. He was much closer than I. Realizing how helpless I was, I stuck my head out from the tarp and clutched the edge of the boat with white-knuckled hands. I watched, hoping disaster would be avoided. My boat began to rock more and more violently as the massive wake fanned in my direction.

After less than a minute, I brought myself back in to center my weight in the boat. The tanker's approaching wake threatened to capsize my tiny craft. I moved crates around, equalizing the weight, placing myself in the dead center. I pulled the tarp back halfway so I could watch for Danny when he bailed out so I could somehow manage a feeble rescue attempt.

I waited and watched, expecting to see him emerge at any second. He never did. I could see Danny's boat now in the ambient lights from the tanker, it bobbed without mercy and the tarp remained shut.

The smell of the salty brine coupled with the exhaust fumes of the tanker filled my lungs. It reminded me that I needed to breathe. Danny's small boat was about to be pulverized and there was not a damn thing I could do about it.

An unexpected rain began to fall, pelting the tarp like a shower of pebbles. Water ran into my eyes making it almost impossible to see through the sheeting torrents of the downpour. I pulled the tarp up over my head and watched Danny's boat, hoping against hope. Hope was not with us tonight.

A few moments later, it happened. Even above the roar of the ship and the relentless pounding of rainfall, I heard it. The dull scraping sound of pulverizing metal and then, for an instant, I heard a scream. Even though I never heard Danny scream before, I knew what I heard. Who else could it be out here? All I could do was sit under the tarp, my heart hammering against my ribs almost in unison with the tanker's strumming engines. As the massive ship passed, I tried everything I could to keep my small boat afloat.

I bobbed about like a cork in a wave pool, water sloshing over the sides, forcing me to bring the tarp back down for fear of my boat being swamped. After what seemed like an eternity, the massive ship finally passed, and the waves began to calm.

The rain subsided to a steady drizzle and I began to scan the water for any sign of Danny or his boat. Visibility was low and I could not see or hear any signs of life.

"Danny!" I shouted through the darkness, my voice swallowed

by the immense body of water. My only response was the roll of the waves, the dissipating murmur of the tanker and the cascading sound of rain. I didn't like the answer they were giving me.

I don't think I have ever felt more alone than I did at that moment. I called out for Danny again. Still, no answer. I considered retrieving a small flashlight in my pocket and scanning the vicinity. I reconsidered when I saw another patrol boat searching the shore in the distance. I didn't know if they could see my tiny light at all. It was best not to risk it.

My heart leapt into my throat when I felt the boat pull against the waves. I almost forgot the hundreds of souls in the depths below. My rope lurched with a deliberate jerk as if someone was trying to get my attention. I reached forward; grasping the rope attached to the front of the boat and gave a quick tug in response. The wet, taught nylon gave my palm a friction burn, which I didn't notice as I waited with anticipation for what would happen next. A few moments later, I could feel the boat start to move forward. Once again, we headed for the tunnel.

The rain started to pick up, pelting my eyes and soaking any dry patch of clothing left. I pulled the tarp over my head and wiped the large drops beading on my face with the damp sleeve of my shirt. The four-inches of water in the bottom of my boat sloshed in unison with the pitch of the ocean, sending streams of water into my boots. It also ate away at the thin cardboard of the battery cases. It would be extremely difficult to unload the batteries with wet and tearing cases.

The bridge leading into the tunnel grew larger as my boat chopped through the waves. I was about to start searching for Danny again when something thudded against the side of the boat. The first thought in my head was a shark. In the same instant, I heard the scrape of metal on metal. It was something else.

Peering out from under the tarp, I feared something was about to jump out at me any second. I knew how irrational it sounded, but all sorts of things run through your mind in an eerie situation such as this. As I strained my eyes in the darkness, not in my wildest nightmare could I have imagined what happened next.

A sudden wave surge brought the mysterious metallic object back for another pass. I shrieked with terror when I realized what it was and what it was trying to show me. The crumpled aluminum hull of Danny's boat bobbed inches from my starboard side. It was as if some giant reached down and wadded it into a ball as if it was made of paper, however I don't think that was what made me scream. I screamed because Danny, my friend and superior officer was in the boat, or at least part of him was. A single mangled hand protruded out from one of the folds in the metal. It flopped about like a morbid buoy; striking the side of my boat at random intervals like it was trying to get my attention.

My stomach lurched and I purged the remains of Martian Burgers all over the bottom of the boat. Coming up for air, I looked back at the crumpled boat. It was gone. I finally spotted the small craft pulling away into the distance, the arm flopping about as if it was waving goodbye.

"Oh my God and sweet Jesus," I thought to myself. "They are still towing the boat."

After one cresting wave, I could see the rope still attached to the area now unrecognizable as the front of the boat. It pulled tight and moved towards the bridge. It was quite possible the Impals were oblivious to what happened on the surface. With a hundred feet of water buffering the sound, it was possible. I couldn't see how they hadn't heard the noise. The God-awful screeching noise of stressed metal and the bloodcurdling scream accompanying it. I would remember the sound for the rest of my life.

Judging by the distance of the two boats, which was only about fifty yards or so, I would guess the two Impal armies were now close enough to see each other. What did I know? The water was so pitch black I didn't know how you could see anything.

As I sat and stared at the water, a strange sensation came over me. It was like sitting in a dark room as your eyes adjust to the darkness. Things once invisible in the blackness slowly seem to materialize in indistinct form and become recognizable.

I could see fish, large ones and small ones swimming below me. I could also see clumps of seaweed drifting by in the tide.

"What the hell is that? I shouldn't be able to see a damn thing right now."

I thought I was hallucinating. All the stress and horror of the evening finally caused me to crack. As I sat staring into the water, the light got brighter. It was like a swimming pool light in a milky, over chlorinated pool. The light bulb in my head started to come on, brightening in unison with the light below me. I knew what it was. The Impals' batteries were dying.

I glanced at the bridge; we were still at least a half-mile away. Then I turned my attention to the distant shore. From my current angle, I could see a patrol boat disappearing around a peninsula to the south. When I checked the shore behind me, my blood ran cold. A patrol boat just came into view and would be parallel to us in less than ten minutes.

I cursed the military, cursed my father, cursed the cosmic storm, cursed the tanker . . . I cursed anything and everything that might have a hand in my current situation. After that was out of my system, I began to pray. As I said a desperate prayer, I dipped my arms over the front of the boat and began to paddle at the water with furious strokes. We had to get the Impals to the tunnel. We must get them there before the patrol boat was close enough to see their collective light. I believed it would be sooner than ten minutes as the inside of the boat began to brighten, enough so that I could read the labels on the battery cases.

I paddled with desperate heaves, as I did when I drifted into the nest of snakes as a child. I did not take my eyes from the bridge. It never occurred to me that my paddling would not spur the Impals on any more quickly; however, desperation lit a fire in me. My single-minded focus pulled my attention from everything except for our destination. That is why I didn't notice anything happening below me. I almost jumped out of my skin when I felt an icy cold hand grasp mine in the water. I shrieked and pulled back, landing on a crate of batteries and sending the contents splashing into the sloshing salt water on the floor. I wiped the misting rain out of my eyes and blinked. My heart leapt and turned to ice in the same instant. The ethereal, Impal form of Danny was climbing over and through the edge of the boat.

CHAPTER 25

THE TUNNEL

"Stop looking for the light at the end of the Tunnel and
Find God in the Darkness."
~Unknown

"Give me some batteries!" he snapped. He was calm and casual as if nothing happened.

I gaped at his glowing form as he finally climbed *and* passed the through the side into the boat. I should have expected this. The shock of the situation dulled my brain back to pure survival instinct. I grabbed a couple of batteries bobbing in the sloshing, salty tide on the bottom of the boat and handed them to him.

He took them and his glow immediately faded. I could see he wore military fatigues in forest camo. His rank insignia stitched on the collar and his name above his left breast pocket. He dropped the batteries in his pocket and then shook his head.

"No, I need more!" he said in a firm tone underscored by the tinny resonance of an Impal's voice. "We've got to dim the light before the patrol boat gets closer!"

I started scooping batteries out of the water and then out of crates as fast as I could manage. Without looking, I handed them to Danny and turned to get more. As I tore open the lid of another crate, I wondered how the Hell he was going to carry these batteries down to the Impals. If he dropped them, they would be lost in the darkness, silt and muck of the bottom of the bay. Turning to hand him an armload of batteries, my heart sank at what I saw. Danny was pitching the batteries over the side as fast as he could get them. Before I could say anything, he stood up and walked through the side of the boat, then dropped into the water.

Sloshing my way to the side on my knees, I brought one knee down on a battery lodged perpendicular in a groove on the floor of the boat. I howled in pain. Lurching sideways, I scooted on my hip until reaching the side. There I pulled myself up and peered over the side. Danny had a large tarp stretched out on the water's surface. Judging by the color and size, it was the one from his boat. The limbs and branches protruding from underneath were a dead giveaway as well. They also helped to keep it afloat. The tarp rocked like a large jellyfish on the pitching sea. The weight of the batteries piled in the center kept it somewhat steady.

Danny folded the four corners over the pile of batteries and then shouted in my direction.

"I'll be back!" he said as he disappeared beneath the waves, followed by a bubbly slurping sound as the tarp submerged behind him.

I watched as Danny and the tarp went under. It now resembled a large misshapen jellyfish descending into the eerie luminescent murkiness. The luminescence seemed to be getting brighter by the second. I saw the silhouette of a couple of large fish pass beneath me. I shuddered and withdrew from the side of the boat when I recognized one of the fish as being a shark. I cautiously peered over my tarp. The patrol boat was still moving on the same course all the others before it. How long would it be before they spotted the massive glow of the Impals and came to investigate . . . one minute, five minutes, ten seconds?

I had no clue. I kept my eyes trained on it, searching for any change, any course correction that might suggest they saw us.

"Why the hell was the Navy wasting this time and energy?"

It was not as if we expected an attack from a foreign enemy. Nor should we expect a flood of Impals sneaking into the country. That would be a foolish move on their part . . . unless forced to do so.

I knew it was a possibility. Some other countries wanted to put their metaphorical trash on our doorstep, knowing they would be put in the ultimate trash compactor. Europe was alleged to be more humane in their treatment of Impals. However, this was not the case with countries in our own hemisphere. Some of them could barely maintain their political and economic structure before the storm arrived. Their capacity was now pushed far past their respective limits. These countries would be beyond desperate.

Yes, my father would want to avoid that as much as he wanted to get rid of the ones already here. He was doing a service for America. He was doing a service for God by getting rid of these deceitful 'demons.' Turning the Navy into a glorified border patrol was no stretch for him. I wondered how long it would be before anxiety overtook Europe. Humanity can become scarce in the presence of desperation. Were we really doing these Impals a favor, or were we delaying the inevitable?

As I watched the patrol boat, I did not notice the water around me was starting to get darker. It was like someone lowering a dimmer switch. When the boat approached our launch site, my heart froze. They almost come to a complete stop. They aimed their spotlights deep into the parking lot of Grandview Natural Preserve. I strained my eyes to see. After several torturous moments, I breathed a sigh of relief. The trucks were all gone.

The plan was that once Danny and I were away, everyone would return to their respective bases. Except for Derek, who would wait on the Hampton Roads side of the bridge for us? It seemed it would only be me slipping out now.

Soon, the patrol boat moved on, mimicking the same course as its predecessors. It wasn't until then I realized that I was sitting in the dark again. My boat still moved toward the bridge/tunnel. I leaned forward and peered into the water; it was as dark and murky as ever.

Looking up, I saw a dark shape looming above me, a short distance away. My blood ran cold with my initial reaction. I thought it was another tanker about to plow into me. When I recognized the large pilings underneath, I knew it was a long pier. It was the long fishing pier on the northwest side of the island marking the beginning of Thimble Shoals Channel. The bridge disappeared in front of me as the road dipped under the water, giving way to the beginning of over a mile of tunnel. A couple of flashing red lights marked the end of the pier, warning off any approaching ships. The pier extended out at least a couple of hundred yards from the rocky shores of the man-made island.

As we pulled even with the end of the pier, Danny's head popped up over the side of the boat. He more came through the edge of the boat than climbed over it. He then sat down across from me with a grin on his face that said, "Well, haven't we just had the shittiest luck?" I think that assessment is the understatement of the century. After several seconds of uncomfortable silence, I asked, "Are you okay?"

He regarded at me with a serene expression and then the corners of his mouth began to slowly turn up. His answer shocked me.

"I am terrific," he said with sincerity. "I don't think I have ever felt better in my whole life."

"Are *you* okay?" I asked, tapping my finger on my forehead.

Almost on cue, a loud metallic scraping echoed underneath the pier. The crumpled remains of Danny's boat banged about on the rocks in the swell of the surf. Even in the shadow of the pier, it was still recognizable from the ambient walkway lighting above. He stared at the twisted hunk of metal with his former arm protruding from it. A frown washed over his face and he turned back to face me.

"I don't know why everyone is so worried about dying," he said in a matter–of-fact tone. "There's nothing to it."

I was incredulous. Aside from taxes, dying was the largest concern of mortal man. Of course, Danny was not mortal anymore. I glanced back over at the wrecked boat as it made contact again with the rocks again.

"What's better?" Danny asked. "That," he said pointing at his boat, the arm flapping against the side. "Or this?" he said, taking his same arm and moving it back and forth through the side of the boat.

I didn't know what to say.

"I don't have an ounce of pain anywhere in me right now and I have never had so much energy. I feel invincible," he said.

I suspect he was right, unless he came up against iron or . . . the Tesla Gate.

"So what are you going to do?" I asked.

The question sounded vague, yet Danny understood my meaning.

"As soon as we get them safely on the boat, I'm retiring from running the Impal Underground Railroad. I'm going with them."

"So what's the plan now?" I asked.

"I left the tarp lying beside the tunnel down there. They are supposed to drop their batteries before going in . . . then I'm going to lug them up here."

"You can see the tunnel?" I asked.

"Not really, but you can tell where it is. There's a rock pile over the top that makes it kinda stick out."

I paused for a moment, trying to recover from my shock and absorb everything Danny was telling me.

"So . . . how are you going to get the batteries up here?" I asked. "Won't the tarp be kinda heavy? The water has to weigh a ton."

"Well . . ." Danny said. "I have that figured out; at least I think I do." He flexed his biceps like a bodybuilder showing off his physique. "I feel a lot stronger now. I haven't put it to the test quite yet. I think between the two of us we can handle it."

I'm pretty sure my face turned white. I couldn't believe Danny wanted me to go down there with him and help him hoist up a tarp full of batteries. I was a decent swimmer, not a strong one. I hadn't participated in a breath holding contest since I was a kid. I think even back then my personal best time was a little over a minute. I didn't see how I could be of any assistance unless I was, well . . . unless I was like Danny. I had no desire to 'give up the ghost' just yet. Besides, I need to get back to my family. Danny read my apprehension and gave a hearty laugh in the metallic Impal timbre. As always, I shivered.

"Relax, Cecil," he said. "With my plan you won't even have to get wet!"

A few moments later, our momentum and the current brought us to an abrupt halt on the rocky shore of the island. To our right, the fishing pier towered about twenty-feet overhead. I could barely make out the rooftop to a brick building beyond it. I recognized the building as the sole restaurant and visitor center on the vast expanse of the Chesapeake Bridge-Tunnel. There was open ocean to our left. In the distance, was the other end of the tunnel where the road snaked out from the water like a sea serpent. The bridge continued a little over a mile away. I was thankful the rain stopped. It made visibility a lot better, but the counterpoint to that was the wind had picked up. The rear of our boat bobbed up and down like a seesaw, as the bow remained lodged on the rocky shore. A cool wind began to blow over the surface of the water, chilling me to the bone in my soaked clothing. I wished more than anything that I was back with Barbara, lying together in some secluded mountain lodge in front of a roaring fireplace. Maybe it would be possible now that this was almost over. It's funny how discomfort and longing can manifest naivety in an otherwise rational mind.

Danny reached up and started messing with the now slack rope tied to the front of my boat. Either the Impals stopped and were waiting for instructions or they were now passing into the tunnel.

After a few frustrating moments, Danny turned to me.

"Can you help me out here?" he asked in a sheepish tone. "First day with the new fingers," he said, wiggling the fingers on both his hands.

I scooted forward as Danny moved out of the way. There was not much room to maneuver in the tight proximity of my little boat and my left side brushed against him. I didn't think my skin could be any more chilled than it already was, but the frigid touch of an Impal was more intense than any cold. Our brief meeting almost took my breath away until Danny moved off, giving me plenty of room to work.

After a few quick tugs, I loosened the rope. Danny sprang forward and took it from me. He stood over me in the boat holding the end of the rope in both hands and scanned the pier above us. After a quick inspection, he turned to me.

"Take this end of the rope and go up there," he said, holding the rope out to me. With the other hand, he pointed to the nearest railing on the pier.

I took the rope and peered up the slope. My heart skipped a beat when I considered having to make a twenty-foot climb on slippery pier pilings. Then I noticed how the rock shore sloped gently upward until the island and the pier met. It should be an easy climb, although it would require sure footing, unless I wanted to assist Danny down under the waves.

"I'm going to take the other end down here and weave it through the grommet holes of the tarp. We should be able to hoist it up using the railing up there like a makeshift block and tackle," Danny said.

I was doubtful. No matter how tight he bound the tarp together, we would still have the issue of water collecting inside and it would increase the weight of our load.

"What about the water weight?" I asked.

Danny held out his hand.

"Give me your knife," he said.

I pulled out my small pocketknife, and handed it to him. He took it and then asked me to open the blade for him. It seemed that tasks requiring nimble fingers were quite a challenge for Impals, at least new ones. I pulled out the longest one and handed it back to him. He reached over and grabbed my tarp, which dangled over the back of the boat, and began to slice chunks out of it. As soon as he carved out five or six substantial pieces, he handed them to me. I stared at him blankly. He held out his hands, palms up.

"Unless you want to burn the hide off your hands when we start pulling the tarp up, I would suggest wrapping your hands with these."

He stood up, and then made a few upward poking motions with the knife. "Don't worry; I'm going to turn our tarp into one big ugly black colander."

Without another word, he stepped through the side of the boat and disappeared beneath the churning waves.

CHAPTER 26

THE PIER AND THE PULLEY

*"Never say goodbye because goodbye means going
away and going away means forgetting."*
~J. M. Barrie

I SAT IN THE BOAT FOR A LONG TIME, unable to move. I was in a compounded state of shock that started when I saw Danny crushed by the tanker. I didn't notice the metallic clang anymore. Still, his crumpled boat bounced about between the pier pilings like a ghoulish pinball. The shock increased when Danny showed up in his luminescent form like it was just another day at the office. However, I think what shocked me the most was he didn't seem to mind one bit. In fact, it might be accurate to say he relished it. I tried to put myself in his shoes and found the task impossible.

I would think I would be shaken up and a little stunned. This was true of the Impals I have witnessed leave their fleshy existence. The one commonality Danny and I did not share was that I had a family. They waited on me to return safely tonight. Danny did not, unless you counted a hostile ex-wife.

Danny was tough as nails and he didn't ascend to the rank of colonel being otherwise. I knew him to possess little fear of death. When we served in a few war zones overseas, he portrayed a calm and collected exterior. I guess that trait made it easier for him to embrace his current situation. I found myself pitying him for what happened and admiring his resolve in the same instant. He was indeed a hero and humanitarian in life and in death.

I knew it was going to take more than a few minutes of pondering to come to grips with the mortal loss of Danny and his curious rebirth. I pushed it to the back of my mind. Focusing on the task, I grasped the rope tight, wrapping it around my hand for purchase. I then stuffed the strips of tarp into my pocket. I felt like a man attempting a net-less tightrope walk as I gingerly stepped out of the boat and onto the wet and slippery shore.

After almost teetering backwards a couple of time, I completed my climb on hands and knees, clinging to the rocks for dear life. The wind whipped through my hair, making it impossible to hear anything. I guess that's why I didn't hear Danny at first when he resurfaced.

I breathed a sigh of relief when I reached the entrance to the pier, then turned around and screwed up eyes as I gazed into the darkness below. Danny brought three Impals up with him. They all apparently carried batteries on their person because I could not see any of them. Only their dark, moving silhouettes were visible. I did recognize Danny because he was the one giving orders.

Danny and another Impal grabbed my boat. They pushed the small craft away from the rocky shore then turned it on its side, swamping it with water. The other two Impals made their way through the choppy water under the pier. They did the same thing with what was left of Danny's boat. The small mass of crushed metal would also be his crypt. I didn't fault Danny for sending the other two out to deal with it. I don't care how tough you are, I don't think anyone wants to be his own undertaker.

Danny scuttled both of the boats to make sure there was no evidence we were here. This was a smart idea. If our boats were discovered in the morning drifting near the bridge it would throw up a red flag, especially if one of the boats contained the corpse of a Myriad Resistance member. In that case, the evacuation boats waiting on the other side of the island wouldn't make it out of United States waters.

Both boats disappeared beneath the waves before I could set up my position on the pier. Danny and his Impal companion, introduced as Horace Wexler, joined me on the pier. The other two took up position below. I still couldn't see the other two. Horace was a middle-aged man from the 1940s. He wore a pinstripe Oxford suit with a red and gold necktie tied in a perfect Winsor knot. This made him seem completely out of place in the middle of the ocean. I couldn't imagine anywhere he wouldn't be out of place except for the newsroom of the Daily Planet.

If Impals came back in whatever clothing they were most fond of or comfortable wearing in life, I couldn't imagine that anyone would be comfortable in a suit, especially not for eternity. Because, aside from my dress uniform, I could count on one hand the number of times I have worn a suit in my life.

The process of hauling the batteries to the surface was both arduous and fascinating. There was no way that just Danny and I could have completed the task. We barely pulled them up with four. It was slow going at first with all the Impals. It took a tremendous amount of concentration to pull the rope without it passing through their hands. Fifteen minutes later, we had the tarp sitting on the rocks a few feet from the water's edge. After letting the water drain through the 'colander' holes Danny poked in the bottom, we easily pulled it up and over the railing of the pier. After a brief rest for me, the two Impals below climbed up to meet us. They grabbed the rope and began to pull the tarp across the large asphalt parking lot of the visitor center. They then turned and headed towards the exit ramp from the bridge.

I froze when I noticed a solitary car in the parking lot. A light was on inside the visitor center, casting a narrow beam through the window facing the parking lot. We would have to go past the window. I motioned for everyone to stop then crept forward and peered inside. A heavyset African American woman had her back to the window as she ran a rather noisy vacuum cleaner. A pair of wires dangled from her ears as she sang to the music coming through her earbuds. I watched her for a moment. When I was satisfied she wouldn't turn around any time soon, I motioned everyone forward. She could not hear a bomb go off between her loud music and vacuum cleaner. I kept my eye on her as they moved past, unsure of exactly what I would do if she turned around and spotted us.

A minute later, we passed the visitor center and headed for the exit ramp. As we passed the little white sedan, which I assumed belonged to the vacuuming woman, a bumper sticker in the back window caught my eye.

"I Brake for Impals!" it proclaimed in red letters on a white background.

Beside the slogan was the smiling face of Casper the Friendly Ghost. His innocent image made me chuckle at first, then it made me think of Seth. A pain of guilt shot through me because I was unable to stop that atrocity, my laughter soon faded. Were he and his father still around or were they shredded out of existence? I wasn't sure if I would ever know.

I did feel a small degree of encouragement in the fact that there were people who stood up for the right thing, even when it might not be popular. Yet, she could just be a fan of the cartoon. It was hard to believe the best in people anymore after all I have witnessed. I guess it was still possible. The Army fatigue clad colonel running ahead of me was proof.

We soon reached the bridge, then took an immediate left toward the tunnel. The two lane north and southbound lanes merged to form a single two-lane stretch through the tunnel. A few minutes later we headed down a steep incline; the entrance to the mile-long passage under the Chesapeake Bay. The lighting was minimal since the bridge was closed to traffic today. It reminded me of the entrance to the haunted house at the state fair. An ever-increasing ethereal glow added to the eeriness as we descended further. A moment later, we were drowned in a blinding light as a horde of Impals approached us from the depth of the tunnel.

I squinted as I stared in amazement at the massive assembly of spirits. This was the first time I had seen them all together and that, coupled with the close quarters, made it appear as if there were thousands. Danny and my Impal companions spread the tarp out in front of them and as they passed, they each picked up a couple of batteries.

I watched as they formed two lines, one on each side of the tarp, as they picked them up. The expression on some of their faces was troubling to say the least. Fear, shock and confusion seemed to be the most common among them. There were many who showed stoic resolve as they scooped up their ration and marched toward the mouth of the tunnel. I felt a cold hand tugging at my arm. I looked down to see Chester, his batteries already in hand.

"I told you I'd do it!" he said proudly.

"You did great, Chester. I'm going to miss you," I said, patting his glacial head.

The truth was, I did not get a chance to know Chester very well. After all, he was only with us a couple of days. I guess I revered him as much as I did Danny. I couldn't imagine what he endured for almost a century and then bounced back with so much resilience. I couldn't imagine being an Impal either. It was beyond my comprehension right now and that's the way I wanted it to be . . . for a long time.

Chester strode forward and then I turned to face Mrs. Fiddler and her daughter.

"Thank you, Mr. Garrison," she said and gave me a peck on the cheek. I felt cold on my waist as her daughter wrapped her arms around me.

"Thank you," she whispered, then turned and followed her mother.

Tesla shook my hand and thanked me. There were few pleasantries exchanged between us. He was a proud man with a quiet demeanor. He studied his hands with intense curiosity. It was as if he had never seen them before. "You know, Mr. Garrison," he began. "Our virtues and our failings are inseparable, like force and matter. When they separate, man is no more."

A lump started to form in my throat. I have heard that quote before, but never in this context. The world was never in this context before. Force and matter, soul and body, virtue and failings, right and wrong . . . never have they been on such prominent display in the course of human history as they were right now. Tesla gave a faint smile then turned and walked up the tunnel. I regretted I would not have the opportunity to know the man better.

Last, and certainly not least, Lincoln, Powhatan and the president, met me. I turned and walked in quiet conversation with the three men until we exited back into the cool night air. There were no profound expressions about the meaning of it all and no quotes to be passed down to posterity. It was just four men talking. We could have been taking an evening stroll around a park. I think deep down that is where each of us wished we could be. As we neared the tunnel exit, something on the wall caught my eye. I am not certain if anyone else noticed, but it lifted my heart. Someone had spray painted the Myriad symbol inside the tunnel.

"Tell your beautiful wife and daughters I said goodbye," Lincoln said.

"I will. Thank you, Mr. President."

At least I would get to go back to my family; these men would probably not see their families again in this lifetime. Lifetime . . . I am not sure if that is the appropriate term to use. It is all I know to call it in my limited experience. So much of man's knowledge and understanding has been turned upside down in the last couple of months. I'm sure a good portion of the dictionary will be rewritten when and *if* this is all over. Of course, it depends on who controls the dictionaries. Soon, we emerged back into the drizzling, cool night air. We then turned left and headed for the other side of the island.

A surge of panic shot through me when it seemed as if my biggest worry was realized . . . the boats were not here. After several moments, the faint ultraviolet light beaming through the wispy clouds revealed the dark outline of two boats. They were anchored a few yards off the steep rocky edge of the shore. All lights were extinguished in order to avoid detection from the shore patrol. I could see a couple of obscure forms moving about on the decks of both boats.

As my eyes became accustomed, I could see the boats were identical. Each was about two stories high above the main deck and half a football field from bow to stern. They resembled small versions of the QE2. There might be enough room for all the Impals to fit on board both ships. As horrifying as it sounds, maybe it was a blessing in disguise that the North Carolina group did not make it. There was no way we would have enough room for twenty more, let alone one hundred twenty.

I have always believed things happen for a reason, regardless of how terrible or unfair the reason seems to be. I said a silent prayer of thanks for getting us this far. I also said one for the group who did not make it.

"Hello, I'm Edgar Andrews!" a man called from the deck in a raspy voice as he tried to whisper his shout. "Where is Sam?"

The man must be Sam Andrews's brother, the one who owned the ships. I swallowed hard when I remembered about my last view of Andrews, shackled in the back seat of one of the SUV's. Danny stepped forward and answered.

"We needed Sam to get everybody safely back to base. I and Cecil Garrison came in a couple of small boats. My name is Danny Bradley. Thank you for meeting us!" he said in a strong, metallic voice.

The figure moved closer and leaned over the railing as if he was trying to get a better look at us. The others on deck froze in place and stared at Danny. As the clouds parted and the surreal moonlight shown on the boat, my heart jumped into my throat. The man was the spitting image of his brother, enough so I thought somehow it *was* him for several seconds. He wore a flannel shirt with rolled up sleeves and dark colored work trousers. Staring at Danny with incredulity, he opened his mouth to speak. "You . . . you're an Impal?" he half asked and half stated.

I stepped in and answered since I was the only non-Impal in the group. "He wasn't when this mission started tonight; we had an accident on the way out. Does his being an Impal now make a difference?"

Edgar Andrews turned his head to me and stared long enough to make me uncomfortable. Finally, he shook his head. "No, just took me by surprise . . . that's all," he said.

Edgar scanned the entire shoreline choked with Impals and then turned back to me.

"Did you bring extra batteries?" he asked.

I shook my head and explained that the batteries were lost in the accident. All that were left was what all the Impals now carried. Even in the dim lighting, I could tell he was upset.

He shook his head, and then turned to talk with some of the other people on deck. My stomach sank into my shoes. Did we come all this way to be turned away for want of extra batteries? What was I going to do with all these Impals? I was confident I could sneak past the guards at the entrance to the bridge. Especially since they were concerned with not letting people on the bridge, they wouldn't be paying as much attention to the bridge itself.

In any case, I knew several places where I could slip off the side and onto the beach before I got to the checkpoint. There was no way I could get this many Impals out. Not if their batteries started wearing out.

Edgar turned around and strode back to the railing. "Very well, then. It's going to be sunrise soon," he said glancing over his shoulder at the faint line of orange light on the eastern horizon. "They won't be as noticeable in the daylight. If we get stopped . . ." he said then trailed off.

We stood silent for several moments, neither of us certain of what to say. Finally, Danny interrupted. "I understand your concern, Edgar, and I appreciate the sacrifice you are making to do what is right. Once we are in International Waters, it shouldn't make a difference."

Edgar shrugged and threw a rope ladder over the side of the boat and motioned for the other ship to do the same. He then made a gesture in our general direction to say, *come on.* Danny immediately took charge and split the Impals into two equal groups then assigned each to a ship. A few minutes later, lines of Impals treaded water towards their designated transport. As I stood over them on the slope, they reminded me of a colony of ants returning to their respective anthill after a hard day's work. Several waved at me before entering the water and several more did so from the deck of the ship. Danny was the last to leave.

"God bless you and your family, Cecil," Danny said as he gave me a bone-chilling hug.

"Take care, colonel," I said. "I appreciate your leadership . . . we all owe you our lives."

It seemed like an odd thing to say under the circumstances. Danny took my meaning and bowed his head in acknowledgement. Without another word, he strode into the water and quickly traversed the distance between the shore and the boat. Once on deck, he gave me a final salute and then disappeared into the throng. I stood alone on the small island as the boats began to move away. I felt more alone than I did in my small boat right after Danny died. At that moment, I wanted nothing more than to be back with my family. Glancing at the orange crescent of the sun rising to the east, I turned and jogged out of the parking lot. I turned left on the bridge, towards the shore. I hoped my friends still waited on me.

CHAPTER 27

THE RETURN TO BASE

"I have, indeed, no abhorrence of danger, except in its
absolute effect—in terror."
~Edgar Allan Poe

I HAD NOT DONE CONDITIONING WORK in a while. It showed on my jaunt
across the bridge. I guess I was no more than a mile along when I
started to get a stitch in my side and my breathing turned to gasps. I
paused for a moment to rest. I squinted back to the southeast to see if
I could see the boats in the distance. The rising sun made it difficult to
tell. I think I could see them far on the horizon. I didn't see any other
boats in their vicinity, which was a good thing.

After a minute of rest, I turned and continued my run, trying to
keep my head down and my breathing steady to avoid another cramp.
After what seemed like a marathon run, the bridge finally made land.
I passed over the tan beach extending for miles in each direction. I
slowed down and began to consider my possibilities. I was still about
twenty-five feet above the beach, a little too far to jump even into the
soft sand.

Traveling a little further, I passed some beachfront condos. They
were taller than the bridge, but too far away to reach. As I rounded a
corner, about a half mile from the toll plaza, my already hammering

heart almost burst out of my chest. A military blockade was set up a couple hundred yards from me; I hadn't expected it until the other side of the toll plaza. I immediately crouched down by the concrete guardrail. If any of the four soldiers manning the blockade turned around, they would have seen me. I was fortunate they continued to face forward . . . at least for a while.

My mind raced as I tried to figure out a way out of this, then it hit me in the face, literally. A large green leaf blew across my cheek and stuck to my face, clinging to me like glue with the moisture of last night's rain. I realized there was a large tree next to the bridge. There were several of them growing along both sides of the bridge with several varieties and sizes. I peered over the side and saw I was still at least twenty feet off the ground. I could also see another tree, a few feet away from me, boasted several good size branches. They should support my weight all the way to the bottom, or at least until I got low enough to where I could jump.

I swung my leg over the guardrail, watching the soldiers. They did not move. I reached out and grabbed a limb. Before I could get it in my grasp, the unthinkable happened. I heard a vehicle approaching from behind and then the sudden squalling of brakes. The soldiers heard it too and wheeled about with their weapons drawn. I was exposed. I was visible and they saw me.

"Hey you, stop!" one of them shouted and began to run in my direction with his weapon trained on me.

I knew if I didn't stop, the top of this tree along with my body would be riddled with bullets in a few seconds. I did the only thing I could do, the only option open to me . . . I jumped. As I flew through the air turned to leap, I glanced over my shoulder to see who had driven up; I saw the car with the Casper bumper sticker a few feet away. The visitor center janitor stared right at me with her eyes and her mouth as round as the tunnel. She leaned forward, her face inches from her windshield.

I think I actually laughed as I took the leap from the bridge. I'm not sure if I was laughing at the absurdity of the situation, or the woman's comical expression. Perhaps it was because I considered I was going to die from a fall and become a forest running Impal. Would my father show up for my Shredder party? I knew he would consider me no different from anyone else. I would be just another demon trying to deceive the living.

I didn't die. Instead, I yelled and cursed as my body bounced from limb to limb. Finally, I managed to grab hold of a medium-sized bough about eight feet off the ground. I held on for a brief moment until I heard the soldier's shouts above. I let go of the limb as if it was on fire and bolted full speed through the woods. It did not take long to realize that I was not in the woods, instead I was in a heavily forested neighborhood. This was much worse. The obstacle course of fences, toys, swing sets, clotheslines and the occasional backyard dog kept me on my toes for the next several minutes. Just when I felt my lungs would explode and my legs collapse, I emerged from between two houses onto a busy four-lane highway.

On my mad dash through suburbia, I did something I was not proud of. I grabbed a red Washington Redskins jersey off one of the clotheslines. Under normal circumstances, I would not have done anything so despicable. Today was anything other than normal circumstances. Moreover, I knew the soldiers saw me so I needed to change my appearance. I slipped the jersey on over my head and was pleased to see that it hung down around mid-thigh, making a change of pants unnecessary.

A large red bandana hung next to the jersey and I grabbed it by accident. I was glad I did. The jersey would not be a sufficient disguise; I would also need something to cover my head. 'Dew rags' were what we once called bandanas tied on one's head, giving the wearer the fashionable appearance of a pirate. I had not worn one since I was in college and was not sure I remembered how to tie it. After a couple of failed attempts, it came back to me. I was soon walking down the street in my dark-red jersey and a serviceable, red dew rag bandana on my head. I felt like a gang member and hoped I wasn't in one of those neighborhoods.

No one bothered me and I was thankful to see no police or military anywhere. Either they hadn't called my incident in or I gave them the slip by heading in a direction they did not expect. I didn't know what direction I headed. My flight or fight instinct told me to run the hell away . . . screw the direction.

It took me a few minutes to get my bearings on the street. Once I did, it seemed I caught my first break today. I was less than a mile from the twenty-four hour grocery store where I was supposed to meet everybody. We all agreed it would probably be the most inconspicuous place for a vehicle to park for a long period. Several minutes later, I arrived in the parking lot and spotted the SUV parked next to a shopping cart return. Burt was in the driver's seat, fidgeting nervously.

I approached with caution and knocked on the passenger side door. Burt jumped as if he were in an ejection seat. He bumped his injured arm and let out a cry of pain. He turned in panic. When he saw me, relief flooded across his face.

"Cecil! Boy am I glad to see you!" he said as I opened the door and slid inside.

His smile drooped into a frown as he looked beyond me, and then in the rear-view mirrors.

"Where's Danny?" he asked.

There was no way to sugarcoat it so I told him the whole story from the tanker to boarding the cruise ships. After I finished, he sat quietly for a while, drumming the fingers of his good hand on the steering wheel. He finally took a deep breath and turned to me.

"He was a good man; he will be missed," he said with misty eyes. Then with an attempt to break the fog of heavy emotion; he turned and started the vehicle. He then switched the radio to a reasonable level. A song was playing I did not recognize.

"They're playing music on the radio now?" I asked.

Burt shook his head as if snapped out of a trance.

"What . . . oh . . . yeah, at least in touristy areas like Virginia Beach," he said. "There will be more propaganda on later, you can count on it."

Burt moved his arm in the sling with a wince. He turned his head and faced out the window. I could see his grimace of pain in the mirror.

"Why don't you let me drive, partner," I said. "I've got two good wings."

The truth was I felt as if I had been clubbed on my arms and torso with a baseball bat. I also suffered several burning cuts and scratches all over my body. Adrenaline deadened my nerves as I jumped from the bridge and ran the neighborhood steeplechase. Now that it was over, my body was starting to erupt into a crescendo of raw nerves. At least I could move both of my arms relatively pain free, for now anyway.

Burt didn't give me the argument I expected and I was glad. I didn't want to waste time arguing, I wanted to get back to my family. We had been gone over twelve hours now and I am sure they were worried sick about me. We exchanged seats and I buckled up, shifted into gear and pulled out of the parking lot.

"Oh, I almost forgot!" Burt said, reaching into the back seat and retrieving a brown paper bag with the grocery store's logo on it. "I took the liberty of getting you breakfast. I know it's not breakfast food, but it is the best I could do without a microwave handy."

"Thanks, it's great!" I said as I peaked in the bag while we waited at a traffic light. I was hungry, hungrier than I realized before he mentioned food. However, when I peaked in the bag, I almost lost my appetite. He bought me a tuna sandwich, a bag of potato chips and a bottle of water. Under normal circumstances, I would consider it a fine meal. Burt knew of my affinity for what we called 'gas station' food. There was just one glaring problem. There was two of everything. He also bought breakfast for Danny.

I tried to divert the attention away from the obvious fact, but it ended up backfiring on me.

"So, where did you get the money?" I asked in a joking tone. "You been holding out on us?"

"Danny," Burt said then turned and stared out the passenger window.

I felt about three inches high.

"Of course it was Danny," I thought to myself. He gave me money to take Steff to Martian Burgers. I would say he was the only one with enough foresight to accumulate cash, yet that wasn't entirely fair. I escaped from jail and fled to the base with no real opportunity to pay my bank a visit.

I said a silent prayer of thanks for my breakfast, and for Danny, as I took a bite out of my tuna sandwich. It was dry and I chased each bite with a swig of semi cold water. It wasn't five star dining, but it satisfied

9

me and gave me a little burst of energy, something I was going to need a lot of today.

We drove in silence for thirty minutes, both of us remembering our friend and pondering numerous questions in our heads. Burt broke the silence with a deliberate clearing of his throat and a deep breath.

"So, do you think everyone got away?" he asked. He sounded like his throat was as dry as sandpaper so I grabbed Danny's water out of the bag and offered it to him. He took it and downed half the bottle before setting it in the cup holder and wiping his mouth with the back of his hand.

"Yes, I do," I said. "I could see them clearing the mouth of the bay while I was still on the bridge."

He pondered this for a while, and then took another drink of his water.

"Will they make it without batteries?" Burt asked.

"They should; they will make International waters by noon and be out of my father's jurisdiction."

"What happens when Europe gets tired of them?" Burt asked.

I shrugged and ran my fingers gingerly across my scalp. It felt as if it had taken a blow from a thorny rose bush. I could feel a warm, wet patch in my bandana and knew it was not sweat. I was glad the dew rag was red.

"We can only worry about what we can control, Burt," I said. "All we can do is hope and pray for the best and then cross that bridge when and if we come to it."

He shrugged then leaned his seat back and closed his eyes.

"I can't wait to get back to Sally," Burt said in a dreamy voice.

I cracked a smile. I felt the same way about Barbara. I also was anxious to see the girls. I glanced over and caught Burt peeking at me out of one eye. He closed his eyes as if he was visualizing Sally. I was glad we had something else to occupy our minds.

It wasn't long before Burt was sound asleep. I found myself wishing I stayed in the passenger seat. It was a long, trying night and the effects were starting to creep up on me. I shook myself awake as I took the bypass exit around Richmond. My eyelids felt as if weighted with sandbags. I knew I was going to need to pullover and get some fresh air or we would wind up in a ditch.

I parked at a small roadside park and stretched my legs before going to make use of the facilities. After a visit to the urinal, I stopped to examine myself in the mirror. There was a large scratch on my right cheek and my left ear. I ducked my head to see a large wet spot on my scalp. I considered removing the bandana, then decided to wait until I had something to replace it.

As I touched my arms and torso, I winced with pain. I knew I must be an unholy sight under this baggy jersey. Before I could examine my wounds further, a man with a small boy came in the door. I washed my hands, and then splashed water on my face before stepping out the restroom door into the bright morning sun.

When I turned towards our vehicle every fiber in me knotted with terror. A state police car pulled up beside us and two officers sat like stone in the front seat. I couldn't tell for sure in the glare from the sun, but I think they were staring at me. Why wouldn't they? I looked like a gang member who had just been in a fight.

As I walked towards the SUV, both officers got out and headed in my direction. I tried to remain casual and avoid eye contact as I stared straight ahead. I could feel their eyes boring into me. I tried to look at anything else. A tree, a bush, the trash can, a couple of sparrows fighting over a half-eaten French fry . . . still, I could still feel their eyes burning holes in me. My mind went to work with desperate fervor, trying to come up with stories and excuses. I knew none of that would matter if they asked for my identification. Fake IDs escaped Danny's advance planning.

Drawing close to the officers, I glanced up. It surprised me to see they weren't even paying attention to me. They eyed a vending machine under a nearby pavilion. The officer closest to me acted as if I wasn't even there. I turned and watched over my shoulder as they attacked the defenseless machine with a handful of change. I wondered if there were donuts in it.

When I got back in the vehicle, Burt sounded like a buzz saw as he slept off the night's adventures. I started the vehicle and pulled back on the highway. I felt a little more rejuvenated, yet still longed for restful sleep. We hadn't been on the road long when a high-pitched noise made me jump. It took a few moments for me to realize that it was the ringing of a phone. I checked in the console and floorboard beside me. I couldn't see any sign of the phone. After about five rings, I realized it was coming from somewhere on Burt, yet he continued to slumber like a baby. I reached over and tapped him on his good arm.

"Hey, wake up!" I said. "Where the hell did you get a phone?"

We were forbidden to carry any personal cell or satellite phones due to the distinct possibility that they would be tracked. However, I knew Danny communicated somehow with the other camps in the region. The phone stopped ringing by the time Burt shook himself awake.

"What?" he said with groggy eyes.

"The phone," I said, getting impatient. "You have a phone on you. It was ringing. Where did you get it?"

His eyes suddenly lit up with recognition and he began to dig in his pockets.

"I bought a disposable phone last night and so did Derek . . . we agreed we wouldn't use it unless it was an emergency."

He finally located the phone and jerked it out of his pocket as it began ringing again. He answered it.

"Hello?"

Burt's face melted like a wax figure near a flame as he listened to the caller. When he finally hung up, he did not say a word. He absently dropped the phone in the seat beside him. His face was ashen white as if every drop of blood drained from his body. He turned to me with a haggard and drawn face.

"It . . . it's the military . . . they raided our camp last night."

CHAPTER 28

THE LOSS

"I am all in a sea of wonders. I doubt; I fear; I think strange things, which I dare not confess to my own soul. God keep me, if only for the sake of those dear to me!"
~Bram Stoker

I FELT LIKE MY INSIDES FROZE SOLID IN AN INSTANT and then rapidly thawed, leaving only an empty void inside of me. It seemed as though I was living in a dream, some bizarre hellish nightmare from which I hoped I would soon wake. I was exhausted . . . yes, that's it, we were exhausted from our all-night mission and I was dreaming. We were sitting at the rest area right now catching a quick nap before heading back to our families.

I attempted to wake myself when a passing truck did it for me. His horn blared as I veered into his lane. It was not a dream. We were on the road and Burt was still staring straight ahead with the same gaunt countenance. He did not even notice the truck.

I suddenly felt adrenaline kick in and my heart began to race. Inhaling the last vestiges of liquid from my water bottle, I pitched the empty container into the back seat. Then I began to accelerate. After several minutes of exceeding the speed limit, Burt reached down and picked up the phone on the seat.

"It's not going to make a difference you know," he said.

"What?" I snapped. My focus was on little else than getting back to the base as quick as we could.

"It's not going to make a difference," he said, a little louder.

I gave him a traitorous glare. I felt as if he turned his back on everyone. At that moment, that is exactly what I believed. Burt rubbed his face with the back of his good hand and stared at an unseen point on the dashboards. Finally, he took a deep breath and continued.

"I mean it does us no good to go storming in there. Everyone there has been rounded up in one form or another," he said.

I felt a sick burning in the pit of my stomach. I knew what he was inferring. If anyone was killed, their Impal was captured and taken to the Tesla Gate. As crazed as I was with rage and terror, the logic of what Burt was saying started to sink in, albeit not fast enough.

"Call Derek back!" I yelled, grabbing Burt's wrist, almost making him drop the phone. "Call him back and find out EVERYTHING he knows, we need information dammit!"

Burt winced with pain as he pulled his wrist free. Anger and fear burned in his eyes, making me feel guilty. In all the years we have known each other; I have never put my hands on him, not like this. Part of me wanted to apologize, however the family protector side of my brain dominated everything now. I stared straight ahead with my jaw locked and my foot on the gas. If he didn't make the call soon, I was liable to backhand him. I was glad when he began to punch numbers in the phone.

Derek answered on the first ring and I spent the next five minutes hearing only one side of the conversation. I didn't like what I was hearing. When he hung up the phone, his expression did not make me feel any better.

"When they were going up the highway to the camp this morning, they met several military trucks coming out of the trail leading to our camp. The trucks were covered so they could not see anyone in the backs. They were pretty sure that one of the Humvees escorting the trucks . . . well, they are pretty sure they saw your father riding in the passenger seat."

A sickening mixture of horror and hope ran through me at the same moment. I was horrified that my father saw fit to personally supervise this raid. The thing that troubled me the most was whether or not he would allow Barbara and the girls to be harmed. Being taken into custody by him was the lesser of two evils. At least they would be alive.

"Have they been able to get close to the camp?" I asked.

"No," Burt said. "They parked about a mile up the road and tried to sneak through the woods. There were patrols searching around the lake. There were several more soldiers at the cabins and mess hall."

"They're waiting," I croaked, wishing for another bottle of water.

"For what?" Burt asked.

"For night . . . they are waiting for night."

"So they can spot any Impals," Burt said in a quiet voice.

"Yes. They are also waiting for us to come back."

We were still about an hour away from the camp, so I pulled off at the next exit and parked in a convenience store lot to collect my thoughts. I got out and walked around for a minute, racking my brain for what we could do. If Barbara and the girls were taken, there was nothing I could do, aside from doing exactly what my father wanted by turning myself in. I considered the plan for a few minutes until I thought about it rationally. We would be incarcerated and, more than likely, separated. I could do them little good if I was locked up as well.

Burt joined me outside after a while and leaned against the vehicle. In the bright sunlight of the ultraviolet sky, he seemed to have aged twenty years since we left the grocery store parking lot.

"You got any money left?" I asked.

He reached in his pocket and retrieved a wad of bills. "This is all I have," he said, handing me the lump of money.

"Thanks," I said as I stuffed it in my pocket. "I'm really thirsty; do you want me to get you something?"

"Gatorade," Burt said, "a big ass, cold Gatorade."

I was thinking of water until the mention of the thirst-quenching drink made me change my mind. I went in, purchased two-quart size bottles from the cooler, and then we were back on the road a few minutes later.

"I gave Barbara instructions," I said after taking a long drink and then propping my Gatorade on the seat beside me. It was too big for the cup holder. "I gave her a map before we left."

"What kind of instructions?" Burt asked.

"I told her that if something happens, she needs to take the girls and hide nearby where I would meet them."

"How on God's green Earth did you know something was going to happen?" Burt asked.

"I didn't; I just wanted to be prepared. The damn camp has made me uncomfortable ever since we have been there. There's only one road in or out . . . I always felt trapped."

"Well, you must be a damn psychic," Burt muttered. "I wish you shared some of your insight with me . . . maybe I could have given Sally a plan to get out."

I glanced at Burt and noticed a tear forming at the corner of his eye. He took a deep shuddering breath. That is when I decided to lie to him.

"I told Barbara to get to Sally and take her with them," I fibbed. I felt terrible for him and I guess I assumed he took precautions of his own.

My heart lifted a little when a spark of hope appeared in his eyes. "Really?" he asked.

I didn't answer. I guess a part of me believed it wasn't a real lie if I didn't say it again. It bothered me to lie to my friend. Nevertheless, it didn't bother me as much as the worry eating away inside me like a malignant cancer. The chances of Barbara and the girls making it out were slim, especially if the soldiers arrived in the middle of the night. Even if they did manage to sneak away, navigating through the woods in the middle of the night would be problematic at best.

We rode in relative silence for the remainder of the drive, each of us sharing a common horror and struggling with it in our own private way. I wanted to cry, I wanted to curse, and I wanted to rage at the heavens . . . I wanted to kill my father. I somehow managed to keep my emotions in check. My adrenaline surge now faded back into a state of physical and emotional exhaustion. The only thing keeping my eyes open and the vehicle on the road was the desire to get to my wife and daughters. There was hope, however small.

Shortly before noon, we passed the Martian Burgers Steff and I visited. The small town was empty as usual with the exception of a dozen cars parked outside the restaurant for lunch. A minute later, we turned onto the highway leading out to our camp.

We scanned the bushes and the trees for any signs of the military. We took every corner on the winding road with gut wrenching anticipation. The only other sign of life we saw was a stray dog chasing a squirrel. I couldn't tell for sure in the noon sun. The dog seemed to have the shimmering luminescence of Impals. I knew it was possible because Thomas Pendleton told me about his son, Seth, finding and befriending an Impal dog. I had never seen any type of animal Impal. He disappeared into a thicket and never reappeared.

Ten minutes later, we approached the turnoff to the single road leading to the mine. It not only rained on me in the Chesapeake Bay last night, it rained here as well. Large tire tracks of heavy vehicles gouged the muddy road. The muddy streaks of tires smeared across the highway like a bad omen. The tracks suggested that all of the vehicles headed back the way we had just come. There were no signs of life anywhere, not even at the general store across the road. It seemed odd to see a single set of Hummer tracks coming out of the dirt parking lot of the old grocery store and gas station.

"What the hell are they doing pulling in over there?" I mumbled.

Maybe they were been officers and used the parking lot as an observation point to watch the troops coming and going. A sickening feeling burned my stomach when I guessed one of the occupants of the Hummer was probably my father.

"I think the coast is clear," Burt said.

"No, it's not. They're in there . . . waiting," I said.

I tried to drive by as casually as possible. Whether I succeeded or not; I didn't know. A minute later, we rounded a corner and passed out of sight of the road. Heading for the designated rendezvous point, I scanned the woods for any sign of Barbara and the girls. It was a fruitless endeavor and I began to sink deeper into despair with each passing second. We reached the place I mapped for Barbara, and then pulled off into the small clearing.

It was the same place where Steff and I turned around on our outing to Martian Burgers. The clearing was only about fifteen feet wide from the edge of the road to the woods and was full of knee-high switch grass. Two very large rhododendrons bordered the road, a few feet from the shoulder. This gave us the perfect place to pull in and remain hidden in a nook of foliage. I could imagine this would be the perfect hiding place for a police speed trap and hoped none showed up today. Anyone would be a fool to speed on this windy and treacherous mountain road.

I backed the vehicle into place, pulling as close to the rhododendrons as possible. I then cranked down the windows and shut off the ignition. This location was well-shaded and a refreshing mountain breeze blew through the vehicle.

"Do you want to get some sleep?" I asked. "I'll take first watch."

Burt grimaced with disbelief. I realized immediately the stupidity of my question. There was no way either of us could sleep. Not now, not until we found our families or our bodies finally reached their limit and forced us to sleep. I turned my attention out the window. A large white rhododendron bloom swayed inches from my face. It emitted a heavy sweet smell that reminded me of Barbara's perfume, something she didn't wear often. I must admit, I sometimes found it a bit overpowering on those rare occasions. Today, I would give anything to smell that overwhelming fragrance again while kissing the nape of her neck. Images of Barbara and the girls flashed through my mind. These images filled me with great joy and then hollowed me out with a feeling of profound loss. I clutched my fist to my chest as it burned with the anguish of a father and a husband.

We sat in silence for a long time listening to the wind, the rustle of the leaves, the chirping of birds and the distant sound of an airplane. We listened and heard everything except for what we wanted to hear . . . some sign that our family members were nearby. I jumped when I felt a sudden poke in my ribs.

I sat up and realized I had been sleeping. The shadows of the trees were now much longer. Burt was watching me with an amused grin.

"How long was I out?" I asked.

"A couple of hours," Burt said. "I would have let you sleep, but a cop just drove past."

"Did he see us?" I asked, craning my neck out the window.

"I don't think so. I wanted to make sure you were alert in case he came back."

A question covered my face, a question that was on both of our minds. He shook his head.

"No, no sign yet," he whispered.

I spent the rest of the afternoon in the midst of a constant battle between my body and my heart. My body wanted sleep, it wanted it bad. My heart wanted my family more. I had no intention of giving in and fought my fatigue with every fiber of my being. When dusk fell, I realized I couldn't sit there anymore, not without my ally of sunlight to keep me awake. I got out of the vehicle to walk around and clear my head. I also had not taken a restroom break in hours. I walked into the tree line on the far side of the clearing and relieved myself. As I walked back toward the truck, something caught my eye in the woods on the far side of the road.

I paused for a moment, thinking it was an animal, perhaps a deer. I was about to start walking again when I saw it a second time. A dark, mysterious form was moving about from tree to tree. I screwed up my eyes and peered into the darkness. An instant later I saw more forms approaching from behind the first.

"It's a military patrol and I have been spotted," I thought to myself. Before I could begin my sprint back to the vehicle, a voice called out to me in a hoarse shout.

"Major Garrison, is that you?" a man called in a hoarse whisper.

I stopped and stared in disbelief, I recognized the voice of Dr. Winder. I almost forgot he was back at camp too.

"Dr. Winder?" I confirmed.

"Yes," he said, stepping a little closer. "Is it safe to come out?"

"Yes!" I called back with excitement and motioned with my hand for him to come forward.

A moment later, Dr. Winder emerged from the woods and into the ethereal nighttime light. Three more people who stepped out behind him as he crossed the road followed him. My heart leapt when I saw Barbara, Abbs and Sally. I was so overjoyed to see them; I didn't notice the absence of one of my own children.

Dr. Winder shook my hand. It was my shortest handshake in history because I was anxious to get to my family.

"Burt is over there," I said motioning with my head to the SUV as I rushed over to embrace Barbara.

We hugged so tight that I might have smothered her. She didn't seem to mind as she kissed me numerous times on my ear and cheek. I looked over her shoulder at Abbs who was watching us with a sad expression on her face. I released my grip a little to reach out to Abbs and bring her into our embrace when Barbara grabbed my arm to stop me. It bewildered me because she would not meet my gaze. Finally, she looked up at me with tears brimming in her eyes.

"Abbs has something to show you," she said, then stepped away, leaving Abbs and me standing a few feet apart.

Abbs stood perfectly still with a quivering lip and mournful eyes. After a few moments, she held out her hand to me with her fist closed and palm facing down as if she wanted to hand something to me. I held out my hand with my palm up and an instant later, I felt a couple of metallic objects drop into my hand. I recognized these smooth cylinders without seeing them. I handled enough of them in the past twenty-four hours. My oldest daughter began to glow with the shimmering luminescence of an Impal.

CHAPTER 29

THE TURNCOAT

*"Perhaps we have been misguided into taking too much
responsibility from our children, leaving them too little
room for discovery."*
~Helen Hays

I ALMOST DROPPED THE BATTERIES on the ground when I saw the radiant form of my daughter. Internal conflict paralyzed me for several moments; I was happy to see Abbs, but not like this . . . this was not supposed to happen. I failed my family; I failed them miserably and now here was my punishment.

Nevertheless, as she stood in front of me in her shimmering translucent form, she had never seemed as tangible as she did now. I felt as if I was seeing her for the first time. My shock and heartache began to dissolve, giving way to my unconditional love for my daughter. When I reached out to embrace her, she stepped backward like a frightened rabbit. Gazing in her eyes, I whispered. "It's okay, Abbs. I love you."

She began to cry. Shining tears streamed from her cheeks like falling stars disappearing into the ground below. She stepped forward and I pulled her in, preparing myself for the freezing cold shock. It only lasted an instant. As I pulled my daughter closer, I started to feel a sensation described to me by Thomas Pendleton, the pleasant warm and cold of a hot fudge sundae. I had made incidental contact with Impals on numerous occasions, never like this, not this close and intimate. As I pulled Abbs closer, I could feel her passing into me as the cold dissipated, giving way to warmth. It was the most perfect warmth I have ever felt, almost as if our souls touched. I guess in a way they were.

My head swam with a thousand questions. I decided they could wait for the moment. When my daughter was comforted, I would talk in private with Barbara. The biggest question was where Steff was. After several long moments, Abbs and I pulled apart. I told her that I loved her again. She smiled and picked up her batteries. Abbs then walked over to join Dr. Winder who was standing on the far side of the clearing. Everyone respected Burt and Sally's privacy in the SUV.

"Where's Steff?" I whispered to Barbara as soon as Abbs reached Dr. Winder.

"I don't know," she said with such hollow despair, it almost paralyzed me. "She ran off again last night, but this was the first time she ever did it after dark."

"Where?" I asked.

"If I knew that, we would have her right now, wouldn't we?" Barbara snapped. She then gasped and said, "I'm sorry."

I shook my head. I knew she was right, and I knew it was a stupid question. "Tell me what you know," I said in a quiet and soothing voice.

Barbara took a deep breath and tears began to stream down her cheeks. In spite of that, she managed to give me a thumbnail sketch of the night's events.

A short time after we left with the Impals, Steff disappeared from the mess hall. They had been sitting there with Sally and Dr. Winder playing a game of Gin Rummy. They went outside and began to call for her. After thirty minutes of shouting her name and checking cabins, they began to get truly worried.

Taylor heard them calling from his guard post in the woods and came down to join the search. After a brief discussion, they agreed to split up into two groups. Taylor and Abbs went in one group and Barbara, Dr. Winder and Sally in the other.

"We must have searched for at least an hour," Barbara sputtered as she wiped her eyes. "That was when it happened."

I waited with patience and let Barbara tell me in her own time about how they heard several heavy vehicles approaching up the road. A minute later, the woods were flooded with lights as the trucks approached along with several soldiers on foot.

"We were almost on the other side of the lake when they arrived," Barbara said. "Taylor and Abbs were trapped. They fired on them without warning," she said in a dry voice, then began to cough.

I pulled her close and patted her back until the coughing subsided.

"The soldiers killed them," she whispered. "I know because I saw them, saw them standing there with their bodies on the ground. Taylor, he—," Barbara trailed off and looked over at Abbs, who was talking with Dr. Winder. She then turned back to me, her eyes swollen and miserable.

"Taylor . . . he charged the soldiers giving Abbs time to run away. She grabbed the flashlight she dropped and ran toward us. Thank God she did because she managed to get the batteries out before they could catch up to her. She hid in the God-awful, dark lake almost the whole night while they searched the woods for her."

"Where did you go?" I asked.

"We tried to get up on the hillside where you found Chester's grave, but it was so damned dark. We couldn't turn our flashlights on. Sally fell into a small rock cave. It was just big enough for all of us to fit in. We waited there the whole night, watching the soldiers pass by a few feet away. Right before dawn, I managed to slip down to the lake to get Abbs and bring her back to us. We stayed in the cave all day watching the soldiers continue to search. When it seemed they had given up, we came here as fast as we could."

"Jesus," I said and pulled her close. "I'm so sorry, honey."

She cried into my shoulder for a long time.

"I don't know where Steff is," she finally said.

We were startled to hear Burt's voice beside us.

"Cecil, I think you might want to hear this. The general is about to be on the radio with an important announcement," he said.

I was thankful he did not say my father would be on the radio; my hatred of the man had grown beyond belief in the past twenty-four hours. It was about to grow even more.

We managed to pack everyone in the SUV. Dr. Winder sat in the back with Burt and Sally, while Abbs sat between Barbara and me.

There was a public-service announcement playing. It advertised the bounty for Impals was now one-thousand dollars a head. Now people had even more of a reason to go out and kill their neighbor. It seemed that law and order was now even more barbaric than the Wild West. To make matters worse, immunity was granted for anyone handing over Impals. I saw no method to this madness, just a blatant disregard for morality and, even more so, sanity. The hypocrisy of the self-righteous had thrown my family into chaos, not to mention the world.

A few moments later, the radio announcer came on.

"We have some breaking news to report this evening," he said with excited anticipation in his voice. "We have none other than the illustrious General Ott Garrison with us to discuss this amazing turn of events."

"Illustrious?" I thought to myself. He might as well have said the great and benevolent Royal Highness, Supreme Leader and Grand Poohbah. After all, he was those things to some people even if not in name. To many he was a savior, sent by God to rid us of a sudden demonic infestation. I could tell the announcer was definitely in that camp. I was of the opinion that the general was a malignant hemorrhoid on the butt of the Statue of Liberty. He needed to be stopped at any cost, father be damned.

"Thank you for having me on tonight, Jack," my father's arrogant voice boomed.

As if he had any choice.

"So, I understand you made a huge breakthrough today in the case of your son?" the announcer asked.

My spine stiffened as I exchanged glances with Barbara. I then turned to Burt who stared straight ahead. Abbs put her head on my shoulder and I found the warm and cold strangely comforting.

"Yes, indeed," he said. "I got an anonymous tip where they were hiding a cave full of demons."

I felt as if the fires of hell bloomed red hot in my belly. We all had the same questions. "*Who the hell was the informant?*"

"So you investigated this tip, I presume?" the host asked, excitement mounting in his voice.

"That we did Jack."

"Any arrests?"

"Well, yes and no," the general said. "All of the rebels defending the camp were killed in the raid. The demons trying to imitate the souls of the fallen were taken into custody."

"How many?" the announcer asked.

"Oh, about a dozen or so."

"I understand, general," the announcer said in a solemn tone. "That you suffered a devastating loss today."

My father paused for several moments as a few sniffs could be heard, and then he spoke in a quivering voice.

"My oldest granddaughter was there. She was gunned down by the reckless gunfire of the rebels. They shot her after numerous requests to stand down. I think they did it to spite me," he said with heavy emotion in his voice. He sounded as if he might cry.

"So . . . she was murdered by the Impal sympathizers," the announcer offered.

"Yes," he said, his voice breaking. The crocodile tears were making me ill.

Abbs shut her eyes tight. She was trying to block the whole world out. She was not succeeding. Tears dropped onto my arm leaving no trace except for a warm sensation like sparks passing through my body. I glanced at Barbara and saw fury blazing in her features. I have never seen my beautiful wife this angry and I shared her wrath. I think we could both tear the man apart with our bare hands and then beat his resulting Impal senseless with iron bars. Was the Tesla Gate a harsh sentence? Perhaps not for some.

"What about your son?" the announcer asked.

"The coward ran away, leaving his daughters behind. I am ashamed to call him my son for more reasons than one. I will never call that cowardly demonic sympathizer son again," he said. His voice was forceful and angry. For an instant, he exposed himself. He forgot he was supposed to be putting on an emotional show.

"I'll never call you father again you lying, murdering, sociopathic zealot," I thought.

"He took the Impals he was harboring with him?" the announcer asked.

"Yes, but we'll find them. It's just a matter of time."

"The hell you will," I muttered. Our refugees should be in International waters right now and steaming straight for the English Channel.

"General Garrison, in spite of the tragedy you endured today, there was also a bright spot that came out of this. Am I right?"

"Yes, indeed," the general piped up, sounding chipper.

"Would you care to elaborate?" the announcer said, almost giddy with excitement.

"Well, Jack . . . I think I can do better than that!" he beamed. "I can introduce you to the brave soul who tipped us off today."

Burt and I exchanged glances as we prepared to hear the identity of this traitorous person. My jaw clenched as I listened to the shuffling noise in the background while someone entered the studio.

We listened for several moments while the microphone remained open. Shuffling and whispers rustled in the background. Finally, the host cleared his throat.

"Well, we do indeed have a special guest here tonight," he said. "And what is your name?" he asked, sounding a little too joyous.

The general interrupted.

"Jack, I would like to make this introduction if you don't mind."

"Of course, General Garrison . . . the mike is yours."

The general cleared his throat and smacked his lips as he sipped on a beverage.

"Jack, it is my great honor to introduce someone who is not only a great human being, they are a true patriot as well. Someone who risked all to do what they believed was the right thing. After they escaped the clutches of the rebels, they called in the report."

I didn't need to hear anymore, I knew who the person was. The realization of the informant's identity sank over me like a dark fog of horror. Was it some sort of psychic insight that told me the identity of this person? No, it was the familiar cough and clearing of the throat that gave it away.

"I am proud," the General continued. "To introduce my grand-daughter, Miss Steffanie Garrison."

I knew my own daughter. Obviously not well enough.

CHAPTER 30

IN THE EYE

"For the waves of death encompassed me, the torrents
of destruction assailed me; the cords of Hell entangled
me; the snares of death confronted me."
~2 Samuel 22:5–6, King James Bible

BARBARA BEGAN TO CRY with a mixture of horror and relief. Abbs was outraged as she sat bolt upright, clenching her fists while she stared at the radio like it was a hateful thing. I don't know what the reaction was in the back seat because I couldn't turn around, couldn't move, so I stared straight ahead. I felt like a father watching his child pulled out to sea by a large shark while standing helpless on the beach. The only difference between my father and a man-eating shark were gills and a dorsal fin. A suffocating dread began to descend on me. My chest began to constrict so I opened the door and stepped outside. I leaned against the vehicle while taking long and labored breaths. Did I expect my father to harm his granddaughter? No, not in the physical sense anyway, but mentally . . . I shuddered to think.

"Welcome to the show, Steffanie, and thank you for your service to our country," the announcer said.

That was a phrase reserved for military members who have served our country, not a naïve twelve-year-old manipulated by a sociopath. I doubted either man made the distinction now, nor did they even care.

"You're welcome," Steff said in a small voice.

"I understand your family was with you at this camp," the announcer said. "Do you know where they are now?"

It was obvious the announcer overstepped his bounds when my father answered. He was slow and distinct as if speaking to an idiot.

"They are all in hiding right now," he said. "I'm sure they will soon see the error of their ways and turn themselves in."

There was no mention of Abbs, which was a good thing. I was certain that her body was recovered and identified along with everyone else slain at the camp. The general knew and he had not said anything to Steff. I didn't think he was trying to protect her from the horrible news. He was withholding that knowledge from her like an ace up his sleeve until it suited his purpose sometime in the future.

"Where are my mom and dad?" Steff asked. Her voice sounded as small and frightened as it did when she was three years old and terrified by a thunderstorm. My heart went out to her and all my anger and resentment I carried towards her attitude melted away in an instant. I would give anything to have her back right now.

"They're safe," the general lied to her. "Why don't you tell everyone how you managed to escape and call me?"

Steff could not speak over a whisper, so the general retold her tale for her.

Steff took the change I gave her from Martian Burgers and slipped down the road leading to camp. After a half hour of fumbling about in the dark, she made it to the main road. She then crossed the highway and used the pay phone at the general store. She called my father and waited on the front porch of the store until he arrived with a convoy of soldiers.

"She waited there, just like I told her, until we arrived," the general said.

The announcer and the general entered into a conversation about the importance of detaining Impals. Neither man heard the comment Steff made as they carried on. I did. It was faint, yet distinguishable, spoken inches from her microphone.

"I just wanted to go home," she said with a sniffle.

Tears began to streak down my cheeks as I walked to the far side of the clearing and stared up at the Moon. The damned lunar monstrosity hung in the night sky like a taunting eye. I once found it beautiful and unique, now it mocked me. It reminded me that the world has changed and it will never be the same again.

The interview didn't last much longer and Steff was taken off to God knows where. I kicked myself for not recognizing the signs. Her constant sneaking away and hoarding change in a place where currency did her no good should have been obvious red flags. However, the most apparent sign of all was her intense curiosity about the purpose and uses of a payphone. I never in a million years considered Steff would do what she did. In her mind, she believed she was doing the right thing. She thought she was going home. Her immaturity turned out to be much more than a mere annoyance; it was a nightmarish catastrophe. Before the radio interview, I wanted to wrap my hands around the neck of the traitor, whoever they were, and squeeze the life out of them. Now, I wanted to wrap my arms around my daughters and never let them go.

"We've got a place to stay tonight," Burt said, making me jump. He got out of the SUV and approached behind me. He was only a few feet away.

"Where?" I asked, turning my head in an attempt to conceal my tears.

"Derek and Andrews got ahold of Charlotte, of all people. I guess her family was somewhat well off and they own a mountain cabin outside of Front Royal. We can use it as long as we need. The best thing is, it has electricity and hot running water . . . God, I swear I will never take it for granted again."

A hot shower and a night on clean sheets sounded good. Even though we were only in the camp for a little less than a month, it felt like a year. As appealing as it sounded, it still didn't make me feel any better. I didn't think anything would ever make me feel better again.

"Let's go," I said.

We turned and walked back to the vehicle. It was time to leave. We couldn't stay here any longer, and we had pressed our luck too far. I walked a few feet when I felt a hand on my shoulder.

"I'm sorry, Cecil. I truly am," Burt said with the empathy only a true friend can relay.

I think I acknowledged him; I am not sure. My mind and emotions floated and bobbed like a rowboat on a stormy sea. I shouldn't be driving; still I slid back into the driver's seat and fired the ignition. We turned onto the road and headed towards town.

Burt wrote the directions down on a piece of scrap paper and called them out at the appropriate times on our journey. When we finally got to our destination an hour later, my heart began to pound out of my chest. I didn't remember a single damn minute of the trip; it was as if an hour of my life vanished like jumping to the next chapter on a DVD. Both my body and my mind, not to mention my soul, were spent. As I rolled myself out the door, I knew I was going to be lucky to walk inside.

Even though we were miles away from the nearest house, or paved road, the cabin contained all the amenities we hoped for. The only disappointment was that a large generator in the back provided the electricity. This meant we would need an ample supply of gasoline to keep the lights on for an extended period.

The cabin was a modern rustic with a log façade that ran from its stone foundation to the green metal roofline two stories up. Derek, Andrews and Charlotte sat on the porch in matching high backed rocking chairs.

"Welcome!" Charlotte said as she got up to greet us.

She abandoned our camp after a few days. Danny said it was stress because she wasn't used to being in the field, in harm's way. She was a self-admitted pencil pusher. What she saw and experienced in her short tenure with us was enough to make even the most battle-hardened person's blood curdle. I couldn't blame her one bit and if I was honest with myself, in another situation I might have done the same thing. God bless her for taking a stand though in a time when not many people would.

Her bubbly personality insisted she hug every one of us. When she got to Abbs, she recoiled in shock. Charlotte stared at Abbs as if she was some disgusting thing that just crawled out of the ground. I knew she didn't mean anything by it. If I hadn't been so tired, I might have found a way to warn her. My fatigue took control of my emotions.

"That's right!" I snapped pulling Abbs close to me. "That's right, she is. I'm damn proud of her, too. Do you have a problem?"

Charlotte shrunk away like a wilting violet, shaking her head in apology. I felt bad, yet I was also too tired to care. Apologies would have to wait until I was better rested.

The next thing I knew I ascended the stairs to the porch and entered the large oak front door. It was almost like I was walking outside of myself.

The house contained three bedrooms, two downstairs and one upstairs. My family and I took the one upstairs while Burt and Sally took one of the downstairs rooms. Derek and Andrews took the one right across the hallway. Poor Dr. Winder took the oversize leather sofa in the den, but I don't think he minded. He was glad to be indoors again and not in some ancient shack.

I didn't have time to take in my surroundings as I made a beeline for the bed and collapsed. I fell asleep before my head hit the pillow. I think I heard Barbara say she was going to get a shower and Abbs say she was going to sleep on the daybed. I'm not certain, I could have been dreaming.

When I awoke the next morning, I was not sleepy, but I still did not feel rested. I was sure my night was full of terrible dreams even though I couldn't remember the details of any of them. Barbara was not in bed so I sat up and stared across the room at the daybed sitting in front of a large bay window. The sleeping, luminescent form of Abbs was resting peacefully, lying on her side with her back to me. I didn't have the common thoughts that most people do about Impals such as, why do they sleep. Instead, I wondered if she blamed me. Who could blame her if she did? Most of all, I wondered if she still loved me. I would rather die and enter the Shredder than to think that my daughter did not love me anymore. I was about to call out to her when there was a knock at the bedroom door. I got up and opened the door to see Dr. Winder standing there with a puzzled expression on his face.

"Have you been outside this morning?" he asked, a hint of fear in his voice.

"No, I just got up . . . why?"

He shook his head as he furrowed his brow.

"I'm not sure. I would like you to come take a look . . . to confirm if I am crazy or not."

I didn't need to worry about getting dressed because I hit the bed fully clothed. I glanced over my shoulder at Abbs. She did not seem to be disturbed by Dr. Winder's visit, so I followed him downstairs. Barbara was in the kitchen cooking breakfast. The delicious aroma that met my nose made my mouth begin to water. I didn't realize how hungry I was until then. I felt a leap of excitement in my belly when I considered the prospect of having real cooking on a regular basis.

"Good morning, sweetheart," she called from the kitchen's arched doorway. "Did you sleep well?"

I knew Barbara better than I knew anybody in the world. I knew beneath the happy Martha Stewart persona, there was a hollow woman. I could see it in her eyes and her demeanor. She was a mother who lost two children in the past twenty-four hours. Maybe not lost to death, or at least death as we have defined it for millennia. Abbs was lost to our limited understanding of life. Steff was in the hands of a zealot lunatic, and I was sure that the brainwashing against us was in full swing. I think I could see Barbara's emotion so clearly because I felt it too. We still had the essence of one of our daughters upstairs and, right now, we must cling to that at all costs.

"Not too bad," I lied. "I feel a little better this morning."

At least a half-truth is better than no truth at all.

In fact, I was so numb that I did not feel the pain of my injuries. Nor did I realize I was still wearing the same bandana and jersey.

Dr. Winder and I went outside and descended the steps to the small gravel parking area. He paused for a moment and then pointed up.

"What do you see?" he asked.

I looked up through the horseshoe shaped ring of behemoth oak and pine trees dominating the woods around the cabin. I stared for several long moments before it dawned on me.

"The sky is a little less lavender and has a very faint reddish tint?" I asked.

"And the clouds?" he asked.

I looked up again, not seeing any clouds at first then one slowly drifted over. I stood in puzzled astonishment as I ran my fingers through my hair. "They are orange!"

"Yes, a very distinct orange," Dr. Winder agreed.

"What does it mean?" I asked.

Dr. Winder frowned for several moments as if considering something unpleasant then shrugged. "I'm not sure, probably nothing," he said. "Perhaps an anomaly related to particulate matter in the ionosphere."

"Huh?"

"Pollution," he said.

In the months since the storm encompassed Earth's atmosphere, I have never ever seen a faint reddish sky, let alone orange clouds. Every day, without exception, the sky was lavender and the clouds were yellow. Maybe pollution increased since the arrival of the storm? I wasn't sure.

I was about to ask Dr. Winder about other possibilities when a bloodcurdling scream erupted from the house. My heart leapt into my throat and the hairs on the back of my neck stood on end. I knew it was Abbs and she was terrified.

I flung the heavy oak front door open as if it was made of paper and bolted up the stairs. Barbara was hot on my heels. Throwing the bedroom door open; it thudded into the wall with a loud bang as Barbara and I tumbled into the room. Abbs was standing beside the daybed. Her horrified expression was more than I could endure.

She walked towards us as if she was in a trance, her arms outstretched and her mouth silently forming the words, *help me*. I reached out to her to pull her tight to my chest.

"What is it baby, are you okay?" I asked.

The next thing I knew, Abbs wasn't in front of me, she was behind me. She reached from me to her mother with horrified desperation. She passed through me and I did not even feel her, no cold, no warmth; only nothingness. Barbara reached for her. She might as well have reached for a tendril of smoke as her arms passed through Abbs as if she wasn't there.

Her semisolid luminescent sheen faded to an opaque outline, her features growing fainter by the second. It was as if she was slowly fading out of existence.

"Mom, Dad . . . what is happening to me?" a faint, otherworldly voice called out in a pitiful plea.

Barbara and I made one more attempt to embrace our daughter, but it was no use. Abbs was gone.

Falling to my knees, I cried out in anguish. I felt a piece of my soul tearing away. We held on to each other as we huddled in the floor and mourned the loss of our daughter.

I never noticed that Derek, Andrews and Dr. Winder stood in the doorway and witnessed the whole thing. They went outside and conducted a fruitless search for Abbs. At least Derek and Andrews searched. Dr. Winder turned on the radio in the kitchen and listened to the news reports. The doctor let Barbara and I mourn as long as he dared before he came back to the room. He could not wait any longer because the situation was too grave.

"Cecil, you need to come listen to this," he said as he helped us off the floor.

It took a while before I could summon the courage and the energy to accept Dr. Winder's invitation. Dr. Winder helped her up and escorted her to the bed where he helped her to lie down. He returned and pulled me to my feet. My body felt heavy and it was a struggle to get up. I followed him down the stairs as if in a trance. I slumped into a chair at the kitchen table as he turned the volume up on the radio.

The announcer sounded like the same one who interviewed the general last night. It was difficult to tell because so many people from television moved over to radio. The government handpicked most of them. I think what made his voice hard to discern was the fear and panic it resonated in spite of his attempt to subdue it; his voice was rapid and shaky.

"Since this cosmic storm entered Earth's atmosphere almost three months ago, there have not been any significant changes . . . well, that has changed today."

He paused and took a deep breath before continuing.

"The color of the sky has definitely changed in this hemisphere. That is to say every place on the planet where it is currently daylight and . . ." he continued with newfound giddiness, "it appears that all the Impals have disappeared or are disappearing as we speak."

"What did he have to be scared of?" I thought to myself. It sounded to me that the government, aka - my father, was getting exactly what they wanted and this person was their mouthpiece. My question was about to be answered.

"One moment. ladies and gentlemen . . . I am receiving some new information," he said then the radio was silent for over a minute. Whispers and shuffling papers could be heard in the background.

"What is happening?" I asked.

He frowned and stroked his chin before responding.

"I would guess the eye of the storm has moved over us."

"The eye?" I asked, incredulous. "You mean like a hurricane?"

"In a way . . . every storm, whether terrestrial or cosmic has a definite shape and a defined center. We were able to measure the size of this storm and its possible duration. Like the storms composition, we have no idea what kind of energy is in the eye . . ." he trailed off with a troubled expression on his face.

"What?" I asked.

We had discussed this one morning by the lake. It now completely slipped my mind. He decided to share some new information with me. Information he selectively omitted in our prior conversation.

"Well . . . the eye should not have arrived until at least two years from now, according to NASA's calculations. Not many of their calculations or guesses have been right."

"What if this isn't the eye, what if the storm has passed completely?" I asked.

Dr. Winder shook his head.

"Impossible! If the storm passed completely, I would think the sky should be normal again."

"How can you be sure?" I asked. "This is uncharted territory for everybody."

Dr. Winder gave me a hardened stare for several moments, and then I saw the confidence melt from his features. He knew I was right. Before either of us could carry the conversation further, the announcer came back on the radio. He cleared his throat and smacked his lips. He seemed uncertain on how he should deliver the new information.

"Ladies and gentlemen, we are receiving reports from several journalists worldwide. One from a journalist in Turkey, and another in Beijing, China," he said, clearing his throat.

"We advise everybody to stay inside until further notice and keep as many lights on as possible, Awar Habib reports from Istanbul."

Again, there was a long pause and another deep breath.

"The accounts we received from numerous sources state . . . and I quote . . . *the very darkness seems to be a living thing, a malignant entity that engulfs and torments anyone it encounters. It is as if a shapeless and faceless devil occupies any area devoid of light.*"

The announcer again cleared his throat.

"Folks, take it for what you will. It is nighttime right now in Turkey and in China."

The sound of shuffling papers rustled again.

"The report coming in from China tells a similar and more disturbing story," he said. "The report from Boqin Zhu reads as follows: *the darkness is a conscious yāomó, thriving anywhere there is absence of light. I have witnessed many people outside my window writhing about in agony as the dark engulfs them, dragging them away to God knows where. Stay inside, stay in as much light as possible because even the shadows are domains for this horror, if not the horror itself.*"

There was a long silence before the announcer spoke again.

"My producer tells me that yāomó roughly translates as an evil entity such as a demon or fiend, I . . ." the announcer was suddenly interrupted as a horrific scream erupted from the speakers.

I couldn't tell if the shriek came from him or someone else in the studio. It was followed by bangs and then the shattering crash of breaking glass. The voice of a woman began to wail with desperation.

"Turn on the lights! Someone turn back on the lights!" she screamed.

Earsplitting screams vibrated the speakers. My stomach churned and my flesh crawled as I listened to this. Then, as fast as it started, it stopped. There was no static, no test tone indicating the station was off the air, only eerie silence.

Dr. Winder and I stared at each other in disbelief for a while then I shook myself out of my trance and bolted outside. The cabin had a number of windows facing every direction. With the curtains opened, there was plenty of light during the daytime; however the woods were a different matter. The cabin rested in an old forest with gargantuan trees that provided a sprawling dark canopy in several places.

My first glance was overhead. The sky was the same as it was a few minutes ago. An instant later, my gaze was drawn to the forest . . . into a very dark area about fifty yards to my left. I was standing in a bright wide beam of sunlight so I screwed up my eyes to peer into the darkness. I felt like a clammy hand stroked my spine; my hair stood on end and my heart began to hammer. Even though I could not see anything tangible, I knew without a doubt something was there. Something was watching me. Whatever it was, it was waiting for the darkness to spread into my circle of light so it could pounce. I could not see anything other than the dark. What I was experiencing was more or less a feeling. It was the most certain feeling I have experienced in my life.

Staring into the blackness among the massive tree trunks, I could have sworn I saw eyes watching me. Dozens of pairs moving rapidly from tree to tree like burning coals. It was only a glimpse, and then it was gone.

I was startled when a deer wandered into the dark area. It approached with caution, sniffing the air. The instant its nose penetrated the darkness it was as if an unseen hand grasped it by the snout and flung it to its back. The terrified creature bellowed and kicked its legs in desperation as it writhed on the ground. After several agonizing moments, it managed to spring to its feet and dash away through the forest. It was as if the darkness spat it out. The poor animal bumped into trees and underbrush as it ran, panicked and confused.

I started to back away, several scenarios playing through my head like a movie on high speed. I glanced over at the generator humming away beside the house. It was our only source of electricity . . . how much gas did we have? The road approaching the house was full of gloomy shade.

I was about to ascend the steps on the porch to discuss our predicament with Dr. Winder when I experienced a horrific sense of déjà vu as another scream erupted from the house. This time it was Barbara. I glanced up at our bedroom window and saw the drapes were drawn. Barbara was up there . . . alone . . . and in the dark.

www.ingramcontent.com/pod-product-compliance
Lightning Source LLC
Chambersburg PA
CBHW030246200626
46816CB00002BA/535